"I can protect you,

"I know you think that," Shayne answered. "But you're the opposition!"

"Look, Shayne," Noah said. "I don't blame you for feeling this way. I wouldn't depend on us either if I was in your position."

"So why should I?"

"Because I've made a promise to you. I will take care of you and make sure you're protected, no matter the outcome."

"Why should I believe you?"

"You have no reason to other than my word."

"Please understand then, this isn't about you."

"Will you give me a chance at least? A chance to prove to you that we're on the same team?"

Shayne took a few steps forward, the pull of being so close to him drawing her like moth to flame.

"Please, Shayne? Will you give me that chance to prove that I will keep you safe?"

"Okay. I can do that if—"

The explosion happened without warning. The kitchen window shattered in a rain of glass.

Shayne barely had time to scream before Noah dragged her to the ground.

Dear Reader,

Welcome back to Midnight Pass, Texas. I bet you thought everything had wrapped up nice and neat with the capture of former FBI director—and now FBI betrayer—Rick Statler. But Rick had a few more connections up his sleeve and has escaped custody, determined to exit Midnight Pass just as he'd always planned—on top. There are only two things standing in his way: his former girlfriend, Shayne Erickson, and the FBI lead determined to bring Rick to justice, Noah Ross.

Noah believes he has a lot to atone for. The death of someone in his past haunts him and missing the depths of Rick's depravity has hit their FBI unit hard. They should have known there was a snake in their midst and no one feels this more than Noah.

Shayne also knows something about regret. She's spent the past month since being rescued desperate to figure out how she could have missed all the signs that the man was a manipulative psychopath. When it's discovered Rick is staying in Midnight Pass out of some sense of unfinished business, Noah knows Shayne is the key.

Danger is mounting once again in Midnight Pass. But this time, it's leading to a showdown of epic proportions. I hope you enjoy this race against time to catch one of the most dangerous men to ever set their sights on the Pass.

Best,

Addison Fox

HER TEXAS LAWMAN

Addison Fox

Recycling programs for this product may not exist in your area.

ISBN-13: 978-1-335-73824-0

Her Texas Lawman

Copyright © 2023 by Frances Karkosak

For questions and comments about the quality of this book, please contact us at CustomerService@Harlequin.com.

Harlequin Enterprises ULC
22 Adelaide St. West, 41st Floor
Toronto, Ontario M5H 4E3, Canada
www.Harlequin.com

Printed in U.S.A.

Addison Fox is a lifelong romance reader, addicted to happily-ever-afters. After discovering she found as much joy writing about romance as she did reading it, she's never looked back. Addison lives in New York with an apartment full of books, a laptop that's rarely out of sight and a wily beagle who keeps her running. You can find her at her home on the web at addisonfox.com or on Facebook (Facebook.com/addisonfoxauthor) and Twitter (@addisonfox).

Books by Addison Fox

Harlequin Romantic Suspense

Midnight Pass, Texas

The Cowboy's Deadly Mission
Special Ops Cowboy
Under the Rancher's Protection
Undercover K-9 Cowboy
Her Texas Lawman

The Coltons of Colorado

Undercover Colton

The Coltons of Grave Gulch

Colton's Covert Witness

The Coltons of Mustang Valley

Deadly Colton Search

Visit the Author Profile page at Harlequin.com

For the sisterhood of cousins—Beth, Katie, Carol, Ellen, Margaret, Heather, Alisha, Ramona and Neeley.

Dancing till we dropped at all the weddings and the Thanksgiving candy basket and impromptu band concerts (apologies forever for my oboe solo) and celebrating the joys of welcoming the next generation.

Some of us have spent our whole lives as cousins and others we've been lucky to pick up along the way. How lovely to know we're also friends.

Chapter 1

Noah Ross looked out over his team in the south Texas FBI field office, headquartered in the heart of Midnight Pass, and mentally cursed their continued bad luck. He counted himself fortunate—he hadn't had a team this good in his decade and a half with the Bureau—and they fought by his side every day. But even with their dedication, expertise and collective smarts, they were no closer to their goal: capturing their former boss and the recent predecessor of Noah's current position, Rick Statler.

"Intel puts him in Juárez on Friday." Ryder Durant gave his report with a steady calm and minimal inflection in his voice. No mean feat considering the man's hatred for their quarry.

Durant was one of the best on the team. He also had a personal interest in this one since Statler had held Durant's fiancée, Arden Reynolds, and Statler's ex-girl-friend, Shayne Erickson, at gunpoint a month prior.

Noah quickly amended his thought. The running assumption had been that Shayne Erickson was Statler's ex, but in the weeks since the hostage situation that proved to be all it was. An assumption.

One they had continued to review, over and over, as they evaluated the time Statler had spent with the woman and what his possible connections might be since he escaped FBI custody two weeks prior.

Arden had sworn up one side and down the other that Shayne wouldn't have helped Statler, but Noah was keeping his options open. He'd managed far too many cases where a hurt, misbegotten woman was left behind, only to pair up with a piece of scum after a few frilly promises.

Hadn't his ex-wife done the same? Or was the proper term *late wife*? The monikers conflated in his mind too often for comfort, and *on the way to being an ex before she died* was too complicated to work through every damn time he thought of Lindsey.

Besides, he preferred *ex*, anyway. While he had desperately wanted her out of his life a decade ago, he'd never wanted her dead.

Ignoring the shot of regret he'd never been able to convince himself to abandon, he refocused on Durant and his report. "So, Mexico is his latest known whereabouts?"

"It's false." Ryder's response was immediate and devoid of emotion. "He knows how to cover his tracks and there's no way he'd let himself be seen that easily on local cameras. He's either stayed close or he's far from here. But the intel feels like a plant."

"Do you think he's close?" Noah asked.

"Yeah." Ryder lifted his cap and ran a hand through his hair. "I think he's got further plans here in Midnight Pass."

"You think he's going to make another play for Shayne Erickson?" Brady Renner spoke up.

"We have to assume that despite showing no signs of attachment behavior before, Statler's attached to Erickson," Durant answered. "That was clear when he kidnapped her. He also doesn't like to lose. He's spent too long and come too far to give it all up now."

Noah cursed the realities of what they were dealing with. An ex-FBI leader who knew intimately how they worked, now with proven mob ties and an ex he'd formed an unhealthy attachment to. Hadn't his escape further attested to his determination? A well-placed bribe against a vulnerable agent assigned to hold him and Statler had escaped into the seeming ether.

And that bribe only scratched the surface of what the man was capable of.

Statler's list of sins was long and growing longer with each discovery the team made. From supporting local criminals when he was still in Boston to the trafficking and criminal underworld he supported once he got his promotion and arrived in Texas, Rick Statler had fooled a lot of important people for a very long time.

Which only added to the crap storm that hovered over them as they worked the case.

Top brass with egg on their face never boded well for anyone.

"Any other sightings?"

"Nothing else in the past week." Durant shook his head before standing and walking to a large dry-erase board they'd set up in their conference-room-slash-war-room. He gestured to the map they'd set up, a trail of surveillance photos tacked beside it. The same board had the supposed sightings to date as well as the safe house where Statler had hidden out. Ryder's K-9, Murphy, had advanced first on that rescue mission and had taken Statler down pretty hard.

Ryder continued, "And even with the few weeks he spent in custody on antibiotics, Murphy'd done a number on him. I know we keep saying he could just as easily be holed up here in town as he could be buried deep somewhere in Mexico while the heat cools off, but my money's on here."

Noah's money was on here, too, but he valued Durant's assessment. He'd also been doing this long enough to know that sometimes it was worth it to talk things out. Put one idea after another, trying them on for size. Which brought them squarely back to Texas or points farther south or any freaking place in between.

That was what they were dealing with.

And they had so little to go on, nothing pointing them in any definitive direction.

So they'd keep working what they did know. Or were still uncovering. A shocking amount continued to come out on Statler's past activities, on top of the exhaustive interrogation they'd done while they had him in custody. The discovery that Statler was working with several drug cartels outside the country had put everyone on edge.

But the biggest surprise—discovered on Shayne Erickson's tech after they'd confiscated it—was that the work with the cartels was the tip of the iceberg. Statler had apparently gone all in with a prominent and multifaceted Russian mob organization, a situation that had only escalated the scrutiny on the case and ensured the highest echelons of government wanted this situation handled PDQ.

What Noah still hadn't pieced together was how Statler had worked it all so far under the radar.

Sure, there were ways around the system. Someone with a determination to do bad things could always find a way. It was harder in the Bureau, but that didn't make it any less true. What he couldn't figure, though, was how the man had fostered the depth of connections that he had and how he had done it with no one the wiser.

They'd yet to find even a whisper that Statler had another inside man helping him. Even the junior agent who'd helped him escape had been nothing but an opportunity on Statler's part—a weak link he leveraged. Nor had the tech team had much luck beyond skimming some search details off Statler's equipment that would raise eyebrows.

Yet somehow Shayne's computer held the key to everything?

It didn't play for him.

Nothing ran nowadays without a digital footprint. Yet Statler had skulked around like a freaking ghost *except* on his girlfriend's devices.

Which brought Noah right back to Shayne Erickson.

Was she the connection? By all accounts the woman was a successful consultant, specializing in wireless communications. She had a home office, extensive electronics and a professional ability to use them.

Which circled him right back around to traitorous-girlfriend territory.

Noah gave the meeting another five minutes before

dismissing everyone to lunch. After they were all gone, he got up and stood before the same board as Durant. His gaze drifted to Shayne Erickson's photo, just as it had so many times over the past month. He skimmed the various images tacked up on the board, one of her on Main Street in a yoga outfit, another of her speaking at a conference and a third of her, also in professional mode, in a headshot that had been pulled off her website.

A distant idea began to take shape, nagging from somewhere deep in his brain that there was a clue to her whereabouts in those photos.

Although she'd been nothing but cooperative after her kidnapping rescue, they ultimately questioned her in every way imaginable and then needed to let her go. But since the news broke of Rick Statler's escape from FBI custody, Shayne had disappeared, too. Was she on the run? Helping Rick?

Or maybe she was running scared, fearful of being the man's next target.

He turned that last one over as he took his fill of the photos on the board: the soft fall of blond hair resting against her petite shoulders, clad in a black business suit. Bright blue eyes stared back at him from the photo, their seemingly clear vision as unsettling as always. He was a good judge of character, damn it. And he didn't give people the benefit of the doubt because they were attractive or because somewhere deep beneath his breastbone he felt a soft tug.

And he sure as hell didn't give them the benefit of the doubt because he could still remember their arms wrapped tightly around his neck as he carried them from the room they'd been locked in as a prisoner for nearly forty-eight hours.

Until proven otherwise, he had to keep up his guard.

And until proven otherwise, he had to believe Shayne Erickson was in league with the enemy.

Shayne Erickson stared at the darkened face of her cell phone and cursed her situation once again. Turned off, it was nothing but an expensive—and useless—screen. Just like her tablet and her computer. Which hadn't kept her from hanging tightly on to all three, each wrapped securely in a bag that rarely left her side. Nor had it stopped her ridiculous vigilance in keeping them charged.

She had no desire to be tracked the moment she turned them on, but she'd be damned if she wasn't going to use them should the need arise.

Only so far, nothing had arisen except for endless hours of boredom and self-recrimination.

The boredom was a steady reminder that she likely spent far too many of her normal waking hours on all three devices.

And the self-recrimination because…well…how in the hell could she have been so stupid?

Over and over, she'd thought through the past months in her relationship with Rick Statler. Every conversation. Every date. Every whisper of their time together. And never, in any of those thousands of moments, had she ever considered that he was a psychotic monster?

Not once?

How could she have been so utterly freaking clueless? The man was a violent criminal, involved in any manner of sordid, horrific crimes.

And now he was a violent criminal on the loose.

She was a smart woman. Hell, she prided herself on being savvy and self-aware. The room she was currently hunkered down in was proof of that. Her business had taken her all over the country and even expanded into the occasional international job. She'd recently taken up a lease to set up an actual office outside her home.

It was a small space—she didn't need much room— in a newly built office complex about twenty minutes outside Midnight Pass, but it did put her closer to the airport when she needed to travel. It had also given her tangible proof of her work. Something that required her to get dressed and do more than sit behind a desk in her home office still clad in her proverbial bunny slippers.

She ran a business. A damn good one.

And because of it, she knew the score. She had experience. Street smarts. And at thirty-two, she'd learned long ago there was no such thing as Prince Charming. There was Prince-Charming-from-Time-to-Time and that was about as good as it got.

For anyone.

So how had she let Rick Statler slip beneath her guard? Because he was attractive? Thoughtful to her? Interested in her work?

What had prompted her complete and total lapse in judgment?

Because Rick Statler wasn't just a run-of-the-mill jerk who'd shown his true colors and ghosted her after they'd had a few dates and a few rounds of sex. The man was certifiably psychotic, with a list of kills to his credit and Russian mob connections. Connections he had used her former computer—still in FBI custody, thank you very much—to contact.

The new laptop secured in her bag was a small, unexpected boon, courtesy of an anxious shot of paranoia. That first night at home, before the FBI had come with their warrants, she'd glanced over at the new laptop she'd purchased for her business. Some strange sixth sense had compelled her to make a full copy of her existing laptop, and she was grateful for it now.

She was quite sure the federal geeks would figure out she'd done it, but for the time being, at least she had something. And the additional paranoia that had her hide the laptop with her next-door neighbor had been the second win. Mrs. Santiago had been so excited for her, watching with hopeful eyes as Shayne's relationship with Rick had progressed. The older woman—now disappointed and irate on her behalf—had been more than willing to stash a few items when asked.

Unfortunately, Shayne wasn't able to get much out of the device because she refused to go online. That was a sure path to discovery, and besides, her expertise involved communications networks, not hacking.

Obviously, her expertise didn't extend to picking solid men to share her life with, either. A point made more than evident as Rick had held her and her friend Arden Reynolds at gunpoint while kidnapped in a government safe house he'd repurposed.

Without warning, she was back in that room, her hands tied behind her with thick plastic zip ties, fear coating her throat in thick, syrupy waves that tasted like metal. Then those moments of freedom when Arden managed to get them out of the restraints as they determined what to do also came back to her. And then the way Rick had stood before her, that easygoing smile somehow twisted into something beyond recognition, as he told her about how good a future they'd have together.

Whatever she'd battled in her own mind, none of it compared to how sick and messed-up he really was. So much had come out since the kidnapping. The endless questioning from the FBI, set up in the guise of "meetings," To determine what she knew. The search and seizure of her home, also under the guise of finding any details Rick might have left behind.

They'd told her little, but she'd put together enough. The questions about Rick's time in Boston and his work in the Midnight Pass office. The suggestions that he knew cartel heads and Russian mobsters. And maybe the saddest of all, the recent discovery that he'd killed an innocent ranch hand on Arden's property, just to incite panic and confusion.

Even now, she could remember his eyes flicking over her in that safe house, washing over her in the same predatory fashion as a snake sizing up its prey. The man she'd felt herself falling for—the man she'd felt lucky to have found—had turned into some sort of super-villain right before her eyes.

The good guys had arrived, like a full cavalry riding in to save them. FBI lead Noah Ross had come to her rescue, along with Arden's fiancé, Ryder Durant, and his faithful K-9, Murphy.

But Rick had still won, finding a way to escape FBI custody and go on the run only a few weeks later.

Noah had remained kind to her through all the questions about Rick. He'd shown the same warmth and support when rescuing her from the safe house—even carrying her from it when she was still struggling with shock and overwhelming fear. But even with the kindness, she sensed underneath it all he believed she was collaborating with Rick.

The thought made her skin crawl.

How could anyone think she could be a part of any of that? Despite her ignorance of Rick's true personality, she'd somehow painted herself into a very bleak corner. Trapped, with no one to believe her.

That was what the days since the kidnapping had taught her. The fear that had blossomed and spread in that small cabin had grown deep roots in the ensuing days as she talked to the FBI. There weren't enough polite platitudes in the world to erase their abundantly obvious lack of belief.

Which meant she was on her own and marinating in feelings of distrust—for others and herself.

Nothing she tried since—no amount of yoga or positive thinking or even her plots and plans to reach back out to law enforcement for help—could stem the bitter tide of acidic fear.

So instead, she fought through it. She forced breaths in and out of her lungs. And she plotted and planned. She might not have her tools ready at her disposal, but she still had her mind. She could map out an action plan. And, if she thought long enough and hard enough and dug down deep enough in her memories, she could find something about Rick Statler to take to the Feds to get them to help her.

Right now, she was the ex-girlfriend on the run. They had no reason to believe her and no reason to help her.

But if she could become a witness with tangible proof they could use, she might get them to believe her.

With that thought foremost in her mind, she grabbed the legal pad off the top of the small stack she'd created over the past few weeks. She'd even built out a calendar, racking her brain to remember every single thing she'd done since meeting Statler, in search of some useful information.

It had been a taxing exercise and had reminded her, more than once, that her dependence on her digital tools was far more foundational than she'd understood. But it had also forced her to think. To remember the various conversations she'd had with Rick as they'd gotten to know each other. To remember the places they'd gone and the times he'd opted to stay in rather than go out, often feigning a need to borrow her computer quickly for work.

Slowly but surely, she'd crafted a picture of her life over the past six months.

She could only hope there was enough actual, tangible proof in her notes and scribbles and remembrances to catch a killer.

Determined, Shayne focused on the recent spate of notes she'd jotted down in a fervor the night before. She reviewed the odd conversations she and Rick had shared in the days leading up to the night she was kidnapped. And then his mad ramblings as he'd held them captive, bragging about how smart and clever he was. She reread the odd, rambling words as a layer of unease swirled over her skin, puckering her flesh with goose bumps.

Then she fought back the scream that crawled up her throat as a loud, heavy knock slammed into the office door.

Noah's free hand drifted over his gun, and he allowed it to hover there as he pounded on the door with his other fist. It was a long shot, but the idea to look into Shayne

Erickson's new professional digs had come to him just as he'd given up staring at his board to head out for lunch.

The idea had kept him company, rolling around in his mind on the walk down to the sub shop, but it was only when he found himself buying two subs, a roast beef sandwich for himself and a turkey club for Shayne, that he'd realized his intent.

"It's Noah Ross. Open up, Shayne." He bent down to pick up the bag of subs he'd set at his feet, hollering as he stood. "I've got lunch and I want to talk to you."

Dead-calm quiet radiated from the other side of the door, but something had Noah staying right where he was.

When he lifted his hand to knock once more, he heard the distinct sound of footsteps. Everything inside Noah stilled as his earlier thoughts came back to him. Although he'd played a hunch, he wasn't entirely convinced Shayne Erickson was innocent.

Was it possible Statler was with her?

The subtle snick of the lock broke through his thoughts before the door drifted open. Still on high alert, Noah surveyed the space in front of him, half-convinced his old boss would be standing there.

Instead, he had the fleeting impression of stale air and an odd hopelessness evident in the pulled blinds and dark atmosphere of the shuttered office.

"What are you doing here?" Shayne stood beside the door, out of sight of the street or anyone who might be in the parking lot.

Or standing guard, watching.

"I came to talk to you."

She made no move to gesture him in, yet something in her stance telegraphed her discomfort standing there with the door wide open. He saw the calculation on her face—should she let him in or slam the door—before she seemed to make a decision in his favor. With that foremost in his mind, Noah pressed his advantage.

"Can I come in?"

She shrugged but didn't answer, moving back in a gesture of welcome.

Well, not quite welcome, Noah amended to himself. *Resigned acceptance* was a more apt term. But he stepped in all the same, removing the hand that had hovered over his gun so that it rested at his side.

He stayed in self-defense range but relaxed enough to not seem threatening.

She closed the door behind him, the snap of the lock echoing in the silence between them. "How'd you find me?"

He considered making something up but went with instinct as he decided the truth might be the way to get close to the answers he needed. And he needed some measure of truth to get her to drop her guard. "No one's seen you, and you haven't used a credit card or logged into your personal accounts. I played a hunch."

Shayne hadn't moved from the door, her tall frame stiff where she blocked the entrance. Her casual outfit of workout pants and a T-shirt couldn't hide the edgy wariness that suffused her. Or the fact that her slim frame had edged toward gaunt after more than two weeks on the run. "So I'm being watched?"

"Yes."

"Because I'm a person of interest?"

"Because Rick Statler is a wanted man and anyone remotely related to him is under watch."

Those thin shoulders slumped, defeated. "Which means you didn't come here to tell me you caught him."

Noah nearly stumbled over the assumption. Was that why she'd answered the door? "No." He held up the bag in his hands. "I did bring lunch, though. Come on and eat with me."

Although her gaze remained wary, she moved away from the door and followed him toward the small kitchenette he could see off the edge of the office space. Curious, he quickly scanned the area. The kitchenette was small, but he saw a coffee maker on, the pot half-full on the counter. An open shelving unit sported office-sized boxes of granola bars, mixed fruit and crackers.

Taking a seat at the table, he watched as Shayne crossed to the fridge. "Regular or diet soda?"

"Regular." He spied a rack full of soda and another that looked rather depleted before she closed the fridge door. "How long have you been living on crackers and fruit?"

"Longer than I ever thought I'd have to." His drink hit the small table with a thunk, hers following behind it before she dropped into the chair opposite him. "But I also never thought a food run before moving in here would come in handy like it has."

Noah considered the trash can. Although he saw a few granola bar wrappers, it was surprisingly empty. "Have you been going out?"

She looked up from where she unwrapped her sandwich. "Only late at night."

"That's the worst time to go out."

"I'm careful." She spoke the words around a mouthful of turkey, and Noah didn't miss how her eyes closed slightly at that first bite.

"I've spoken to any number of victims who've said the same."

"I'm not a victim. And since I was the first to buy in here and this place is still under construction, I'm not at risk of running into people, so I won't inadvertently make someone else a victim."

"This isn't living—it's surviving. Hiding out in a few darkened rooms. If that's not living like a victim, what would you call it?"

She laid the sandwich down on the paper in front of her and reached for her soda. "*Victim* suggests an innocence lost. While I'm innocent of knowledge of Rick Statler's crimes, I let the man into my home and into my life." She stopped but sheer grit reflected back out of those deep blue depths. "That's on me."

Noah slowly unwrapped his own sandwich, giving her comment time to hover between them before replying, "That's awfully understanding of you."

"It's got nothing to do with understanding. It's the truth. I'm a grown woman. I know my own mind. I run my own business. I had no business getting involved with Statler."

Noah considered the harsh tones and couldn't deny they ticked another mark in the innocent column.

Only he hadn't come here to determine innocence or guilt.

Then why did you come?

He'd come here, damn it, to find her and find out what she'd been up to. No credit cards, no digital signals. It was like she'd vanished, and it was his job to make sure she didn't go on the run.

"What are you going to do when the food runs out?"

"I keep hoping you and your team will catch him before that's a problem. And if not, I'll stick to my late-night runs to the mini-mart up the road."

Noah set his sandwich down. "Shayne. That's not smart and you know it. Staying here isn't smart."

"What other choice do I have?"

"There has to be something you can do. Family? Friends?"

"There's nothing. And there's no way I'd drag into this the few people I do talk to." Her voice was flat, the lack of emotion adding one more check to that innocent column.

But it was the bleakness in those captivating eyes, turning them a troubled shade that edged toward gray, that pulled somewhere deep inside him. He knew what it was to care for someone. Worse, he also knew what it meant to have that affection betrayed by a person you believed you knew.

What did Shayne Erickson know?

And despite everything he'd learned in his career—hell, in his life—why was something tugging at him so hard to believe her?

Chapter 2

Shayne finished the last bite of her sandwich and marveled at how wonderful it felt to have something in her stomach besides a granola bar or a small container of mixed fruit.

Definitely an odd and shocking reminder of how much she'd taken for granted before this entire mess started.

She'd never been a person who dwelled on the past or on things that couldn't be changed. She believed in forward movement and hard work and the value of putting on your big-girl panties and taking care of yourself. She had believed deeply in the power of movement and staying in motion and hadn't ever given much credence to the idea that part of the beauty of staying in motion was that you didn't have to think about all the things that crowded in on you when you stopped.

So it was only in the past month that she'd begun to

question all she'd ever thought or believed. Terrible still-ness had descended after the whirlwind of the kidnapping and the endless days of being questioned by the Feds. All that wonderful, active motion had simply ceased, and she was left alone with her thoughts.

If someone as horrible as Rick Statler could get under her defenses so easily, what could she possibly depend on?

Or, more to the point, who?

She couldn't even depend on herself.

Depend on him. Trust Noah.

So tempting. Way down, bone-deep tempting to con-sider giving her problems over to the strong, attractive, capable agent. That was the last thought she needed to entertain.

Yet that one thought seemed to dig in, determined to scream the loudest.

He hadn't responded to her suggestion that there wasn't anyone in her personal life she'd want to drag into this mess, and she wasn't all that interested in going down that path with him anyway. Wadding up her sand-wich wrapper, she picked it up and her now-empty soda can and headed for the counter. She considered her dwindling supplies as she stared up at the shelves and wondered if she'd ever look at the large containers at a wholesale club store the same way again.

As a single woman, she'd never even considered buy-ing so much food in bulk.

And now?

Shayne shook the idea off, as well as the endlessly dark, wending train of her thoughts. She'd worry about what to do with an empty shelf when she got there.

Crossing back to the small table, she considered Noah

Ross once more. She'd known of him, from when he'd first come to The Pass. Almost every single woman in town had noticed the man. The tall, slim lawman who, on the rare occasions he came in, never had more than one drink down at the Border Line pool hall and carried himself with a quiet stoicism more like the local cowboys than hometown law enforcement.

Only he wasn't hometown. He was a federal agent, placed in The Pass to manage and root out the criminal activity that swirled beneath the surface. A man determined to mete out justice until he was suddenly replaced by Rick Statler.

Rick's arrival had been met with little fanfare, and other than those occasional sightings out at the bar, Noah's departure was met with little notice as well. Bigger things going on in town had captured everyone's attention.

Much bigger things, as Shayne's friend Arden Reynolds had learned with shocking clarity.

Arden's family had seen it all firsthand over the past year. She and her three brothers had each battled evil people intent on doing them harm. And while those experiences had brought each of Arden's brothers their new wives—and a baby for her youngest brother, Hoyt—there had been a pervasive sense of menace beneath those experiences.

Shayne had observed it all, sadly seeing those crimes play out in close proximity as a student at Arden's yoga studio.

And then the madness had visited itself on Arden. And, eventually, on Shayne.

Arden's fiancé, Ryder, worked for Rick and was the first to realize things were not as they seemed under

Rick's leadership. Ryder was ultimately responsible for uncovering the man's crimes—a years-deep betrayal of the FBI and all his colleagues—causing Noah to come back.

Admittedly, while she hadn't forgotten about Noah, a man she knew only by sight hadn't taken up too much room in her thoughts. She'd moved on, as had the other single women in town, seeking new special someones to set their sights on.

It was only once he'd come back, rescuing her out of Rick's clutches and carrying her from the scene, that she'd remembered.

Remembered those strong arms. The broad shoulders. And the commanding way he held himself that suggested not one single thing could touch him.

Ignorant of her rambling thoughts, Noah stood up from the table, wadding up his own sandwich wrapper. He neatly three-pointed the paper into the garbage before turning his always-intense focus back on her. "What have you been doing with yourself here?"

"Thinking. Remembering. And doing my best to write down any and every scrap of memory I can dig through."

"You've got notes?"

"Pages of them."

"Go get them." As if he sensed her issue with being ordered around, a wry smile ghosted his lips. "Please go get them."

The quick shift was unexpected, and she was already heading for her office before she could reconsider. It was only when she had her stack of legal pads in hand, walking back to the kitchen, that she wondered if she was being too hasty.

Was she really thinking of handing all her notes over to the Feds?

All her work—all that she'd focused on for the past month—was on those legal pads. No, she quickly corrected herself as she thought of some of the intimate details she'd written on those sheets.

Her life was on those notepads.

Was she really comfortable putting it all on display?

Trust Noah.

While frustrated over her inner voice's discernment when it came to men, Shayne had to admit that there was some value in making the exchange. No matter how kind his demeanor toward her, Shayne knew Noah Ross still had reservations about her innocence.

Her stack of legal pads might go a slight bit further toward changing his mind.

They certainly couldn't go in reverse.

She'd been damn honest in her notes, writing down her feelings and innermost thoughts at the time of each occurrence, as well as what had actually happened.

From her thoughts on Rick's dismal computer skills to the dress she'd picked for Valentine's Day to her ex's wildly varied sexual prowess, it was all in there.

And now she was handing it over.

Trust Noah.

With that last, lingering idea, Shayne laid the stack on the kitchen table.

Noah spread out the stack of legal pads, the bold scrawl visible on page after page, and considered what Shayne Erickson must have gone through over the past few weeks. Each entry was meticulously captured— with the date she wrote the words and the date she was writing about. Although there were lapses in some specifics—he could see question marks near a specific date but a confirmation beneath that something had actually happened in January, for instance—her notes were incredibly complete.

She was handing over to him a treasure trove of information on his most hated enemy.

He glanced up at her as she stood beside the table, her arms crossed over her chest. That same impression he'd had when she'd opened the door—of a slim frame gone gaunt—was still there, but beneath it he saw rigid strength and determination to get through whatever was staring her dead in the face. "How many of these are there?" Noah tapped on one of the legal pads.

"Six." Her arms remained resolutely folded. "One for each of the six months we were dating."

Noah had no idea why, but the word *dating* stuck somewhere deep in his chest. Which was ridiculous since he knew damn well Shayne had dated Statler. More, that she'd been intimately involved with the man.

Why did that chafe so badly?

If she was as innocent as she claimed—and these notepads added one more of those tick boxes his mind seemed insistent on tallying up—then she was a victim of Statler's betrayal, too. Just like the Bureau. Just like the men and women who worked day in and day out under Rick's leadership.

Emotional betrayal. Physical betrayal. Professional betrayal. Statler had done it all, carving a deep wound into the department and the men and women who'd looked up to him and his leadership.

He knew himself well enough to know his mind

would chew on all of it, so Noah deliberately pushed it aside. He'd worry on it later.

For now, he had something new to consider as he hunted Statler down.

Flipping through the legal pads, he reviewed the dates on each entry. The timing and notes were a fit for the same window of events he'd built on his own. Statler had transferred him out of the Midnight Pass field office and up to Fort Worth, under the guise of a promotion, nine months ago. Noah hadn't been in The Pass for long, but he had covered the kidnapping of Midnight Pass PD detective Belle Granger. She'd ultimately been the one to trap her captain after discovering he was the one murdering drug runners as vengeance for his own son's death by an overdose years before.

After that incident, Statler had come in claiming that a federal presence was not only warranted but necessary. And then he'd pushed Noah out with the promotion, making a big fuss in the process. Although he'd never doubted his ability to handle a case or considered himself undeserving of a career milestone, something had never sat well with him about the way everything had gone down.

That feeling had only been reinforced when he'd arrived in Fort Worth and the IT department didn't even know about the transfer.

It had been a little thing—a nuisance, really—but it had stuck, burrowing deep as Noah bided his time in Fort Worth. Oh, he'd been plenty busy. A larger territory and a much bigger population meant he had more than enough on his plate.

But he wasn't quite ready to give up that insistent jangle that refused to quiet in the back of his mind. Why had he been removed so quickly?

That question had nagged at him long enough that he'd finally begun to look for more.

Any missed details or the opposite, the oversharing of minute details in reports as a way to pad the materials and distract from the minimal intel actually gathered. A review of ops run out of the Midnight Pass field office, looking for patterns or clues to what was really happening. It had taken some time, but even Rick couldn't fully hide his actions, especially from someone tenacious enough to look for the small, inevitable holes. Now he had Shayne's notes. Even in a casual skim, he noticed they were like a mirror to his own.

"How long did it take you to do this?"

"A few weeks. Since I found out Rick escaped and I decided to hole up here. I was going stir-crazy and realized that this was something I could do to keep myself busy."

"What else have you done?"

She stared down at the legal pads, for the first time not really meeting his gaze. "Not much. I've been sleeping a lot."

"Where?"

"Under my desk. With the door locked."

Noah filed that news away, the idea that she'd spent so much time in sleep suggested she was battling some serious depression as an aftereffect of the kidnapping. It was understandable, even if the thought of her holed up here alone left that raw, achy feeling dead center in his chest once more.

Whatever else he discovered today, that needed to stop. He was putting an end to it, here and now. "Sounds uncomfortable. Which is why we're going to find you a new place to bunk down."

That seemed to stop her, the head of steam he saw flushing her cheekbones dying on a hard exhale. "You will?"

"Of course." He kept his gaze level with hers, the wariness in those blue eyes easy to read. "You're not staying here."

"What if I want to?"

"Too bad. I'm not going to leave you here."

"Why do you care, anyway? It was your organization that left me with no other choice." She finally took a seat, some of that anger fading as she got out what she'd obviously needed to say.

"We could have helped if you'd asked."

"That's BS and you know it. You all think I'm working with him. Well, I'm not looking to prove myself to a bunch of suspicious jerks who refuse to listen to me."

"I listened to you."

"Because it was your job. I know you don't believe me."

Since he'd had that very thought himself not more than a few hours before, Noah could hardly argue with her.

But what if she was telling the truth?

It was as easy to run through guilty scenarios as it was innocent ones. After restacking the legal pads, one on top of another, he folded his hands on the treasure trove and gave her his full attention.

"Go ahead then. Prove it to me."

Rick Statler crouched down behind the earthmoving equipment and wondered where the lazy slobs who were supposed to be running it all had vanished to. It was the middle of the afternoon. On a Wednesday.

Not that he was in a position to complain. He was doing his level best to stay hidden, and if a bunch of people wanted to knock off the job for a late lunch and leave large equipment out in the open, creating an easy surveillance position, who was he to argue.

He'd been watching Shayne's house off and on for the better part of ten days. It had taken him that long to surface from his escape from the inept junior agents holding him. His leg and side were still a frigging mess, but he was at least mobile. And he was pretty sure he'd fought off the infection that had hit after Ryder Durant's dog had done a number on him.

"Damn mutt," he muttered to himself, thinking the highly trained animal was just an ignorant mongrel. Ryder had always taken such pride in that dog, and after meeting the business end of the K-9's teeth, Statler had to admit that the pride was well-placed.

He'd had plenty of time to think about that fact as he waited for Shayne to come home. It had been last night, as he was doing one more stakeout, that it had finally hit him. He hadn't seen Shayne yet because she was lying low somewhere.

Which, if he were operating at optimal capacity, he'd have realized, but damn it, those bites just weren't healing fast enough. Even with the antibiotics the Feds were kind enough to pump him full of, his wounds were itchy and raw, the skin puckered and painful as he healed.

He hadn't seen her since that last day in the safe house. He hadn't wanted to subdue her like that, but he couldn't afford to have her go on the run before he could ascertain if she was with him or not. Their relationship had progressed nicely, and he was pretty sure she'd stick with him if he told her what sort of future they could have together. Or he could have gotten them there, with a few more weeks of work on their relationship.

It was a risk, but she was worth it.

Why had it taken him so long to recognize it? He'd been so damn worried about getting in too deep that he hadn't recognized he was in over his head until it was too late.

If only he'd recognized it sooner. Before his contacts had gone sideways. Before Vasily Baslikova had caught wind of his work and decided Rick could join him or perish.

Before his team had finally decided to put some scrutiny on his actions.

Ignoring the stab of pain that only added to how bad he physically felt, he focused on the recently built office building across the way. The pain was his only excuse for not considering that Shayne might have hunkered down and gone to ground in her new office. She'd only bought into it recently, excited by the prospect of moving her expanding business to an office space. He'd listened with half an ear, but she'd gone on and on about it long enough that it really shouldn't have taken him so long to come up with it.

Rick kept low to the ground but looked around to see if the work crew had left anything behind he could use. Although the equipment was in place, the crew had done a good job of locking up their tools. He couldn't find a damn thing that might prove effective in heading into that office after Shayne.

As he crept back toward his hiding spot, he saw a small glint of metal flash in the sun. There, just be-

neath the edge of a tire. Ignoring the pain in his side
that still lingered despite the course of antibiotics and
a second round of stitches he'd needed to do himself,
Rick stooped low, his fingers closing over the metal.

He came back up with the keys to the earthmover.

Talk about a jobsite violation. But damn if it didn't
work to his advantage. What did he care if some lazy
slob got his ass handed to him by management?

He had a way in.

With one last glance at the building across the way,
Rick reached up and unlocked the door to the earthmover. There really was no question about it. Shayne
was inside that building.

Now all he needed to do was set a trap to get her out.

Prove it to me.

Noah's words still lingered between them as Shayne
considered the man, back arrow straight, in one of her
office kitchen chairs.

Where to start?

The beginning was a good place but also opened up
a vulnerability she wasn't crazy about divulging. She
didn't talk about her family to anyone. She hadn't even
mentioned them to Rick beyond minimal references, a
small miracle she'd been grateful for every single day
since the kidnapping.

"What do you want to know?"

Noah leaned forward and reached for her hand. The
move was so unexpected, Shayne allowed him the lib-
erty, realizing her mistake only when her fingers cra-
dled gently beneath his large, strong ones. "Whatever
you want to tell me."

A ball of emotion lodged almost immediately in her

throat, that gentle touch a surprise. She nearly bent forward at the simple kindness. But his light squeeze of her fingers had the opposite effect.

That ball of emotion still stuck hard in her throat, but something stronger took its place.

Strength.

Support.

And the possibility—even though it was only a tiny glimmer—that someone might believe her.

"I told you I dated Rick for about six months."

"Right. So that would be October?"

"September. Six months before the kidnapping."

"Of course." Noah dropped her hand before gesturing toward the chair. "Now it's April."

She took the understanding he seemingly offered and started in.

"We met at a bar. I don't usually meet men that way, but there was something about him that caught my attention. He's attractive." There was a slight darkening in Noah's deep brown gaze, but she resolved to think on it later. "In a self-confident, larger-than-life way."

It was how she'd thought of him at the time. That sort of man didn't usually appeal to her, often turning out to be too much of an insufferable jerk once the conversation started, but Rick Statler had been different. He spoke of starting his career in Boston and how much of a culture shock it was moving down to Texas. He'd been polite and interested in her work, asking her real questions about what she did instead of brushing off her ambition or her own drive to succeed.

In the end, he'd said all the right things and been all the right things she was looking for.

When he'd followed up and asked her out on a date, she'd gone. Willingly.

She told Noah all of that, establishing how they'd met and the timeline of the early days of their relationship. Although it embarrassed her now, she spoke of how she'd felt, fluttery inside and believing that someone actually saw her, not the exterior package.

"You've mentioned that a few times now." Noah stopped her, probing a bit. "The way Rick wasn't like other men who hit on you in bars and then you mentioned how he saw you. What do you mean by that?"

The question only proved what Shayne already knew. Noah Ross was frightfully observant, and little missed his radar. At the laser focus in his gaze, Shayne amended the thought.

Nothing escaped the man.

This only made her that much more irritated that she hadn't thought through that part of her story a bit better.

"It sounds pompous."

"It's not pompous if it's true."

She considered how to play this. World-weary or innocent, neither exactly fit. So she opted for her truth instead. "I'm usually hit on for one reason and one reason only."

"Aren't most women?" Although his lips barely moved, she didn't miss the light smile that tinged his dark gaze.

"Most women aren't beauty pageant contestants, either."

"That's why you get asked out?"

"Usually. Men don't know the pageant part, but they do notice the exterior package. And they give little consideration to what's beneath it."

"I'm sure it doesn't take long before they do."

He would think that.

Was it because he was so observant? Or something else? A small part of her—the silly part that still had a few sparks of hope left—wanted to believe that was just who he was.

Noah.

Strong. Secure. Trustworthy. Innately a gentleman and good man.

A bigger part of her, though, was determined to squelch any bit of that hope beneath the heel of her very learned boot. "You'd be surprised. Your gender looks first and considers later." She snorted. "Or never."

That same internal urge that told her to trust him knew the simple fact, too, that Noah had noticed her.

While she'd caught his appreciative gaze during those long days of questioning after the kidnapping, she'd always seen his compassion, too.

He listened to her when she'd answered question after question—many of them the same, only rephrased in endlessly different ways. But he'd also answered her when she'd had questions of her own.

His bureau colleagues hadn't been quite as forth-coming, but Noah had tried. The things he could an-swer, he did.

And the rest…

Well, she'd set out to find those answers on her own.

She was no one's fool, and that was the biggest pain in her relationship with Rick. She wasn't—

Something sharp and high-pitched echoed through the room, the very floor beneath her shaking with the impact. "What is that?"

The words were barely out when Noah stood and

raced around the table, grabbing her by the arm. "A problem and we need to move."

"But what is it?"

The walls shook around her as another raging wave of energy seemed to slam into the very fabric of the building. The impact reverberated around her seconds before the lights winked out. The kitchen was on an interior wall, and the entire room went black, minimal light filtering in from the outer office.

Abstractly, she registered Noah's hand over her forearm as he dragged her toward the door. "We need to get out of here!"

"What's happening?"

"I don't know, but we can't stay here." He shifted, wrapping an arm around her shoulders. Shayne heard the distinct rustle of papers as he grabbed the legal pads with his free hand. "Let's go."

"Wait! I need my stuff."

His voice was urgent against her ear as he pulled her tight against his chest, just as another hard slam reverberated through the room. "What stuff?"

"My tech."

"We need to go."

Blind fear at being left without her lifelines whipped through her with the same force as the shaking walls around them. "I need my things."

Before he could stop her, she slunk low, dropping beneath his arm. Although the lack of light made it almost too dark to see, she had the benefit of two solid weeks in the small, confining space to guide her toward her office.

The bag that held her computer, cell phone and tablet

lay on the floor beside her desk. She just needed to run in and run out.

That was her last thought as one final hit slammed against the walls, echoing with the sound of metal scraping against metal, falling in on itself. Shayne vaguely registered the sound, her focus totally on the bag in her office.

She let out a loud, agonizing scream as the roof collapsed in on her.

Chapter 3

"Shayne!"

Her name—and only her name—tore from his lips as Noah fought through the dust and the shaking floor as he attempted to follow Shayne's path through the dark.

Why hadn't he grabbed her and held on?

Why did he let her go?

Whatever she'd deemed so important couldn't possibly be more important than her life.

But he had let her go, even as he struggled to understand what was happening around them.

The walls continued to reverberate, and though an instinctive part of him wondered if it was an earthquake, his finely honed police sense screamed intruder. And one in particular was at the top of his list.

Rick Statler.

Shayne's scream had him on the move, and he continued working his way through the ash and rubble that littered the path from the kitchen to her office. He only had the benefit of broad impressions of the total office layout from when he'd walked in. Noah stilled. Everything told him to keep moving, but he employed a tactic he'd learned early on in the Bureau.

A moment of stillness often paid far bigger dividends than action without purpose.

Reorienting himself, he pictured the path they'd taken to the kitchen from the open lobby area. His mind followed the memory, the doors to rooms along the hallway that had suggested a conference room followed by office space. And the door at the end of the hall that intimated the boss stayed there.

Mental map in hand, Noah followed the path. Shayne yelled again, but this time to get his attention instead of in shock. He took heart in the distinction and moved determinedly on. "I hear you! Cover your head and nose and mouth if you can!"

Ash and thick dust filled the air, and he pulled his shirt up over his nose and mouth to protect his lungs as much as he could. Noah knew the next few minutes were crucial. They had no idea how much damage the building had sustained, and it was possible fire or a further collapse would come next.

They had to get out, even if what was waiting for them was as big a danger as the collapsing office.

Stepping gingerly over the rubble, he moved step-by-step closer to that back office. The damage in this part of the building wasn't as bad, but that didn't mean they were safe. What it did imply was that the destructive force was coming from a specific direction.

The front of the building.

"Noah! Back here!" Shayne appeared through the rubble before him, a fine white mist raining down from the ceiling tiles.

He took her in, her slim form and blond hair covered in a layer of white that matched the ceiling. A backpack was slung over her shoulder, and her gaze was focused as she gingerly picked her way through the destruction.

She was okay.

Now she had to stay that way.

"Are you hurt?"

"Several ceiling tiles fell on me. They didn't feel great, but I was able to keep my balance and keep moving."

A heavy echo rumbled from the front of the building again. The impact was fainter back here but still a problem, especially as Noah looked back and realized the entire front entrance to her office had caved in." Put those in your bag." He handed her the legal pads.

She began to move with him. "Where are you going?"

"Wait! Don't follow me yet." Noah hollered out the order, unconcerned it would be heeded, and retraced his steps back toward the kitchen.

He came face-to-face with a wall of rubble blocking the front door, ensuring he wasn't leaving the way he came in.

Working his way back to Shayne, Noah moved as fast as he could. The insistent banging into the outer wall had stopped, but he held little hope it would stay that way for long.

Shayne had her nose and mouth covered as he'd instructed and waved him back to her. He made it to her, his hands searching her shoulders before he could check the impulse. "You sure you're okay?"

Her blue eyes, bloodshot from the dust in the air, were steady on him. "I'm fine. But we need to find a way out of here."

"The front's blocked."

"There's no back entrance. And my office windows are heavy double-paned glass."

Noah thought of the bulletproof windows in his Fort Worth office and offered up a silent prayer of thanks that a regular-issue office building in south Texas didn't require the same. Energy-efficient window choices, yes. Bulletproof glass? Nope. Not worth the expense.

She gestured him back into her office. She was already hefting an office chair in her hands when he laid a hand on her arm.

With a grim smile, he took his government-issued weapon firmly in hand and aimed for the windows. "Cover your face and put your head down."

Those blue eyes were wide and solemn before she nodded, moving to the wall and covering her face as he'd asked.

Satisfied she was as protected as possible, he dug his sunglasses out to protect his eyes and lined up the shot.

The glass cracked on one.

It moaned on two.

And shattered on three.

Shayne waited for the heavy wave of shattering glass to subside before she stood from her protective crouched position against the wall. The thought might have been misplaced, but she had a very severe vision of sitting opposite her insurance agent and attempting to explain this one.

There was no time to consider the man's aged scowl or even the possibility that she'd ever see her office again.

They needed to move.

Now.

Noah was already at the window, dragging hard on the shades before kicking the small shards still in the frame with his foot. "I can't get it all."

Shayne eyed the empty windows and remembered the curtain samples she'd looked at a few weeks ago. "Hang on."

"Shayne!"

She ignored him as she ran to the small credenza on the far side of the room. The samples were just where she'd left them, and she lifted the gaudy brocade, way happier to see the material now than when she'd stuffed it in the drawer.

"We'll use this."

Noah grabbed the free end of the curtains and helped her spread them out. They worked quickly, doubling the heavy material, then doubling it again to provide as much cushioning as possible.

Although she was on the first floor, the drop out the back of the building was more than a single story. Midnight Pass and the surrounding towns were built on craggy land, varied in elevation, making it desirable to criminals since the land provided natural depressions to hide in.

That was what ensured a twelve-foot drop out the back window of her office now.

Shayne stared down at it and imagined the stacked electronics equipment in her backpack.

Did she dare jump? What if she crushed some of it?

"Can you do it?" Noah asked.

"I can do it, but I can't risk losing my equipment."

Another violent slam echoed from the front of the building. Shayne heard the heavy groan of the building and felt the way her office shook.

Noah glanced at the backpack she had in hand. "That it?" Before she could answer, he was already taking it from her. "We need to move."

"But it's a steep drop out that window."

"I know. But there's no other choice." Noah had one leg over the sill, then the other before holding tight. Before she could even let out a breath, he was out the window and hanging from the covered sill. "Toss the bag out to me as soon as I'm down."

Then he was gone, his hands vanishing from the top of the curtain-covered sill as if they'd never been there.

Shayne quickly scrambled to look out, his solid form falling into a crouch before he stood again. "Throw it!"

She eyed the backpack once more and prayed he was as sharp and solid as he looked.

She let the heavy pack drop.

A part of her wanted to watch, curious to see how accurate he'd be, but the bigger part of her knew that she needed to focus on getting herself out.

Ignoring the drop from the window that awaited her—and the insistently sunny thought that she'd loved that view and had signed an early lease because she wanted the office that overlooked the ravine—she tossed one leg over the sill, just as Noah had done. She hesitated to swing her other leg, the image of falling out whipping a wave of ice through her midsection.

What if she broke something?

Noah's shoulders might be impressive, but there was

no way they were strong enough to catch a full-grown woman dropping on top of him.

Worse, the predator after them—and she knew to her marrow that it was Rick—had determination and a willingness for destruction on his side. What if she did get hurt? They'd be sitting ducks if she landed in the ravine with a broken leg. Or worse, a broken back.

"Shayne! You need to get out of there!"

Noah's holler floated up from the ground below, and she wanted to trust him. She wanted to believe that he knew best.

But he hadn't helped her before today. In fact, he'd arrived here looking for guilt.

Did she dare trust him now?

The walls shuddered once more, and Shayne slipped, her body slamming hard on the window frame and the sill between her legs. A cry spilled from her lips as she struggled to right herself, her hands gripping tight to the window frame. Although Noah had gotten most of the glass, a few shards still poked out at the edge of the curtain fabric and her wrist stung as one of them pressed sharp and hard at the edge of her flesh.

"Shayne! Get out of there!"

That same wash of cold that had curled in her belly spread out, seeping into her bones. A fear unlike anything she'd ever known took root in her soul, and somehow all she could focus on was the pain of that glass at her wrist.

And the fear that any further movement would cause it to slice right through, ending her leap before the ground could.

"Shayne!"

Dimly, Shayne heard Noah's scream, the forceful,

commanding tones that she imagined brooked no arguments. Even with the knowledge that he led good men and women day in and day out, under the most stressful of circumstances, she couldn't force herself to move.

"Shayne Erickson. Listen to me." When she only continued to hold on, her body convulsing in cold shudders, he spoke even louder. "Shayne! You can do this. You've been through so much. You escaped a cold-blooded madman. You stared down a room full of embarrassed, dead-eyed federal agents and met them unblinking stare for unblinking stare. You've started your own company. You've managed this all on your own. You can do this!"

His words were strangely hypnotic, everything he described coming to vivid life in her mind's eye.

Those endless hours when Rick had her and Arden Reynolds locked up.

The endless days that came after when the FBI pressed her for anything—even the tiniest detail—she might know.

The endless weeks since as she tried to find some shred of her former life.

And for the first time since it all began, she wondered what she was fighting so hard for. No one believed her. And no one really cared that she was on the run. Her sister certainly didn't, and their parents were both gone, long dead and unable to care.

"Shayne Erickson! You will climb over that sill, and you will get down here!"

Noah's voice punctured through her dismal thoughts.

"There is a madman mere feet from where you are, and I'm not letting you go like this. You don't deserve what has happened to you. And you sure as hell don't deserve what is going to happen to you if he gets through that wall."

Trust Noah.

Her hands trembled and still held tight to the sill, but Shayne risked a glance at the shard that pressed against her wrist. Blood had pooled on the glass, but she could see the cut from the shard was embedded in the thin flesh at the side of her wrist, not the center.

Not arterial.

Could she let go?

Did she have a choice?

The wall shuddered once more, the ceiling tiles crumbling like stale bread, crumbs falling like sheets of snow to her office floor.

With careful movements, she pulled her wrist from harm's way, resetting her hands more tightly on the window frame. Her wrist still throbbed from the cut, but she could wrap it after.

After she let go.

With the foremost thought that she really didn't have any other choice, Shayne pulled the leg still inside the room over the sill. Noah was on the other side.

And he might even believe her.

Maybe it would be enough.

Noah breathed his first easy breath as he saw Shayne's other leg come over the sill, her body dropping as she hung by her hands. He nearly hollered additional words but knew they were meaningless. He'd achieved his objective.

She was out.

Now he had to focus on the problem that awaited him once she was on the ground. He'd already set her backpack far enough away that even if she rolled after the fall, she wasn't at risk of rolling over the equipment she'd so carefully preserved.

The next few minutes were crucial.

She might be over the sill, but she still wasn't on the ground. But hell and damn, the woman was a warrior. And this small hiccup aside, she continued to fill him with shock and a hell of a lot of awe.

Shayne Erickson was no one's fool.

Nor was she an airhead with nothing between her ears but fluff.

She owned her own tech-consulting business, which had been given a solid stamp of approval from the Bureau's geek squad. She held her own no matter who questioned her. And she was sharp enough to recognize that her future safety depended on helping them catch Statler.

It would have been easy enough to sit back and leave the work to Noah and his team, but she'd taken the time. And she'd understood that copious pages of notes and dates and impressions could go a long way toward helping them put Statler away for good.

Yet here she was, panic setting in as she realized it was all coming to a head.

He hadn't seen any inkling of it while they ate lunch, but something had distinctly changed after he'd dropped to the ground.

She'd had time to think? No, he corrected himself. Time to realize.

She'd spent the past weeks alone with her thoughts, thinking through every angle and an endless number of scenarios.

Thinking wasn't Shayne's problem.

The realization that she'd put her trust in the wrong man was what sat squarely at the heart of her panic.

He couldn't give her a reason to doubt herself again.

Moving forward, he took in the slim form that hung from the window. Her feet were about six feet off the ground. Not so far that she was likely to break something, but far enough that she risked a tough landing.

"I'm right here, Shayne. You can do this."

"I can't." The words were small and quiet, drifting on the wavering breeze that still carried the sound of the building shuddering from Statler's attack. He literally heard the building groaning and knew there wasn't a lot of time.

"You're strong, Shayne. So strong."

"I used to think so."

"I know so."

His words seemed to float away, an ineffective weapon against the fear that had her in its claws. She hung there, stuck in an odd limbo state that offered neither safety nor freedom.

It only left her stuck.

Noah racked his brain for some way through the problem. He'd believed going first would give her the courage to follow, especially once she saw how easy the drop was. He hadn't calculated on the intense pressure of the past few weeks picking this exact moment to catch up with her.

It was only as he stared up at her that the answer became clear.

Should he use it? More, did he dare give her access to the vulnerability that lurked in his soul to this day?

"I know what it means to be stuck, Shayne."

She still hung there, but he thought he saw some

movement, her head tilting toward him. It wasn't much, but at this point the physical challenge of holding herself like that had to be taking its toll.

"I know how it hurts to realize that you've been played for a fool."

Her head tilted again, as if she was trying to see him—to focus on him—as he spoke.

"And I know how it forces you to question yourself and all the self-belief you hold locked tight inside."

"I was so wrong."

Once again, her words weren't more than a whisper, but as they floated down to him, Noah heard the truth as loud as a gong. Rick Statler had betrayed her in every way, and now she was stuck puzzling through the aftermath.

"Come on, baby. Let go. You'll be okay. I promise."

Her hands flexed against the sill, and for a fleeting instant Noah didn't think he'd gotten through.

And then she was floating through the air, falling toward him.

Noah had little time to react, moving instinctively toward her but not nearly fast enough to intercept her. She had enough wherewithal to brace for the fall, moving into an immediate crouch once she hit the ground. He dived toward her, holding her tight and rolling with her body wrapped in his, cushioning any additional impact.

He felt the sobs before he heard them, her entire body shuddering against him. With as much gentleness as he could muster—and without breaking his hold on her—he rolled them to a stop a few feet from her backpack, crooning to her as he slowed their momentum. "Shhh now. Shhh. It's okay."

Her body only shook harder, the force of her sobs taking over.

"Shhh now."

Noah knew how adrenaline worked and was well aware it was a reaction almost beyond the body. The sheer force of an event simply had to be felt. No amount of training or preparation or even rational thinking could stop it.

Sooner or later, the body took over from the mind, forcing that release of pressure and stress.

He understood it, but in this exact moment, he couldn't give any of it the runway it needed to begin the healing.

"Shayne. We need to move."

His words had no effect, her body shaking more at his insistence they needed to get out of there.

The building shook behind them again, and Noah acknowledged they were out of time. There was no way they'd come this far only to be caught in the falling debris of a somehow-weaponized building.

Standing, he got the backpack and slipped it on his shoulders, then bent back to her. He mentally cycled through his extensive training but discarded every bit of it and went with instinct. Reaching down, he picked her up, gentle yet firm in his movements. Her knees quivered but didn't buckle as she stood before him.

"Shayne!" Keeping his voice crisp and sharp, he kept his gaze laser focused on her dull blue one. "You will move. You will follow me. And you will not give Rick Statler one single moment of advantage."

Something shifted in that gaze.

He saw a little bit of acknowledgment and maybe even a little bit of hope.

And a hell of a lot of determination.

"I'm not going to let that bastard win."

"Damn straight, we're not." He layered every bit of force he possessed on the *we're* part and reached for her hand.

He finally took an easy breath as she clasped his fingers in hers and squeezed. "Let's go."

Chapter 4

Come on, baby. Let go. You'll be okay. I promise.

Shayne couldn't stop those words from cycling over and over through her mind as she and Noah crossed the rugged land behind her office building.

Or what was left of her office building.

Baby.

It was an endearment. More, it was one used with a lover.

Hadn't Rick used it often?

Even as that thought left a small shiver rippling through her midsection, Shayne had to admit that coming from Noah, it felt different.

The endearment had been encouraging. Supportive. And in that moment, proof that he believed in her.

It got you moving out the window, she reminded herself. An essential truth that caused embarrassment to course through her system, beating in time with the adrenaline. It pulsed through her body like the heartbeat fluttering where her palm lay pressed against Noah's.

He'd come for her.

That knowledge had been faint, underneath the frustration and anger at her situation, but found room in her overtaxed thoughts.

Noah Ross had come for her. And unlike everyone else in her life since Rick's crimes had been uncovered, Noah actually believed what she was saying.

Or he did a damn fine job of making her think so.

The thought was discordant and at odds with the man who'd brought her lunch and protected her as her office collapsed under the deranged actions of a mad criminal. A man who'd seemed genuinely interested in what she had to share and took her detailed notes seriously. A man who, even now, was helping her to safety.

Was it wrong to think that Noah Ross might really believe her?

That someone finally did?

With those questions still echoing in her mind, she keyed in on the tall man cutting across the rocky land, his hand firmly holding hers as the other effortlessly kept her backpack over his shoulder.

He'd already called in the situation with Rick, his pace unrelenting even as he gave quick orders, followed by a set of directions, to his team.

She waited until he'd hung up, his phone stuffed back in his pocket, before asking, "Where are we going?"

"Away, first." He tossed a quick look over his shoulder, his smile encouraging even as he kept their rapid pace.

"And after we're away?" Shayne knew they'd get wherever "away" was eventually, but questions had begun coursing from her mind straight out of her mouth, and she didn't seem to have the willpower to hold them back. It was like she'd woken up from her catatonic state and now couldn't stop asking questions.

"We'll reassess then. Backup should be here by then, too."

"Do you think Rick's following us?"

Noah's stride remained relentlessly steady, oddly matched to his evenly paced words. "He was still banging the hell out of the building by the time we took off. And he's injured. I'd say that gives us a decent head start. It also gives law enforcement a shot at him."

A decent head start.

But how much of an actual advantage was that against a monster? Rick had proven he wasn't going down easily, his escape from the FBI a flashing signal he'd reached the point where he had nothing to lose. And then there was today's show of force.

Real proof he hadn't forgotten about her.

Hadn't that been her fondest wish? That she was just some stupid shill Rick had hidden behind.

Yes, she'd believed herself in love—or at least falling toward it—but over the past several weeks, since his crimes had come to light, she'd used her anger at his deception.

Channeled it, really.

Now she had to accept that she was a part of this. Not just collateral damage, but a part of the whole.

Shayne mentally shook her head at that thought. At the unreality of it all.

And, not for the first time since discovering who he really was, she was forced to question just how deep Rick's connections went. He was supposed to be in

FBI custody, rotting away in a federal prison. Yet he'd escaped.

How many other corrupt federal agents were in on his work?

For all their eager questions directed at her, Shayne had to wonder how hard the Feds were looking in their own house. While she didn't know all the details—everyone had clammed up each time she posed a question of her own—she'd figured out enough.

And the biggest detail no one wanted to admit was that Rick had run an evil enterprise for himself using the authority of the FBI but flying under its radar.

She might work for herself, but she knew that sort of insult didn't go well in any sort of organization, let alone one as bureaucratic as the FBI.

"You okay back there?"

Noah's question penetrated her thoughts, and she glanced up. Although he'd looked back quickly when speaking, his focus had returned to the ground as they navigated the land. They hadn't stopped moving, but they had gotten into something of a rhythm, keeping low to the craggy landscape and stepping carefully through the rocky land to avoid piles of sliding stones or sharp, jagged edges.

"I'm fine."

She might not be, but it didn't really matter anymore. Right now, getting away was all that mattered.

"We've gone at least a mile. I think we can find a place to stop for a few minutes."

"Are you sure?" Shayne glanced around, assessing where they were and trying to visualize it in her mind. The front of her building was accessible from the highway that ran outside Midnight Pass, but they'd been moving away from the building and the highway.

"I think so. At least so we can stop and get our bearings."

More grateful than she could say for the lunch Noah had brought along with him to her office, she realized that while she'd welcome a break, at least she wasn't starving. "I think we're headed in the direction of Mesa Creek."

Noah stopped and gently laid the backpack on the ground before making a full circle as he took in their surroundings. Vast acres of land spread out around them, but she could still make out the faint, distant sounds of the highway.

The town of Mesa Creek was about twenty minutes away from Midnight Pass, and while she didn't typically travel there through unpopulated wildlands, her sense of direction suggested they were definitely headed toward the bigger town where she and her friends often went for a meal or a night out.

Where she and Rick used to go out for an evening.

Shutting down the direction of her thoughts, she was pleased when Noah picked up the conversation, oblivious to the seemingly ever-present pressure of her memories.

"I stayed at a hotel in Mesa Creek when I first came back down to The Pass."

"Why did you come back? You weren't reassigned here, right?"

"No, I wasn't. But I knew something wasn't right."

He shrugged before dropping down to the ground and gesturing for her to do the same. "I was settled down here in the field office for a few years. I was building a solid team and making a good name for myself. The Grantham case was a big win for us, as well as for the Midnight Pass PD, and it felt like I was doing good work."

It was good work, albeit sad work, Shayne knew. She might not know the inner workings of law enforcement, but everyone in Midnight Pass remembered what had gone down a little over a year ago with their town police captain, Russ Grantham. His insistence on taking justice into his own hands, killing drug dealers in a twisted attempt to avenge his son's death from an overdose, had been big news.

The fact that Russ had nearly taken down one of Midnight Pass PD's own, Belle Granger, now Belle Reynolds, before taking his own life had only added to the sadness of the entire story. A sad story that had a bit of a happy ending when Belle found her way back to her first love, Tate Reynolds, and when Grantham's daughter, Reese, found her way to love with Tate's brother Hoyt.

"You were part of the team that saved Belle."

Noah smiled faintly. "Belle saved herself, if we're being fair, but yes, I was part of it all. And then to be yanked unceremoniously from The Pass a few weeks later never sat well."

"A promotion?"

"It was certainly positioned that way. Rick showed up and all of a sudden, I'm being moved out of The Pass and up to a bigger office in Dallas–Fort Worth."

"But you earned it."

"I did and it meant a lot. A heck of a lot. But the speed of it all and the way it happened, so abruptly, never sat well with me."

"Sometimes opportunities just happen that way."

"And sometimes you're blindsided for a reason." His dark gaze shuttered, and for the oddest moment, Shayne had the impression Noah wasn't talking about work or his unceremonious removal from Midnight Pass.

That idea lodged somewhere deep, even as the cadence of his voice never lost that steady, even, "trust me" quality she associated with him.

But it stuck a hard landing when he neatly changed the subject.

"I didn't intend for us to head this way, but now that we are, I think the best thing we can do is get you into a hotel in Mesa Creek and have you lay low for a few days."

Noah mentally counted off how long it would take for Shayne to explode with agitation. He'd arbitrarily given her ten seconds.

She was already taking off a layer of skin in seven.

"What the hell, Noah? What do you take me for?"

"A smart woman who should lay low until the FBI, in conjunction with local law enforcement, takes care of Rick Statler."

"The same FBI who let him run amok in the first place?" She shook her head and was already scrambling to stand up. "I'll take my chances on my own."

He reached for her hand, surprised the gesture was enough to get her to still. And he jolted, if he were honest with himself, from the soft feel of her skin beneath his palm. "You need to let me do my job."

"And you need to read the damn room. I'm not sitting around, in FBI custody, while your prize ghost continues to stay off the radar as he hunts me down.

You said you called for backup, but how do you know they're not just going to help him stay off the radar and get farther away?"

"I trust the people coming to help us."

"That doesn't mean I do. A sentiment I'm well aware goes both ways."

He considered how to play things. Normally, he'd defend his FBI teammates with everything he was, but Shayne's anger and fear were not only fair but accurate.

Rick had escaped.

And since they hadn't plugged the leak that had allowed that to happen, the FBI did have a situation that needed handling. But he also trusted Ryder Durant and Brady Renner implicitly, and they were the colleagues coming to help.

"Ryder Durant has as big a stake as I do in seeing Statler taken down. And the other field operative with him is one of the best men I know. So no, I don't need to rethink my decision."

He might be sure to his core that his call was the right one, but he was still puzzled by the odd direction of their conversation.

And sometimes you're blindsided for a reason.

Where had that come from?

Although their conversation while walking had veered surprisingly close to memories he actively ignored, he was more surprised those memories had surfaced at all. His thoughts had swerved dangerously close to Lindsey of late, and he wasn't sure what to do about it other than push through.

Shayne's safety was his priority, and there wasn't room for anything else. Especially not deeply buried memories that had no place in his present. It was imperative he get her to a place where Statler couldn't find her.

He'd considered their next move as they walked away from the destroyed office building and kept circling around the plans he could make to keep her safe and out of the way. He should have expected her skepticism.

"I'm not asking you to go this alone, Shayne. My office can help you."

"Like they have so far? No way." She shook her head, pulling her hand from where it was still captured in his grip. "All you're doing is signing my death warrant if you try to put me into FBI custody. The man wielding an earthmover as a weapon of destruction a mere hour ago should have clued you in."

"Give me a little more credit."

"Why?" The anger that had swelled up over and over since he'd found her in her office seemed to deflate like a balloon. "Why should I give you any more credit than you've given me?"

"I haven't—" He stopped himself, recognizing he not only didn't have a leg to stand on, but that he worked for an organization that had refused to give her any benefit of the doubt. "Your situation has been unfortunate."

"Unfortunate?" Her laugh was bitter, and the darkness that swirled around her was at odds with the vision of airy lightness that surrounded her. "That's one way to put it."

He'd observed humans and human nature long enough to know that what a person looked like had very little to do with how they acted. But he had to admit Shayne's beauty-queen good looks and regal bearing risked masking the truth to the casual observer. She was an incredibly bright woman with a strong sense of self and the world around her.

And he was embarrassed to admit that he hadn't put those personality traits at the top of his list.

What he and his colleagues had initially suspected—that she was either in league with Statler or had been too besotted to know that he was manipulating her—was hardly the right approach. Hadn't those notebooks proven that? She had used everything at her disposal to help and to make some attempt to figure out what had happened since Statler had come into her life.

The work was invaluable.

"Yes," he finally said. "It is unfortunate. You deserved better than being betrayed by a piece of trash like Rick Statler. Any relationship steeped in betrayal is hurtful."

Her gaze narrowed, but she appeared to give him the runway to finish his thoughts. "Why do I hear a *but* in there?"

"There's a big *but*. Any betrayal is hard to get over. But given the criminal implications and the access Rick has had for years to secret information, this is a situation with significant risk."

"Which is exactly my point. If he found me once and if he fooled an entire division of the federal government known for catching bad guys, holing up in a hotel room for a few days hardly feels like a safe solution for me."

"We'll protect you."

"Like you already have? No, Noah." She shook her head. "I've been protecting me. And I'm all I've got."

He considered her and realized that even in his recent rush to give her more credit, he hadn't given her nearly enough.

And with that realization came another.

"Do you have family? Or somewhere you could go?" Before she could debate him on that or dismiss the question again, he added, "We could ensure their protection."

Her gaze searched his, and Noah couldn't ignore the distinct sense he was being sized up. "Even if I did believe the part about our safety, it's moot. My parents are both gone."

"Any siblings?"

"Isn't all this in my file?"

"I'm not going to pretend I don't know what you mean. But I'm not sure what any of that has to do with the discussion we're having."

"In the FBI file on me that is no doubt a mile thick by now, it must say that my parents have both been gone for a long time. And you also must know I have a sister who lives outside of Austin. And that we're estran—" She broke off before amending her point. "We rarely talk."

He must have known all of it, but in the moment, he hadn't been able to recollect a single bit about her family. Which was odd and unsettling because he committed his case files to memory, usually after the first read.

So why had he forgotten?

And why did it suddenly seem important to defend his question?

"It probably is in your file. But I'm here. Now. Asking you directly. And family doesn't have to just mean nuclear family."

"So we would or would not put Rick Statler on the list then?"

He'd maintained a fairly even keel up to now. Partially because it was a rhythm and a style that worked

for him and more because it was how he was wired. He
wasn't a big mouth or full of big energy that had to spill
out at every turn. Instead, he chose to focus on his goals
and work like a fiend to accomplish them.

He didn't need applause or fanfare.

Hadn't that been one of the things Lindsey came to
hate about him?

He'd never argued the point with her. Instead, he just
kept on like he always did.

Strong. Sure. Steady.

Which made the heated fire that shot out of his mouth
as much a surprise to him as to Shayne, whose eyes
suddenly widened.

"Bastards who don't deserve a moment of your time
let alone any room in your thoughts don't count. So answer the damn question, Shayne. Do you have someone
you can go to instead of a hotel?"

"No, Noah. I'm on my own."

The admission burned, Shayne admitted to herself.
As sharp as a hornet sting and twice as deep.

She had no one.

Which was also a nasty knock on her sister, who
would do her duty and help, but Shayne couldn't go
there.

Not yet.

Caroline had reached out a few times to see how she
was holding up. Her little sister had checked in with
her in the initial days, after the kidnapping and before
Shayne had gone off the grid with her electronics.

Had Caroline kept asking? Or had the silent treat-
ment been enough to hold her at bay? There was no way
of knowing since Shayne had kept her electronics off.

And even as she let that thought turn over in her mind, Shayne knew it for a lie. She'd never let Caroline get close enough. Not since they'd lost their brother to a freak accident at school and their mom had turned in on herself in grief.

Shayne had done the same, unwilling to engage with her sister for longer than simple platitudes or surface conversation. She'd now spent the majority of her life doing it, and the pattern defined their relationship and created the continued anger that perpetually simmered on low between her and Caroline.

It was also her biggest regret, one that had only magnified as she'd spent the past few weeks alone with her thoughts.

"Then we'll have to come up with plan B."

The heat and fire that had shot out only moments ago had been fully banked, replaced with the calm, steady version of Noah she recognized.

"You mean you're not going to do it anyway?"

"Do what?"

"Lock me up in a hotel room for my own good?"

He frowned and she was surprised by the quick hurt that lined his face in the bright afternoon sunshine. "Contrary to popular belief, the FBI isn't all-powerful. And despite Rick Statler's behavior, we don't act above the law. I have a lot of jurisdiction, but you're not in my custody, Shayne. I hope I haven't given you the impression that you are."

"No. You haven't."

"That doesn't mean I've ignored your situation. I've thought from the beginning that you were one of the keys to solving this. After today, I'm more convinced than ever. I'm not going to apologize for that."

"I'm not asking you to."

"Then what are you asking?"

It was a fair question. One she hadn't actually spent much time thinking about. Oh sure, she was resentful about her situation and her circumstances. Resentful that she seemed to get an outsize set of attention from the FBI, even after being kidnapped and terrorized by a man she thought she cared about.

Thought she loved—

Shayne broke off at that, acknowledging what she hadn't wanted to for so many months. She had cared about Rick while they were dating. She'd enjoyed being in a relationship after a long period of not being in one, and he had certainly been attentive. But if she were honest, she'd never felt they fully clicked.

Sexually they'd been compatible, and she'd had an enjoyable enough time on dates, but she hadn't ever really longed for him when they weren't together. It was silly, and she'd told herself how ridiculous she was being each time that thought crossed her mind.

Yet it had still troubled her.

Shouldn't a woman in love feel more... She mentally shook her head. Just *more*. Wasn't love about more? About needing someone and wanting someone, even when they weren't around?

Or was that the fantasy of it all?

She'd batted that one back and forth in the months she'd dated Rick. That maybe the idea of love was far more powerful than the actual reality of a relationship. And with her family history and her lack of a productive relationship with her only living blood relative, she'd further convinced herself that the great big swelling-music sort of love that you saw in the movies or read about in books wasn't real.

Love might not be real but her instincts were.

A fact she'd finally understood when she'd woken up, blindfolded and chained to a bed in the FBI safe house Rick had commandeered for his own use.

It was the one piece in all of this where she'd finally given herself the benefit of the doubt. Or at least a bit of a pass that maybe her subconscious was working through the puzzle of Rick Statler because there was an actual problem to solve. Not the pop culture nuances of modern romance, but an honest concern that the man wasn't who he said he was.

That he was too good to be true.

Noah still stared at her, his gaze steady as he waited for an answer.

What did she want from Noah?

If any man seemed too good to be true, Noah Ross was it.

That admission had her getting to her feet, unable to just sit there any longer.

"I don't want you to pity me, Noah. Or think less of me because I got in over my head with a bad man. I know what it looks like from the outside, and I know being in a relationship with Rick doesn't give me a hell of a lot of credibility. But damn it—" she heard her tone rising even as something tightened in her chest "—I'm not stupid. Or guilty. Or delusional. I know I made a mistake."

"Shayne—" Noah was on his feet, moving a few steps closer even as she stepped back, determined to get it out.

All the frustration.

All the anger.

And all the roiling, furious embarrassment that she carried like Atlas holding up the damn freaking world.

"I know I screwed up. I know! But I'm more than that. I'm more than all of it."

When he stepped closer, she nearly danced out of reach again, but he was faster this time.

His arms snaked out and wrapped around her, pulling her close.

For a fleeting moment, Shayne considered moving away from him. Noah was a fine man, and he wouldn't hold her against her will. Wouldn't force her to stand there and accept any physical contact, no matter how innocent.

But as those arms came around her—fully around her—and her cheek met his chest, she wasn't able to move.

Even more stunning, she realized as she wrapped her arms around his waist, was that, for the first time in weeks, she didn't want to run.

It felt safer to stay exactly where she stood.

Chapter 5

Noah knew he should pull back.

Away.

Hadn't that been the theme of the day? Get away from the office. Get away from Statler. Now he needed to get away from Shayne.

Only the warm woman wrapped in his arms needed him. And she needed this.

He knew she was hanging on by a very thin thread, but once again, he was forced to admit he'd underestimated her. What he'd assumed had been fear of her situation and the risks to her safety were there, of course.

But she was also grappling with how others saw her and, if he had to guess, how she saw herself.

And damn it if he didn't know what that felt like.

What it felt like when the world around you tilted fully on its axis, and the legs you believed sturdy and self-assured were cut out from underneath you.

It sat uncomfortably with him how quickly he was able to conjure those feelings, as if they'd happened last week instead of years before. He'd believed that pain had faded, but was he only deluding himself?

Burying himself in work had seemed like the answer, so it was jarring to consider that perhaps he'd simply used work as an excuse to run.

Away.

Vowing to think about it later, Noah tilted back so he could look at Shayne. She was a tall woman, and it took only a slight shift of his gaze for their eyes to meet.

But the heartbreaking sadness he saw there nearly felled him.

Life had done its best to hurt her, and yet there was a line of steel in her spine, holding her up and pushing her forward. Despite it all, she had the determination to be heard and to take Statler down.

Impressive as hell.

Tempted to stand there ignoring the danger that still bore down on them, Noah finally broke the quiet. "You are more than that, Shayne. You're more than all of it."

"Thank you."

"But you don't believe me."

A small smile tilted the corner of her mouth. "I'm working on that part."

"You do that."

The fact that it felt so good to hold her got him finally moving away from her. And the sudden ringing of his phone gave him an excuse to take a few additional steps.

Ryder Durant's name lit up the face of his phone, and Noah quickly got down to it. "What do you have, Durant?"

"Mesa Creek cops have already been to Shayne's jobsite. The destruction is significant, but no one else there was hurt. The fact that she's got the corner of the building that he focused on as well as the fact she was one of the first to buy in on the real estate helped. Not all the offices have people yet."

"What about Statler?"

"He's vanished again."

"Damn it."

Noah shook his head and, not for the first time, wondered how Rick Statler was doing it. The man wasn't invisible, and he still carried injuries from the take down in the safe house.

So how was he getting around?

And more, how was he disappearing as quickly as he showed up?

"Any news yet on how he escaped?"

"Nothing. And Renner's lunch interview with one of Statler's former field agents in Boston didn't shed any new light, either. The man's a freaking ghost, Noah, and everywhere we look is a dead end."

Noah heard the frustration in Ryder's tone and knew it was a match for his own. The calls into Statler's old jurisdiction in Boston were one of the latest lines they'd decided to tug, looking into some of the men and women Rick had worked with prior to his transfer to Texas.

Noah knew the top brass had already spoken with them, but a call to the field lead in Boston had given Noah some of the access he'd craved. He might trust his leaders to ask questions, but they weren't as close to the problem, and it was quite possible there were elements they might miss.

Sheila Johnson was as mad as anyone that Rick Statler had gotten the better of them all and was more than willing to have her people help in any way they could. Promoted into Statler's position after Rick left Boston, she carried the weight of what the man had left behind and the mere suggestion her people were crooked had her bending over backwards to help Noah's investigation.

It just sucked that they were looking so hard at their own.

"There's way too many dead ends," Noah agreed, keying back into the conversation. "But there's no way he's covered every base. It's impossible, especially since he's been on the run now for a few weeks. He hasn't left the area, which means he's got some unfinished business here."

"With Shayne?"

"Maybe," Noah glanced over at Shayne, who stood staring out at the land that surrounded them. He'd kept his glances to a minimum, not wanting her to think that he was eyeing her for fear she'd run, but the fact that her back was to him and her attention on the distance gave him a bit of freedom to look his fill.

She had scuffs on her forearms and some dried blood down the back of her arm from where she'd cut her wrist, but all in all she looked rather amazing for a woman who'd dropped out an office window then proceeded to hike another mile over dried scrub grass and uneven ground. She still carried that tense set to her shoulders—one he could feel with her in his arms—but there wasn't much to be done for it right now. The woman was in danger, and suggesting she should relax or feel as if she'd just walked out of a spa was as disingenuous as it was dangerous.

She needed to feel this.

Needed to stay on high alert and be acutely attuned to what was going on around her.

"You think it's something else?" Durant pressed.

"I think Statler's key to surviving this is why he hasn't run. Whatever or whoever that key is to him," Noah paused, considering Shayne once again, "is keeping him here."

"You've got a point and a few more lines to tug. Look, I'm almost to the office complex. Where are you right now?"

"We're on foot. Call me when you've wrapped up and come get us. We'll lay low here for a while."

As options went, it wasn't all that great, but it gave him a bit more time to think through the ideas swirling in his mind that he wanted to discuss with Shayne.

Her notes. Those amazing legal pads had a wealth of information, and they could make good use of their wait time going through them again.

"You want to just sit there?" Ryder asked.

"We're fine. Get whatever intel you can get out of the site and then come get us."

"See you later."

Ryder disconnected the call, and Noah moved closer to Shayne, not at all surprised when she summed up his call with Durant.

"That didn't sound very good."

"It wasn't. Statler's in the wind again."

The relatively calm visage that had taken in the landscape shifted immediately at the news, her gaze darting to the wide-open space around them. "Do you think he followed us?"

Noah was less frantic, his gaze moving over the same

landscape. While he put nothing past the madman, he'd kept sharp focus on the surrounding area throughout their walk away from her building.

Was it impossible Statler had followed them? No.

Was he pretty confident they were alone for the moment? Absolutely.

"How does he keep doing this?"

"He's a trained federal agent. It gives him an advantage."

It was a stark admission, but it was true. And as he took in Shayne's wide-eyed stare, full of a fear he couldn't assuage, Noah knew another truth.

Shayne Erickson wasn't a job any longer. She wasn't just an asset to keep safe, and she wasn't simply a sad soul in a tough situation.

She mattered.

He'd sensed it the day he rescued her out of that safe house and in the days after when she answered endless questions from him and his colleagues. He'd seen that inner core of strength and her conviction to keep pressing for the truth. Her determination to ask questions in return about the man she'd trusted and now knew as a deeply depraved soul.

But that determination had become something real and tangible over the past few hours. Her notes. Her willingness—even in her panic—to escape the office building. How she worked so hard to keep her righteous fear in check and keep moving.

She mattered to him, this amazing woman who refused to let a terrible set of experiences keep her down.

And Noah knew he'd use every ounce of his training and every bit of personal strength he possessed to keep her safe.

* * *

A trained agent.

Of course.

Why did she keep forgetting that?

Whatever the spectrum of her feelings toward Rick Statler, from the romantic to the horrified, she couldn't lose sight of who he was.

"Why are you being so blunt with me?"

While she appreciated it more than she could say, was there something more behind Noah's aw-shucks wholesomeness?

Her gaze caught on the solid cords of his neck and where they descended beneath the collar of his shirt. They were a match for the also solid, muscled forearms she'd noticed when they sat in her small kitchenette eating lunch.

So perhaps *wholesome* wasn't quite the right word.

Or maybe it was just her body's traitorous awareness of how sexy that lean, ropy muscle really was.

All of which seemed off and ill-placed considering she'd just come out of a relationship where her instincts were not only wrong but so magnificently broken she ended up kidnapped.

"I realize your experiences up to now haven't been positive or forthright when dealing with the FBI, but I don't have anything to hide. And keeping you in the dark when you're already well aware of the dangerous situation you're in is wrong in every way."

"I—" She stopped, the urge to make yet another jab at the FBI nearly out of her mouth before she pulled it back.

Noah was being honest with her. Continuing to take pot shots at his profession and his colleagues wasn't the right path forward. Hadn't that been one of her biggest frustrations about her own profession? So often she'd walk into a client's office and have to sell herself and her skills over and over because of a bad experience someone had had in the past with a consultant.

Yet she'd borne the blame and the client's mistrust. Those jobs had been more fraught than they needed to be and, inevitably, getting to a successful end result was way more challenging than necessary.

But she'd persevered on those and she'd keep doing it now when her own life and future was on the line.

She wanted to get out of this alive, and the only real shot she had at that was working with Noah and the FBI. However she might feel about how she'd been treated up to now, they were still her best shot at surviving this.

"Thank you for that."

His gaze never left hers. "You're welcome."

Suddenly afraid far too much lingered in her own eyes, she tore her gaze off of his and glanced toward the backpack they'd settled on the grass just before Noah took his call. "What do we do now?"

"We're going to wait here until Ryder finishes up at your office complex. He's going to come get us and drive me back to my SUV. I'd like to get you home so you can clean up, and then we'll figure out what to do from there."

"You think it's safe to go back to my place?"

She was surprised by the shot of excitement that rushed through her at the thought of actually walking back into her home. She'd only been gone a few weeks, but she missed the comfort and the familiarity desperately.

"For starters, you're not going alone. I'm going with

you, and I'll get some of the team on it. And we'll see that it's swept for bugs and bombs before we get there."

The idea of a bomb in her home caused a wave of nerves to rumble through her body. The sensation had been utterly foreign until the day she was kidnapped. Sadly, in the time since, it had become a near-daily occurrence.

"That's an awful lot of effort."

"Rick's an awful big priority."

Shayne figured she was asking plenty, but since Noah seemed in a sharing mood, she wasn't going to pass up the opportunity to find out as much as possible. "Who do you think he's connected to?"

Noah gestured toward the ground near her backpack before dropping down onto a small patch of scrub grass.

"Best we can tell, he's opened up several drug corridors for the bosses who control the area."

Shayne settled down opposite Noah and abstractly realized they'd positioned themselves so that they had a 360-degree view between the two of them. "Controls the area? South Texas, you mean?"

"Yes, as well as the corridors that pass through here and on into the rest of the US. That's the bigger question. The drugs move up from South America and Mexico, but the bosses aren't always the drug cartels. Several mob groups have gotten involved as well as several drug gangs here in the States."

"A multiheaded hydra."

"And growing heads every day."

She heard the disgust in his voice and saw it in his face. "Doesn't that get to you?"

"What?"

"The hopelessness of it all? You cut off one head only to have three more spring up in its place."

"It's discouraging and—" Noah sighed heavily before nodding. "Yeah. It does feel hopeless some days."

"Yet you keep coming back."

"It's my job."

The sudden rush of shyness that had her looking away before vanished, replaced with an urgency as she caught his gaze once more. "No, Noah. It's a calling. A damn fine one."

"Thank you."

While his gratitude seemed sincere, she wasn't sure he fully understood how special he was. Or how that sort of dedication and devotion—even when the cause seemed beyond lost—drew a person in.

With that realization came another.

For as horrible as the past few weeks had been, including and up to jumping out of her office window, she felt safe with Noah. There was a calmness in his presence that allowed her to hear her own thoughts through the clamoring that had filled her mind since discovering the truth about Rick.

It was stunning to finally feel that silence in her head. And amazing to know the core of who she was still remained somewhere in there.

"What about you?" he asked.

"What about me?"

"You're no slouch in the professional department. A communications consultant with her own business. It takes a lot to work for yourself. Create a business out of your own ideas and imagination. Your own grit and determination."

"I'm not quite sure I'd compare it to running down bad guys."

"Thank goodness for that. I'd hate to think everyone worked in the same field I did. That there was so much crime and so many depraved individuals no one had a chance to build things. To create something out of ideas and gumption."

"That's a nice way to think of it."

"It's true." Noah resettled himself, extending those long legs out in front of him.

Once again, Shayne couldn't deny the appeal of Noah Ross. Long and lean, he had a strength to him that was deceptive on the surface. He was a slender man. One who, if she used a lifetime of Texas-bred football fandom to assess his build, was more the graceful wide receiver than the bull-like linebacker. But just like those receivers who knew how to run and jump as well as block and tackle when necessary, he was well-muscled and you'd sorely underestimate him if you didn't realize how much strength was housed in that lean frame.

Shayne had felt that wrapped in his arms. She'd also felt it in the firm grip of his palm against hers as he led her farther away from her office.

It wasn't just physical, though. She also detected that sense of strength in the calm, steady way he handled himself. She used to feel that in herself, too. That belief in her own inner power and grit that gave her the ability to work through any problem.

Now?

Not so much.

"I used to think I had a strong business sense. A strong sense of self and my ability to read people and situations. Rick's betrayal has made me rethink that."

"I understand. But—" He squinted against the late afternoon sun, his mouth set in firm lines as if he was considering something.

"But what?"

"I think people like Rick thrive on that feeling. They may not realize they do, but it's built in their DNA."

"What feeling?"

"That sense of manipulation. The knowing that others are missing the signs of their behavior. It's easy to look at your relationship with Rick and blame yourself for the outcome."

"Who else should I blame?"

"Rick Statler, the man who betrayed you."

"I'm not blameless, Noah."

"Maybe yes, maybe no. But from where I'm sitting? It sounds like you're taking all the blame, and I just don't understand that."

Way to dish it out, Ross.

Noah ignored the small, insistent voice that kept telling him he had no business going down this path with Shayne if he wasn't prepared to take his own advice. And yet…

His situation was different. His relationship with Lindsey was different.

And betrayal was still betrayal, no matter how you sliced it.

"I'm not taking the blame."

He heard a small spark of flame beneath Shayne's tone and figured that was a decent sign some of his message might have gotten through. "You sure?"

"Of course. All I'm saying is that I should have seen

this coming. Should have sensed this. Or at least listened to my instincts."

"Your instincts suggested you were dating a psychopath?"

"No, but—"

"Then what?"

"I wanted the relationship to be more than it was."

The admission was a surprise, his ingoing assumption up to now was that Shayne had been blissfully happy before the truth of Rick Statler's secret life surfaced. But this?

It sounded like a few cracks in the dam.

And for reasons he didn't want to consider too closely, something in that admission shot through him like wildfire.

His voice was sharper than he wanted when he finally spoke, but he wanted her to see reason. "Then lean into that feeling and don't assume the fact you couldn't decipher the work of a sociopath means what happened is all on you."

He let out a harsh bark of laughter, even though the situation wasn't remotely funny. "He hoodwinked his employer for more than a decade."

"Rick only worked for the FBI for ten years?"

"More like twenty, but all the digging we've done into his background suggests his side business didn't start until he was settled in for some time."

Shayne's mouth thinned before dropping into a small *O*. "You really think he didn't do anything illegal before then? Then suddenly ten years in he starts skimming where he can?"

Noah had wondered the same, even as the brass had maintained the problems didn't go back through Rick's full employment. "It's hard to say, so we're looking for a trigger that could have pushed him down this path."

"Maybe he did his deeds outside the FBI?"

As theories went, it was a good one. Although the FBI tried to keep to itself, maintaining a demarcation between federal jurisdiction and what was owned at the local and state level, there were still connection points. His work in The Pass was a perfect example of that. He worked closely with Belle Reynolds and her team, their work often overlapping. More than was comfortable, he had to admit, over the past year.

Was it possible Rick's activities had begun with the locals when he was still in Boston? If he'd kept his activities on the down low, outside of the resources of the FBI, it would be harder to trace.

"You're good at this."

"I've had a lot of time to think." A small smile creased her lips. "And to settle a hell of a lot of blame on Rick Statler's clueless employer."

"We've earned that fair and square."

She cocked her head. "I'd say you're doing a damn fine job trying to make up for it."

"Thank you."

"I mean that, Noah. I've spent the past few weeks angry and hurt and looking for a place to lay blame. But you're not to blame. People who do bad things are to blame. Your top leaders, if they somehow ignored Rick's behavior, are to blame. But it's not fair to paint every person dedicated and devoted to their job with the same brush. You've reminded me of that."

"Then I'll also thank you on behalf of my dedicated and hardworking colleagues."

Quiet descended between them, not awkward, but

filled with a heavy sense of…awareness. He'd be lying to himself if he didn't admit that he saw the woman sitting opposite him. It was inconvenient in the extreme, but he was aware of her on a visceral level.

He had a job to do when it came to her, and he couldn't lose his focus. Yet at the same time, the work had become personal.

Deeply so.

The strangest temptation filled him to go back to their earlier conversation and the topic of her doubts about her relationship with Rick. But he was prevented from taking that left turn by the ringing of his phone. "It's Durant."

He lifted the phone. "What've you got?"

"No sign of him here at the office, but a hell of a lot of damage, Noah." Durant let out a long, low whistle. "You guys are all sorts of lucky you got out of that. And the fact that he did it all with an earthmover shows a sort of sick determination I'm starting to wonder if we've underestimated."

Noah had considered the same. They'd assumed Rick had a strong desire to stay alive, but his level of determination to stay in his old stomping grounds instead of just vanishing was keeping them on their toes.

Noah nearly said as much before the sound of gunshots filled the air.

Clods of dirt whipped up all around them as bullets hit the ground beside him and Shayne. At an agonized shout, Noah threw himself over her, yelling for backup into the phone before once again wrapping her tight in his arms.

Chapter 6

Shayne heard Noah's heavy breathing and recognized it matched her own somewhat labored exhales. That unmistakable popping, followed by the screaming of birds taking flight, had faded, and in its place was a strangely calm sense of quiet.

Except for the heavy breaths.

"Noah." Her voice came out in a whisper, again a result of the weight of him spread out over every inch of her body. He'd covered her like a human shield, and while grateful, she couldn't help but fear for his own safety. "Noah!"

"Shhh. I'm trying to listen."

"You need to let me up. Or give me a bit of breathing room."

"I don't want you exposed."

"I can't breathe between the weight of you and the hard-packed ground."

Whether it was her words or the strangled tone of them, she didn't know, but Noah did shift slightly, moving off her. He still covered her as much as possible, but the heavy weight of his torso now pressed tightly against her side instead of directly on top of her.

It was intimate, and the breath that came easier with the lifting of his weight became strangled for an entirely different reason.

Get. It. Together. This is not the time to let your hormones wake up.

Rationally, Shayne was well aware this wasn't the right setting for any thoughts other than survival. And intimacy in any form had seemed almost distasteful after Rick's betrayal, so it was even more startling to experience those strong, stirring notes of attraction.

"Noah!" Ryder's voice echoed out of Noah's phone where it lay beside the two of them.

"Can you reach it?" Shayne asked.

"Yeah." Noah lifted his hand, tapping the screen to turn on the speaker. "We're here."

"What happened?"

"We're out here like sitting ducks and the shooting started."

"You make out what direction it's coming from?"

"Southwest direction based on where the bullets hit the ground relative to our position."

"I'm on my way to you." Ryder barked out details before adding, "Chopper was already en route to survey the office from above. They'll cover us."

As if Ryder's words conjured it up, the distinct sound of helicopter rotors filled the air, growing closer with each second.

"Chopper's almost here," Noah said.

"So am I."

Ryder's voice was grim, and Shayne was struck yet again by the raw grit and determination Noah and his colleagues lived with every day.

"You're out in the open here, Noah," Shayne said as she clutched his back.

"We both are."

"At least get the pack and cover as much of your back as you can."

It was little solace—it was just a backpack after all—but it seemed like it might provide them some cover if the bullets started up again.

The whirl of helicopter blades grew steadily louder, and Noah leaned close to her ear. "He'd be a fool to expose himself any further. Not with the eyes in the sky."

"You seem awfully sure of that."

"We have the same training, and it's what I'd do."

"He's not exactly a solid, upstanding agent."

"No, but he's desperate to survive. That's got to work in our favor."

Desperate to survive.

That might be true, but if Rick were so determined to stay alive, why was he taking these chances? Shayne had no interest in making herself the center of all this, but why was he so focused on coming after her?

What did she have that would make him stick around?

She considered her computer and tablet. Although she'd deliberately avoided turning them on while in hiding, she had to believe the tech was clean. The main laptop she'd worked from had already been taken by the Feds, so if Rick had left something on that machine, he'd have to know it was one of the first things the FBI took from her.

His training would ensure he knew that.

So what else?

What wasn't she connecting?

She nearly asked Noah when a rush of air from the helicopter kicked up a load of dust around them. She turned her face back into his chest before he shifted against her, tugging on her shoulders to pull her into a sitting position. "Come on, Shayne. Our ride's here."

Noah looked out over the ground from his perch in the helicopter, scanning in widening concentric circles from where he and Shayne had so recently stopped for a break. Brady Renner was in the chopper with the pilot and had given Noah a quick update as they got buckled in and moving. Two snipers flanked either side of the interior of the helicopter, their laser focus on the ground.

But there was no sign of Rick or even a sense of where he'd been hiding.

Or where he could have hidden himself in the last ten minutes after taking determined pot shots at his former girlfriend.

Brady had already sent out a field team to check out a couple hunting cabins they'd noted from the air, but both had turned up empty and looked as if they hadn't been touched in weeks.

So where the hell was Statler?

Although he'd pushed every ounce of calm he possessed into his tone as he spoke with Shayne, Noah felt anything but. The unexpected shots, while the two of them sat like sitting ducks, was bad enough. But the fact that he'd blithely underestimated Rick Statler's determination to come after them?

Damn it to hell, she could have been hit.

The feeling of her strong body pressed head-to-toe to his where he lay covering her was still imprinted on his skin. The husky notes of her voice as she struggled beneath him echoed in his mind. And the bleak shadows that filled her eyes as they waited those last few minutes for backup to arrive—those shadows damn near broke his heart.

For a man who'd believed himself immune to softer feelings, it was jarring to realize something still remained inside. Despite her best efforts, Lindsey's death hadn't killed every last one of them.

And why was he so intent on treading that old ground again? Why was it all so close to the surface when he was with Shayne?

Because you understand betrayal at a cellular level. You know what it does to a person, and you know it's the kind of damage a person doesn't walk away from.

Once again telling himself—lying to himself?—that he'd give the lingering thoughts about Lindsey their due later, he focused on his team. Brady Renner was as strong an agent as Ryder Durant, and they both helped the Midnight Pass field office shine brightly. Their work was recognized across the state and further on to the top brass in Washington.

The situation with Statler was personal to them. Hell, it was personal to all of them.

Which didn't help when their quarry kept disappearing.

"Did Ryder find anything else with the field team?"

"Nope," Renner shook his head. "They've fanned

out in pairs over the same ground you and Shayne traversed and haven't seen a thing."

"Damn it."

Late-afternoon sun streamed into the helicopter, making it difficult to see through its front windows, but the pilot moved them assuredly toward the FBI field office in Midnight Pass. Noah counted how many team members they had out of the office and considered calling in backup out of Austin or Houston. His boss's boss was already fuming up in DC about the entire Statler situation. What was one more ask against the budget?

"How the hell is he doing this?" Brady asked.

"No clue. Not one damn clue." Noah said.

He had tried so hard not to show his disgust in front of his team, but the situation kept getting worse, and they had no leads to show for it.

"How is Miss Erickson doing?"

"She's hanging in. She's strong and she's solid." Noah's gaze shifted to where Shayne sat in the back of the copter. "And she's going to need every bit of that fortitude to get through this."

"I think we all will."

What were they missing?

It was the question Noah kept asking himself because Rick Statler seemed to melt in and out of the ether at will. And was doing it all with injuries that, while not fully debilitating, would slow him down.

Brady had already turned his attention back to the window, and Noah puzzled through the mystery as the chopper slowly touched down, but Brady's last comment stuck with him long after they got back into the office and through the team debrief on what happened at Shayne's office complex.

His team was giving the Statler case every last bit of effort, but it was easy to see everyone was running on fumes. Between the pressure of the case, the anger of the top brass and the real, earned fury of everyone who was managed by Statler, emotions were running high. For a group of people trained to keep every bit of those emotions in check, it was unsettling to feel them so close to the surface.

Which made the arrival of ten pizzas around seven o'clock both a surprise and a much-needed break.

"Mandatory dinner break!" Arden Reynolds, Ryder's fiancée, came into the conference room, her high ponytail swinging and her vivid blue eyes immediately latching onto Shayne. She'd gotten Ryder and Brady to help with the food but, at Ryder's subtle nod, settled her boxes of pizza on the conference room table and ran over to talk to her friend.

The palpable relief on Shayne's face as the two women hugged was as comforting as the food.

"Arden needed this," Ryder said casually as he moved over beside Noah. The room had moved into action at the arrival of pizza, and the two of them had a natural bit of privacy huddled in the corner, their voices inaudible beneath the din of the room.

"They haven't seen each other since the kidnapping?" Noah asked.

"No, not after that first day of questioning. It's bothered Arden that she couldn't get a hold of her. Her mother-hen gene is strong, but this carries a layer of shared experience, too."

"They went through a lot together."

"Shayne continues to go through a lot."

"She does. Statler's fixated on her for some reason."

When Ryder didn't respond, Noah took his distracted gaze off the women and turned it fully on Ryder. "You don't agree?"

"I think it's something that needs careful consideration."

"Of what, exactly?"

"It all keeps circling back around to the idea that she's got information." Before Noah could push back, Ryder added, "Knowingly or not."

"You really think she has information? Something she hasn't told us after weeks of investigating her, questioning her and now even seeing her on the run from the man who is determined to get to her?"

"I'm playing angles, Noah. All of them. Aren't you?"

He thought about those moments, when Shayne hung from the window of her office, indecision and fear paralyzing her. Whatever angles he had to consider in his job, the one that suggested she was in this with Statler dead-ended in that moment.

"Of course I am. But the angle that says she's helping Statler isn't viable."

"You sure?"

"You think otherwise?"

"He's got no reason to stay here. No matter how frustrating his disappearing act is, he's going to trip up sooner or later. That's how we caught him the first time, when he was using one of our safe houses to do his work. He only has so many connections. So many options. So why does he stay?"

"Maybe something's keeping him here."

"Shayne Erickson's keeping him here."

The biggest risk to his objectivity was to close his mind to options. But in this, Noah just couldn't see the connection. They'd been through all of Shayne's tech, the digital forensics team stripping every byte of data off her computer they could possibly find. Same with her internet files and same with Statler's Bureau-issued tech as well as the cell phones they confiscated from his home.

All of it only to confirm he'd used her computer to log into the Bureau's secure system remotely, a fact Shayne had affirmed from the start.

"You don't think he's staying to hook up with whoever's been paying the freight for his information?" Noah asked. No matter how his own instincts were clamoring, he welcomed his colleague's views.

"Maybe, but why go after the girlfriend? He wants something from her, and until he gets it, she's not safe."

"So, what are you saying?"

"I'm asking if we're all in danger because she's the wild card in all this, Noah. She's the question we can't find the answer to."

He trusted his team, and Ryder Durant was the agent he trusted most of all. So when the man spoke, Noah listened. Something had tickled the man's instincts, and it would do him well to remember that.

But Ryder hadn't seen the fear haunting those blue eyes as Shayne hung from that window.

And Ryder hadn't felt the tremors that flowed through every inch of her as he covered her body with his for fear of rampant gunfire.

Noah trusted his men, but he trusted his instincts, too.

And he had to hope like hell this persistent, increasingly insistent, attraction to Shayne Erickson wasn't blurring his focus.

* * *

Shayne was no closer to figuring out Rick's agenda three hours later but was mentally more settled after a glorious half hour in her shower and a thorough scrubbing. A stomach full of pizza and a good long conversation with her friend Arden Reynolds had helped, too.

The FBI agents had given her a wide berth in the field office conference room, but she'd ignored it, her conversation with Arden keeping the two of them focused on their dinner and catching up. Although they did speak briefly about their kidnapping—her friend wanted to understand how Shayne was doing in the aftermath of that experience—they found other things to talk of as well.

Joyful things.

The normally even-keeled yoga instructor spoke in frazzled tones of her training escapades with her new puppy, Newman, before moving on to a delighted, sigh-filled discussion of her new nephew, William.

Arden was happy.

Despite all that had happened with the kidnapping, her friend had come out the other side. Stronger. More settled. And deeply in love with Ryder Durant.

The two of them were well on their way to forever, and nothing had been able to break that bond.

She'd known Arden since moving to The Pass, and there had always been a subtle loneliness in her friend. She might not have put it that way before, but seeing Arden now—happy and vividly bright—Shayne recognized that assessment for the truth. Even with all the pain and suffering, now she was happy and quite obviously whole.

It levied a shot of envy straight through Shayne's

midsection, and she fought against it as she blow-dried her hair.

She wasn't a person who coveted others' happiness. It flew in the face of how she chose to live her life—with positive intention and a deep desire to see the good in others.

But damn, that attitude had taken a lot of hits over the past month.

Rick. The endless FBI questions. Even the internal blame game had taken its toll. Wasn't that the worst of it?

She already carried a fair amount of guilt over her family relationships, especially with her sister, and now she was forced to question her instincts once again.

Clad in a comfortable old UT sweatshirt and yoga pants, she headed back for her kitchen, where Noah was waiting for her. He'd insisted on coming in and staying with her while she cleaned up. A small, tempting voice had teased her in the shower, wondering what was going to come next and what they'd talk about in the calmer, more intimate setting of her home, but she fought to keep her focus. That stirring attraction she'd felt while they were being shot at had no place in her thoughts.

How much time she would spend with Noah Ross in the coming days had no place, either.

Her only focus needed to be on survival.

That focus had carried her through the past few weeks, and she couldn't lose it now.

Although Rick had spent a lot of time in her home over the past six months, it was still jarring to walk into her kitchen and see a man occupying a seat at the table. He worked on a thin tablet with a keyboard, a steaming mug of coffee next to him.

"I'm glad you fixed the coffee. Thank you."

"I left you a mug but didn't want to pour you a cup until you were back."

She waved him off. "I'll get it. I can refill yours, too." She snagged his mug on her way to the coffee maker, the subtle notes of domesticity bringing back the reasons she needed those steady admonishments in the shower.

This is not some homey scene. A trained killer is after you, and this man is your protector.

The trained killer part should have gotten through to her, but as she took the two mugs back to the table, settling Noah's beside him, she caught his steady gaze. Felt his quiet strength as she stared into those deep brown eyes.

And acknowledged those little flutters that kept mixing up her insides weren't going anywhere.

"You look busy. I can leave you to it."

"There's never a lack of work. Which means it can wait." As if to emphasize that, he folded the keyboard into the tablet cover and moved the device to the edge of the table. "I want to know how you're doing. I have to imagine the shower helped some."

"It did. Arden's pizza delivery didn't hurt, either."

"Everyone needed that. It's been a long few weeks. It's amazing how a break for food can restore in unexpected ways."

"She's a caretaker. It's one of the nicest traits I can think of, and Arden Reynolds has it in spades."

"Ryder sweetly referred to her as a mother hen."

"She's that, but it's something more. She sees what people need. It's a real gift, and I've always seen her bring that to her yoga instruction, too."

"She's good for Ryder. He's an exceptional agent, but the past few years he's gotten more and more isolated. She's brought him out of that, and it's good to see."

For reasons she couldn't explain, Noah's description took hold. "Is that a risk of the job? Isolation?"

He was quiet for a minute, and while he obviously considered her question, Shayne got the distinct sense he was trying to find a way not to answer.

Until he did, with a level of honesty she wasn't anticipating.

"The people who take this job all find some solace in that trait in their lives." He shrugged before offering up a small, lopsided smile. "Or the people who stick with the job, is maybe a better way to put it."

"It's lonely?"

"Sometimes. Most of the time, it's just isolating. You have a job you can't talk to people about. It's not something well understood from the outside, either."

"I bet people think it's all big bad agents, saving the world." She hesitated briefly before adding, "Which was certainly something I observed today. It's not every day, after all, a girl gets rescued in a helicopter."

That lopsided grin grew a bit broader. "There is some of that, yeah. But it's also the mix of secrecy and underlying chaos."

"Yet you do it anyway."

"It's a part of me." As if he sensed her question before she could ask it, he pressed on. "It's an active choice, Shayne. I didn't fall into this, nor do I do the job because I feel some sort of emotional debt to rid the world of crappy people."

"Then why do you do it?"

"Because while I actually do want to rid the world of

bad people, there's no guilt or sense of debt involved. I want to make sure the bad actors pay for their crimes so that the good people of the world can live without fear or worry or loss of personal freedom."

"That's rather lofty."

"I do get regular rides in a helicopter, too, so there is that." The statement was meant to lighten the mood, even as he quickly returned them back to the rational and the serious. "As one of those good people who've lived with fear and worry and loss of personal freedom, what do you think?"

"I'm glad to know there are people in the world like you. Ones who put their own well-being and time and lives on the line to make sure others are safe."

"Good."

"What else don't people understand? About your job?" *What don't they understand about you, Noah?*

"It's moments of high stress interlaced with extended hours of what feels like toiling in doubt."

"You don't strike me as a man who doubts much."

"In the middle of an op? When all we know is the target and little else? You flatter me, but I doubt all the time. The trick," he leaned forward and laid a hand over hers, "is to make sure no one knows."

The large palm that covered the back of her hand was warm and solid, the skin of his palm slightly rough-worn. Shayne had no idea why she suddenly felt so overwhelmed, but the calm she'd felt since getting home and cleaning up faded away. Only instead of the panic she'd experienced earlier as Rick pursued them, this tension was different.

It was exciting. Enticing. And sweet, somehow. A moment in time that simply enveloped them both.

Lifting her gaze from where their hands met, she finally asked, "So why are you telling me?"

"Because I made a promise to myself to tell you the truth." His thumb traced the edge of her hand before he pulled away. "It's a promise I intend to keep."

Chapter 7

Noah's words haunted her.

They'd continued talking about the day and all the potential ways Rick was eluding capture, but even as they poured second cups of coffee and batted ideas back and forth and discussed the damage to her office building, his words kept up a rapt tattoo in the back of her mind.

I made a promise to myself to tell you the truth.

Did he have any idea what that meant to her?

Of all the admissions Noah could have made, that one meant the most. Over the past few weeks, she'd been forced to accept how duped she'd been by Rick's lies. Add on the time spent with the FBI, with their endless questions suggesting they believed she lied, and her faith in the value of honesty had taken a beating.

So yeah, Noah's faith in her meant a lot.

It also made her even more determined to help him, to share whatever she could think of, no matter how obscure or strange it seemed.

"Have you looked into Rick's background?"

"His employment files have been reviewed extensively." Noah's gaze was sharp, suggesting he was already keying into the bigger thought underlying her question. "Why?"

"He and I dated. You talk about growing up and your life in the get-to-know-you process. It would be interesting to see if he lied to me and gave you the truth or possibly the other way around."

"And either way, if there's a gap in the story it's something else for us to dig into." Noah's excitement was palpable. "Let me pull the file with those specifics."

He opened the tablet once more and ran his fingertip across the screen. A subtle hum descended over the kitchen, and a halo of excitement practically rippled off him in waves. "Got it."

"What does it say?"

"Born in Topeka. Went to the University of Kansas. He worked in local law enforcement in Topeka after college, ultimately applying to the Bureau when he was in his late twenties. He started in a Kansas field office but spent most of his career in Boston before getting the transfer down here."

"That's mostly a match."

"Only mostly?"

"He told me he traveled extensively when he was in college and in the years after he got out."

Noah's eyebrows shot up, before his narrowed gaze grew speculative. "Backpack on a student's salary sort of travel?"

"I got the sense it was a bit more glamorous than that. He talked of the Côte d'Azur and castles in Eastern Europe and hiking in Tibet. It's very possible he did it on the cheap, but I never got that sense."

"That's not something you just shake off, either. Not once you have the travel bug."

Shayne agreed. Love of travel wasn't something that just vanished. It might have to be delayed for financial reasons, but that love of heading off to a new destination wasn't something that just faded away. "Especially that sort of exotic travel."

"One of the positive flags in his employment file was that he was fluent in two languages besides English."

"Spanish and Russian?"

Noah's eyes narrowed once more as he looked up from the tablet. "Spanish and French. Nothing about that popped since they're both Romance languages. The Russian? It would have popped. It's a prized skill."

"Yet he didn't share it?" Shayne asked.

"No." Noah tapped a few more screens on the tablet before shaking his head. "Nope, nothing flagged."

"That's odd."

"How did you know about it?"

"He randomly spoke it one day. We were on our way to a weekend festival, and as we were heading out of town we got caught in a traffic jam. Classic Midnight Pass sort of stuff. Someone's cattle had gotten out of a hole in their fence line and were blocking the entrance to the highway."

The day shimmered back to life in her mind, the large herd blocking the road and Rick's indignant muttering and hollering at the animals when he came to a stop.

"Zhalkiye zveri."

Amused, Shayne shifted in the passenger seat to look at Rick. The hard lines of his jaw, lightly stubbled, looked delicious in the early morning light, but that attractive visage was strangely marred by his frustration.

"What does that mean?"

"Nothing." He shook his head, an oddly dark look seeming to paint his features.

"Oh come on, you can't say something sexy in another language and not tell me." Shayne laid a hand over his forearm, softening her voice. "And how didn't I know you speak another language?"

"Job hazard." He flashed a grin at her, any hint of that darkness draining away. He never seemed to stay tense or irritated when she mentioned anything related to sex. A thought that oddly stuck in her gut, even as she was determined to enjoy the day. Those ridiculous, creeping moments of doubt had lingered of late, and she was sick of them.

Even if she was increasingly frustrated with herself when she pushed that sexy, throaty purr into her voice to calm him down.

He was a federal agent, for Pete's sake. An attractive, capable federal agent at that. Why was she so determined to see problems that weren't there?

"So what does it mean?"

"Miserable beasts."

"In what language? It sounded like Russian."

"It was."

"No way! You speak Russian?"

"A bit here and there."

The memory of that darkness riding his features as well as the strange, somewhat overwhelming sense he didn't want to talk about it had her next question sticking in the back of her throat.

How did he know Russian? And while it was possible miserable beasts was a random term he'd picked up somewhere, it wasn't in the realm of the ordinary or a standard sort of curse. Which suggested he knew more Russian than he was letting on.

Was it classified?

Since the cattle had begun to move on at Rick's honking, he inched the car forward, and she switched back to that teasing, slightly breathy tone that she used to mollify. "Well consider me impressed."

Shayne quickly recapped the story for Noah, his attention unwavering as she gave the scenario as well as her impressions.

"He was bothered by the slip."

"Yes! Exactly." It wasn't how she'd defined it at the time, but now, in retrospect, that was what had happened. "I played up the 'isn't it sexy my boyfriend speaks another language' to diffuse the situation, but that's definitely the vibe he gave off."

Noah frowned and, just like those moments with Rick, she sensed that Noah's displeasure was for another reason. But when he spoke, his tone was cool, calm, professional. "He's not one who slips character often."

"No, he doesn't. I don't, either, for that matter."

"You don't what?"

I made a promise to myself to tell you the truth.

Shayne considered his earlier comments and knew she owed him nothing less. More, she wanted to give him the truth.

"I don't come off particularly well in that retelling. The breathy sweet-talk voice and the manipulation to get him to ease up on whatever bothered him." She traced the handle of her coffee mug. "It's not me. I mean, it never has been. I've never had any interest in using sex as a way to bring a man to heel."

When he didn't say anything, she continued. "And while I'm not quite suggesting I was trading sexual favors to have him, I did play up the breathy, feminine qualities when I needed to. They were strangely effective on him, but I hated doing it. No," she shook her head. "I hated how I felt after I did it."

"So why do it?"

"When I figure that out, I'll tell you. All I do know is my instincts kept telling me Rick Statler was off, yet my brain kept telling me I was being dumb. That he was a federal agent, tasked to protect people. That he was a good, solid, decent man who was interested in me. That I was in my thirties now, and I couldn't afford to be picky."

Shayne looked up from the mug, that lingering anger at herself she hadn't fully exorcised still clearly there. "I used every one of those excuses. I'm not proud of it, and I'm still working on figuring it all out."

"Before you beat yourself up too hard about it, do me a favor and consider one thing."

"What's that?"

"Rick Statler showed you what he wanted you to see. He did it to his colleagues and the top brass and likely every person who came into his orbit."

A small sigh escaped before Shayne could check it. "So you're saying I should feel happy I was duped like everyone else?"

"No, I'm suggesting your instincts were telling you something that didn't jibe with the rest of the story. And you were trying to work through it all without thinking the worst of someone in the process."

"You make it sound more plausible that way."

"Because it is plausible. And it's why he's gotten this far. It's also why he won't get any further."

It was impossible to miss the feral gleam in his dark gaze; even more impossible to miss the tenacity that grooved deep lines into his face.

"Because the jig is up?"

"Because no matter how clever Statler thinks he is, his web of lies is unraveling. He's had to work awfully damn hard to keep all this a secret, but there are cracks. There always are when you apply the volume of his lies across a lot of years. His travel. His job responsibilities. The languages. They're all just the start."

"The start of what?"

"The start of the path to take him down. We've got all the puzzle pieces to do it. We just need to put them together."

Rick hunkered down in the small hidey-hole he'd found in the nether reaches of Midnight Pass. Although he'd made a highly lucrative game for himself out of hiding in plain sight, he'd always known it wasn't a strategy that would work forever. It was why he'd used the pretense of being an avid outdoorsman and hiker as a way to traverse the area and find small places he could use if needed.

It was how he'd gotten out of sight earlier that day when his former colleagues put eyes in the sky. It was how he'd stayed off the radar for the past few weeks since his escape. And it was how he was going to keep his sights on Shayne until he could get her alone.

Damn Noah Ross.

The man had been a thorn in his side from day one. Day. Freaking. One.

He saw too much. He worked too hard. And now he was making moves he had no business making.

Which brought him right back around to the reasons he'd risked overplaying his hand and shot at the man anyway.

What the hell was he doing with Shayne?

Rick fully expected Shayne had faced a bad few weeks being questioned by his former colleagues. What did she know? What was she hiding? How had she helped him over the past six months?

They were the same questions he'd have asked if he were conducting the investigation, and despite the fact she was innocent, the Bureau wouldn't believe it. On some level, he'd been counting on them not to believe it. The more they focused on her and what they thought she knew, the more distracted they'd be.

Split focus worked to his advantage.

Yet Ross seemed totally focused on Shayne.

He'd watched them from a distance, the way the two of them had sat there, nestled in that rugged patch of land. Something hard had pooled in his gut. Yes, he still wanted Shayne. But what type of disloyal woman moved on, cozying up to someone new, so soon after her last relationship ended?

He'd stuck around because he'd believed he needed her. That she was not only necessary to getting through this, but that she could help him make things right again.

But what if she had a different purpose?

The outreach last month from Vasily Baslikova was impossible to ignore. The man wanted Rick's access routes back and forth from Texas down through Mexico and on into South America, and he wasn't taking no for an answer. The mobster was making his own business and edging out the cartels for dominance in the US. And somehow—some way—the man had figured out Rick's connection and side job building his own nest egg.

The painful beating had been as convincing as intended. Rick would either get on board or he was a dead man. A fact that had only become truer with his Bureau access cut off.

But maybe he wasn't as defenseless as he'd believed.

He knew the region and knew all the areas the Feds were keeping a close watch on. Which meant he could help Baslikova's network in other ways. And if he handed Shayne over on a silver platter—an offering, if you will—Baslikova would know that Rick was committed to the man's cause.

It was the only way, really. And likely the reason he hadn't run yet.

He'd believed he needed Shayne as some sort of talisman. A sign that the time they'd spent together had not only meant something but had laid the path toward his future.

After seeing her with Noah Ross, he now knew better.

Shayne Erickson was the key to staying alive.

And if he got a shot at killing Noah Ross on the way to capturing Shayne? Well, that would be an outcome worth celebrating.

Noah considered the woman sitting opposite him at the table and marveled once more at her mind, her fortitude and her overall resilience. None of it, however, could hide the fact that she was exhausted.

"Why don't you head to bed. I'll take a spot on the couch."

"You don't—" She looked up abruptly from her coffee mug, which she'd been staring into in a semi-trance. "I mean, you don't have to stay here."

"I'm not leaving you alone. And I can see how being in your own home has been good for you. Lean into that comfort and sleep in your own bed."

"But you don't have clothes. Though I do have extra toiletries in my spare bathroom."

"Then I should be all set."

"Noah, I—" She stumbled again, but this time he wasn't sure if it was from the fatigue or something else. Something that might be a match for his own suddenly thundering heartbeat.

He was sleeping at Shayne's house.

It wasn't a usual ask for his job, but it wasn't so far out of the realm of consideration, either. His job was to keep her safe, and he already knew there was an external threat against her. Under normal circumstances, he'd look to get her into a safe house, but that plan was shot to hell since the very person they were hiding her from knew all the safe houses in the area.

A situation the Bureau was hard at work fixing but hadn't been fully solved yet.

"I've asked a lot of you today. Asking you to bunk on my couch feels wrong, somehow. At least take the spare room."

"While I appreciate it, I'd rather be close to the front door."

She had an alarm system, one he'd checked out while she was in the shower. It was a good, solid unit, and he'd normally have said that was enough to allow him to stay in the spare room, but, again, the threat against them wasn't a typical one.

Rick Statler had stayed here.

And while Noah didn't want to think too hard about that fact—or the subtle anger that coursed through him each time he thought of the man in this house—it was one more piece that needed to be addressed before the alarm would be truly useful.

"I set the alarm when we got here."

"An alarm Statler has the code to, no?"

Her eyes widened on that, the move only highlighting the dark circles that filled the hollows above her cheekbones. "Oh my God, how could I not think of that? He could come and go here as he pleased."

"A situation we'll fix with the alarm company tomorrow. For tonight, I'm more than fine on the couch."

"It's at least a pullout," she added before considering him. "Though you are tall."

"I'll sleep on an angle."

The comment was enough to draw a small smile, and he took it as a solid victory. "Come on. Show me where the linens are, and we'll get the bed made up."

"Okay."

She stood, reaching for his mug when he stopped her, laying a hand over hers. "I'll take care of those. You go get the linens."

Her gaze locked with his, and he made no move to lift his hand. Instead, he took full advantage of the soft feel of her skin beneath his and the quiet moment that stretched out between the two of them.

There really was no place for this between them. The touch over the coffee mug was an accident, with both of them reaching for the cup, but standing there, leaving his hand over hers, was a choice.

One he had no business making.

"Thank you." She placed her free hand over his and squeezed. "For the mugs. For staying. For everything."

"You're welcome."

She slipped her hands from his and padded out of the kitchen, and he forced himself to pick up the mugs and head for the sink. He made quick work of both mugs before washing the coffee pot and setting all of it on the drain board next to the sink.

The few minutes gave him time to collect himself, as well as a chance to look once more out her window. He'd inspected the house fully when they first arrived, but he took another moment to mentally map out any and all external threats before he lay down to sleep.

She lived in a small neighborhood, and it was late enough that most of the houses had extinguished their lights for the evening. A few had single bulbs burning over the porch or a garage, and as he took in the view from the kitchen window, her street looked calm and serene. Empty, really.

There was no way of knowing Rick's next move, but for now, Noah would take that emptiness as a good sign and hope like hell it stayed that way. He deftly pulled the shade over the kitchen window and finished checking all the entrance points in the rest of the kitchen and on into the living room. They were all as secure as on his first walk through, and by the time he'd finished his checks, Shayne was back in the living room with sheets for the bed.

"Here," he walked over to grip the handles on the hidden bed. "I'll get it."

In one smooth move, the bed pulled out. She'd assessed correctly—his feet would likely spill out over the bottom—but he'd figure it out. He'd slept in worse, and the thick eggcrate cushion she'd brought with the linens ensured the bed would be comfortable on his back, even if a bit short.

He helped situate the cushion first, followed by the fitted sheet and then the top sheet. They worked swiftly, in a sort of simple unison that spoke of a quiet domesticity. One he hadn't experienced in a very long time. Hell, when was the last time he'd made a bed?

He lived the proverbial bachelor's life, and that included paying for a housekeeping service. But now that he thought about it, he couldn't even remember making a bed with Lindsey. The act was strangely intimate.

And it was also time to give in and acknowledge Shayne wasn't the only one in the room who was running on fumes. He'd already been working tirelessly these past few weeks to get ahead of Rick, and then today ended up off the charts with the escape from Shayne's office and then going on the run.

It was the only reason—really the only one—that excused what came next.

As he looked up, he caught sight of Shayne staring down at the bed with twin trails of tears flowing down her cheeks.

"Shayne?"

"I'm sorry. I'm fine. Really." She shook her head, a small hiccup marring her protests.

"Of course you're fine." He meant the words to be reassuring—and meant pulling her close for a hug to reassure even further, but when she moved into his arms, something short-circuited in his brain.

He'd held her earlier and didn't have an issue. Or he'd at least held himself in check.

But something about the hour and his own exhaustion and the sheer temptation that he couldn't seem to escape suddenly descended with a fierce sort of madness.

He pressed his lips to hers in a kiss. What he'd intended—even in his short-circuited state—to be something simple and quick, changed immediately.

Exploded, really.

Her arms lifted to wrap around his neck, and she leaned into him and into the meeting of lips. Electricity crackled and arced between them, the simple act of comfort instantly morphing into something more. Something so all-encompassing it blew through him like a tornado in spring.

Tightening his arms around her, Noah held her close as he explored her mouth. Tongues met and tangled, an act of intimacy that belied all the effort they'd both made to remain neutral.

Unaffected.

Distinctly separate.

Because the heat between them in the kiss proved what he'd known all along. And likely what she had, too.

They shared an attraction. One that might be heightening in the rush of danger surrounding them, but which was also wholly its own magic.

Noah indulged himself a few moments longer—he'd already cursed himself for this decision so why not give in and enjoy a bit more?—tasting her and teasing them both mercilessly with the erotic play of lips and teeth and tongue. Willing himself to keep it to just that, his hands practically trembled from the need to roam over her back, to feel the warmth beneath the lived-in, washed-out old sweatshirt she wore.

But he did hold back.

And when he finally lifted his head, questions filled her blue eyes that he knew filled his own.

Why her? Why now?

And the hardest question of all.

What if he couldn't keep her safe?

Chapter 8

The man kissed like a horse thief. Or what her fanciful heart imagined a nineteenth-century rogue cowboy would kiss like. Because nothing in her life had prepared her for what it would feel like to kiss Noah Ross.

And damn him for it because she had no reason to be crying on Noah or staring up at him with what nearly bordered on hero worship. And she sure as hell didn't need to be kissing him.

So damn him.

And double damn him for defying her expectations.

The man seemed so innocent, with his hardworking, aw-shucks demeanor and natural protector qualities and his laser-sharp focus on his duty to serve and protect. He was the long, tall, strong lawman who looked like he belonged walking the streets of an Old West town, keeping it safe.

But now, she was convinced he would have been far more capable of robbing one.

That man—the upstanding one Shayne imagined—would give kisses that were tepid and uninspired. Only he'd turned the tables on her. And the person she'd judged on the surface to be so upstanding, possibly boring, was anything but.

Even if somewhere deep down inside, she inwardly acknowledged, she'd never honestly seen Noah as boring at all.

She'd escaped the living room quickly after that, making an excuse about being tired. Which was both true and a complete lie since she'd now been lying in bed over an hour—wide awake—reliving every moment of that kiss.

What was she going to do about this?

She had no business taking advantage of his professional kindness. And while she might own her behavior, she sure as hell wasn't the only one in that kiss, so she had to believe that he was battling his own concerns. She might not know all the ins and outs of an FBI job, but most workplaces frowned on anything that smacked of a relationship, sex or even mild flirtation.

That had to go double for romantic leanings in the line of duty.

But even with that big no-no, Shayne knew there was even more to the problem. While Noah might be willing to believe her, she was quite sure the rest of his team hadn't fully come around to the same conclusion.

Although Arden had kept her quite occupied in their conversation over pizza at the FBI field office, it hadn't done anything to diffuse the looks Shayne had received from the various agents in the conference room. Their respect for Noah was obvious—and more than enough to keep them from overtly mistreating her—but she was aware no one harbored any soft feelings for her.

For her part, Arden remained neutral, her usual warmth overriding any discussion beyond a cursory mention of what had happened at Shayne's office earlier. Arden had been far more concerned about Shayne's overall health and well-being than poking into the facets of her now-dead relationship with Rick Statler.

But the insinuation of guilt had hovered over the room all the same.

Rolling over in bed and slamming a fist into her pillow to fluff it up as well as to release some of this damnable frustration, Shayne considered her next step. And no matter how tempting, that next step could not involve kissing Noah again.

But what was the next step?

Rick was still out there.

The majority of the FBI still thought she had intel.

And she was still living in limbo until this situation came to any type of conclusion.

A small idea she'd flirted with during her many days in isolation drifted through her mind again and instead of dismissing it as she had so many times, Shayne decided to give it a bit of air and see if it might make sense.

Her sister, Caroline, was a computer expert. Shayne had always considered her own skills fairly advanced, but Caroline's work with algorithms, programming languages and cyber intelligence made Shayne look like a gorilla tapping in basic commands on a keyboard. Caroline had made herself a nice career working in the state capitol in Austin and managing several government databases before going out on her own a few years ago as a cyber-forensics expert. And still, Shayne suspected her sister's skills were far deeper than she could ever understand.

Perhaps it was time Shayne took advantage of that.

She hated the idea of putting her little sister at risk and hated even more coming into Caroline's life only because she needed something.

But she needed help, and Caroline had the skills to get them there.

To get *her* there, Shayne corrected. Why was she assuming Noah would even want to be a part of this?

The real question was what she actually expected on the other side. It wasn't like the FBI didn't have its own well-honed technological forensics experts who were managing the Statler case. But if she pulled in her sister, Caroline would go into it on her side.

Or so Shayne had been telling herself each time she considered the idea.

That was the real danger, she knew. She wanted to believe the Bureau's agents were focused on finding the truth, but she couldn't ignore the fact that they were also under pressure to find a scapegoat. One who hadn't been employed by a highly elite government agency for more than a decade and who could excuse some of the embarrassment coursing through the FBI's top brass right now.

She was the perfect target.

Which meant she needed to protect herself in whatever way she could find.

Noah finished folding the last blanket on top of the now-closed hide-a-bed and wondered at the lack of pain in his back. He'd never had much luck with couch beds, the length of his body ensuring he either contorted himself into a small ball on the rickety metal-based bed or stretched out so far his feet hung off, usually going numb sometime during the night.

The eggcrate had been a revelation.

But the kiss had been the real distraction, keeping him awake long after he should have fallen to sleep.

His thoughts were so full of kissing Shayne that his night had passed in a blur of mental ass kicking and a heated desire so sharp he wasn't entirely sure what to do with it.

Under normal circumstances, he knew exactly what to do with all that pent-up attraction. He might not be looking for anything permanent in his life when it came to relationships, but there were ways to have discreet, adult evenings when needed.

Yet somehow, Noah thought as he added the last pillow to the top of the folded pile, those tepid, functional evenings he'd practiced up to now felt empty.

And flat-out unappealing.

Despite his best intentions, the conversation the day before with Ryder slammed into him.

"He's got no reason to stay here. No matter how frustrating his disappearing act is, he's going to trip up sooner or later. That's how we caught him the first time, when he was using one of our safe houses to do his work. He only has so many connections. So many options. So why does he stay?"

"Maybe something's keeping him here."

"Shayne Erickson's keeping him here."

Noah was sure Shayne wasn't involved.

But was it finally time to admit he might have lost a bit of focus?

"You up for coffee?"

As if he'd conjured her, Shayne came into the living room. She looked even fresher than she had the night before, her hair pulled up in a high ponytail and her body clad in the same sort of workout outfits Arden Reynolds usually wore. Shayne's was a bit more subdued than Arden's normal array of pinks, purples and greens, but there was no denying the firm muscles under the muted gray she wore.

Or how good it was to see some color in her cheeks.

"You look like you're ready to tackle the day."

"I had an idea I wanted to run past you."

Intrigued, he followed her into the kitchen. He'd already made use of the toiletries she'd offered the night before, and while he'd prefer a change of clothes, it had been good to shower off the day before.

"Tell me more about this idea."

"First," she said, a small moue of apology creasing her lips, "I should have thought of this last night. I have some promo T-shirts for my business. I realize you've been stuck in the same clothes, and the least I can do is offer you a fresh shirt." She rummaged in a bottom cabinet in the corner of the kitchen, next to a built-in desk, and came up with a black T-shirt with a white logo discreetly over the breast pocket.

"These are nice."

"They will be if I ever get back to my business."

Although he'd managed to put those aspects of her life out of his mind, it was yet another reminder that Shayne had lost far more than her sense of security. She ran a small business, most of which she handled on her own. And potentially losing it and her livelihood, after this mess with Rick was over, was a legitimate fear.

It was one more thing he was determined to help her with.

One more thing to make right.

In the meantime, he could at least goad her into a smile.

"Come on, now. Where's fresh-faced and optimistic?"

Shayne frowned before that small smile he was hoping for tilted the corner of her mouth. "She vanished for a bit, but grumpy and unoptimistic can be subdued with some coffee."

"There you go."

Noah glanced down at the T-shirt and the woman who busied herself across the room, suddenly aware he was in an awkward spot. Leaving to change would look weird but stripping off his shirt in the middle of her kitchen wasn't much better.

Stay?

Leave?

Since her back was turned to him as she made coffee, he opted to stay put and not draw attention to the quick change.

He realized his mistake the moment his head popped through the top of the T-shirt. Shayne had turned from the coffee maker, her blue gaze hot on him where she stood at the counter.

"Thanks. This feels much better."

"Um, sure. Right. You're welcome." She turned back to the counter quickly, nearly toppling a mug into the sink before catching the porcelain.

Noah wanted to smile, the two of them standing on opposite sides of the kitchen no doubt as strange to watch as it was to experience, but something held him back. He was red-blooded and male enough to subtly preen under her attention, but he was also a federal agent, tasked with a serious set of duties tied to an even more serious set of outcomes.

The lingering remembrances of how she'd felt in his arms when Statler had shot at them.

The kiss last night.

Now the heated glances across the kitchen.

None of it had a place here. He could honestly acknowledge she was an attractive woman whom he had an attraction to and not act on it.

He'd have to.

It was the only way to get through the next few days. And it was the only way to stay on point and make sure Rick Statler never got a shot at this woman again.

"While we wait for the coffee, tell me about this idea." Noah considered the shirt he'd worn since the day before. Holes were ripped in the fabric he'd never fix, so he tossed it into the garbage before taking a seat at the table.

"I'd like to go to my sister's."

He cycled through what they'd already discussed when he'd brought up her family, a bit surprised at the change of heart. "I thought you didn't have much of a relationship with your family."

"I don't."

"But you can go there to stay?"

"Yes. Sure. Of course." She turned away at the sound of the gurgling coffee maker as it came to the end of its brew, and Noah couldn't tamp down on the sudden sense she was hiding something.

"Is there another reason you want to go?"

"There isn't one."

"Shayne." It was just her name, but he heard the world of meaning in his use of it. Both the question at what she was considering as well as the plea that she trust him.

"It's just for a little while. And you'll know where I am. And I'd hope you would have someone keep an eye on us so that I don't have to worry that my baby sister is in danger."

"Why do you really want to do this?"

She'd already poured him a cup of coffee and set the mug down on the table before heading back to the counter for her own. She was quiet when she finally spoke, her gaze on the counter and her voice low, but her words had all the power of gunshots.

"To figure out what Rick knows and find a way to hunt him."

Shayne expected anger. Possibly fury. Even a degree of disappointment.

What she never expected was the sheer regret lacing his tone when he finally spoke.

"Have we let you down that badly?"

She turned from the counter, nearly jostling her mug in the process. "What? I mean no, well, I mean I—"

I made a promise to myself to tell you the truth.

Shayne took a breath, fortifying herself. She knew she owed him her honesty if nothing else. "Yes, Noah. The FBI let me down. Not you, but the organization you're a part of has been more than willing to leave me as suspect number one, easily scapegoating the dumb girlfriend as the problem here."

"That's not true. It's not—"

"No? I spent days talking to the agents in your office after surviving a kidnapping. I was tired and terrified and sadder than I've ever been in my life, but I hung in there. I answered the same questions over and over, believing that if I just told the truth the nightmare would end. And what did it get me? A group of skeptical agents who still think I did it, all while they let the real problem get away."

"That's a problem. I know. But it's not tied to you, Shayne. The handling of Rick's custody was a screwup, plain and simple. But it has nothing to do with you."

"Sorry if I'm not over it yet, but if the FBI let him get away, they're not going to be all that upset if I somehow have the ability to draw him out. I'm disposable, Noah. Don't you see that?"

"No," he shook his head. "You're nothing remotely close to disposable. And we won't let anything happen to you."

"You say that. Right now, you say that, and I know you believe every word. But your colleagues don't believe me. And your top brass is looking for a scapegoat. That's me."

"I won't let that happen."

"It's beyond you, Noah. Just like Rick's behavior is beyond you. There are forces at work here, and they're all playing out before our eyes. I'm not going to sit around and get taken down by a web of deceit I had no part in creating."

"The FBI is not in the habit of placing blame on the wrong people. This isn't some TV crime drama or movie-of-the-week suggesting otherwise."

"No, it's my life. And I've been watching all of this unfold, and none of it looks good for me." She sighed and picked up her mug, walking over to take a seat at the table. "Ignore, for a moment, what you think you know about me. Ignore the part that's even about me."

"But this is about you."

She held up a hand. "Hear me out."

"Fine. Okay, I'm listening."

"Rick infiltrated my life for six months. He did the same to the Bureau for more than ten years. He's got tentacles and connections and ways, Noah. Deeply embedded ways of doing his deeds. I am innocent, but that doesn't mean Rick won't be able to play on the existing uncertainty of the team and use it to his advantage. Falsify information. Drop in small hints that point to me."

"The team's already been through the digital forensics. On your machine as well. No one's found anything like that."

"Until they do. Until he drops something or changes something or just gives enough circumstantial evidence to close the noose around my neck. I need an ally in this. Someone who's just as talented as the FBI digital team, if not more, and who can protect me if I need it."

"I can protect you, Shayne."

She heard the conviction in his words and wanted to believe him. God, how she so desperately wanted to believe that he was knight and protector and able to combat her enemies.

But he wasn't. His job ensured that.

"I know you think that."

"I know that."

"You're the opposition!" She leaped out of her chair, unable to sit still and face him. Unable to face more of that disappointment.

Hadn't she lived with that look most of her life?

Oh, Noah wasn't the same as her family, and she wasn't about to start conflating the two, but she'd spent most of her life—and certainly all her adult years—living with the reality that she had no one to depend on but herself.

"I'm not your enemy."

"That's not what I said."

"It's how you're acting."

Noah was on his feet then, his own agitation pushing him into a steady pace back and forth across her kitchen. When he finally stopped, those compelling eyes on her, Shayne's own thoughts stilled.

Calmed, oddly, in the face of that seeming willingness to make her understand how committed he was.

To her safety.

To bringing down Rick.

To seeing this nightmare through.

"Look, Shayne. I don't blame you for feeling this way. We've done nothing to earn your trust, and I wouldn't depend on us either if I was in the same position."

"So why should I?"

"Because I've made a promise to you, and I won't go back on it. I will take care of you and make sure you're protected. In all of this, no matter the outcome."

"And what if you get moved again? Pulled onto other projects. Or what if your boss and their boss and whoever else has been embarrassed by all this thinks you're not objective any longer? Statler operated in the shadows. Others can do the same."

"I won't let that happen."

"That's an awful big promise, Noah."

"I know."

"Again, why should I believe you?"

Even as she asked the question, Shayne knew the truth. She wanted to believe. In him and in those convictions he held so close to his chest.

"You have no reason to other than my word."

"It's not your word that worries me. It's the people you work with. The organization you're a part of."

"I know, Shayne. Damn it." He ran a hand through his hair before rubbing the back of his head. "To hell and back, I know."

Shayne knew he was such a good man in an abstract yet deeply tangible way. She got a feeling and a sense of him, balanced against how hard he worked and how much he cared, along with his obvious conviction to do the right thing.

How could those two ideas coexist so easily?

Yet they did.

"Please understand then, this isn't about you. This is about me doing what I need to do to take care of me."

"Will you give me a chance at least? A chance to prove to you that we're on the same team, working toward the same outcome?"

Her gaze drifted over the pocket of his T-shirt, the logo of her business emblazoned over his heart.

She had a life. One she wanted to get back to, even as she remembered how hard she worked and how easily it had all been disrupted and—if they didn't find him—potentially ruined by Rick.

But in all that hard work, she recognized something else. It was the fleeting need she'd projected onto her relationship with Rick. That deep-seated need to belong to someone.

More, to belong *with* someone.

In retrospect, it angered her to think about how much time she'd wasted projecting that onto Rick. Even if he hadn't turned out to be the horrible person she now knew him to be, what sort of existence was that? For herself or for the person she was dating.

And now?

As she spent time with Noah and came to understand what drove him and made him tick?

Shayne could only admit that she should have held out. She'd always believed that when you found someone you wanted to spend your life with, you'd know it. Feel it. A heady drug that infused the senses and helped you see the best in the world.

She saw that in Noah.

They'd only shared one kiss, but their experiences over the past day, since he'd shown up with the sandwich at her office, had been some of the most intimate of her life.

It wasn't just heightened emotions.

Nor was it hurt feelings, rebounding from one relationship and trying to find solace in another.

It was him.

Noah.

Shayne took a few steps forward, the pull of being so close to him drawing her like moth to flame.

She shouldn't do this.

They couldn't do this.

But as she moved closer, she couldn't help herself. Laying a hand on his shoulder, she stared up into his eyes. Fathoms deep, she saw trust and respect and the reflection of all the promises he'd made to her.

"Please, Shayne? Will you give me that chance? If it means taking you to your sister, then I'll do that. But will you give me a chance to prove that I will keep you safe?"

"Okay. I can do that if—"

The explosion happened without warning. The kitchen window, still covered by the shade pulled the night before, shattered in a rain of glass and broken slats.

Shayne barely had time to scream before Noah's body came over hers, dragging her to the ground.

And once again, as she lay wrapped in his arms, chaos descending around her, Shayne was forced to face the truth.

She was prey.

And the man hunting her wasn't going to rest until he'd caught her.

Chapter 9

Noah quickly ran his hands over Shayne, looking for any sign she'd been hit, before he got to his feet. When he was satisfied she was simply startled, not struck by a bullet or raining glass, he moved into action. "Call 911 and then go hide in the bedroom! I'm going after him."

He didn't wait for her answer, just assumed she'd do as he asked as he raced toward the front door.

And once again cursed himself for being so damned complacent when it came to Rick Statler. Whatever lingering feelings the man had for Shayne, he and his colleagues needed to get away from the idea that it was calm or rational.

Or, worst of all, even about self-preservation any longer.

By all logical thought, the man should be long gone by now. Yet he was still here, his actions growing bolder by the hour.

Why?

Statler had kidnapped Shayne a few weeks ago for some reason only he understood. Because he felt his colleagues closing in? Because he thought her presence would throw them off the scent?

Who knew?

But now it was evident that Rick wanted to hurt her. And whatever rationale he had for the actions had to be some fabrication in his mind.

Noah mentally raced through it all, even as he physically braced for a showdown.

Welcomed it, actually.

Once outside, Noah looked around. Shayne's street was quiet, no sign of anyone or any cars he hadn't seen the night before.

So where was Rick?

Noah sprinted around the side of the house, in the direction of the kitchen window. Some broken glass littered the ground, and he could just make out the edge of a footprint in a patch of grass near the exterior brick, but nothing else.

Nor could he see any trail of footprints leading away from the house.

Continuing on, he moved toward the backyard, careful to keep his spine pressed as near to the brick as he could for as much protection as possible. A small privacy fence enclosed Shayne's backyard, just like all the other houses on her block. There was the slightest space between her fence and her neighbor's—barely wide enough for a lawnmower to get through to keep it trimmed—but no sign of Rick.

"Damn it."

He swung back around, a new wave of panic coursing through his stomach. What if this was a ploy to get him out of the house? And what if neighbors came running out at the sound of gunshots? Even if no one else ended up in the crossfire, his car was in the driveway, and he'd been with Shayne when Rick shot at them the day before. It would stand to reason the man knew he had spent the night, too.

"Shayne!" Her name tore from his throat as Noah took off for the front door.

She had to be okay.

She had to be.

But as he came around the front of the house, he didn't miss that the door was closed. And as he shoved his shoulder against the thick wood, Noah knew sheer, raw terror.

The door he'd purposely left open was not only closed. It was locked tight.

Shayne huddled in her closet like Noah had told her to, the 911 dispatcher requesting that she stay on the line. Shayne had already told the woman she was hiding and that she didn't want to speak. The dispatcher affirmed her understanding of the danger and kept her voice low and calm as she talked Shayne through the call and the steps with the police.

A call for emergency services had gone out, and there was already a response, a team out on patrol accepting the dispatch and heading toward her housing development. Shayne strained to listen for the sirens but so far hadn't heard anything.

Until she heard a thud.

A hard inhale of breath knocked through her lungs.

"Ma'am. Are you okay?" asked the dispatcher.

"I heard something," she whispered on a heavy exhale.

"I'll alert the team on their way."

"Wait!" She scrambled to give more information. "There's an FBI agent with me, Noah Ross. He's already gone out to look for the intruder, too. He's armed. The police can't shoot him."

"Of course. Of course, I'll tell them. Please wait while I share the information."

Shayne registered the change as the line went quiet. The volume was low enough that she could still hear the woman and call out to her if needed, but she also heard the dispatcher giving distinct instructions to the police unit on its way, alerting them to the potential threat as well as Noah's presence on her property.

That heavy thud sounded again, and Shayne nearly burrowed deeper into her closet before she stopped, recognizing the truth.

Rick had found her.

And hiding in her closet, armed with nothing but her clothes and a few purses, wasn't the way to protect herself. Although...

Her gaze shot around the walk-in closet. It had been one of the selling points of the house, and she admittedly used the closet for clothes as well as any number of items that she likely should have purged long ago.

But in that moment, she could hardly hate herself for hoarding several things she now might be able to use to her benefit. The slow cooker she'd bought during a housewares sale the prior spring still sat in its shopping bag in the corner, unused. And the heavy leather work bag she'd bought on a trip up to the outlets one weekend—which was completely frivolous but had felt necessary—had a deep well she could stuff weight into and use as a swinging weapon.

It wasn't ideal, but it might work.

Or it might at least give her a chance to hold Rick off until the police got there to help.

"Shayne!" Rick's voice rumbled from somewhere inside the house.

Based on where her bedroom was toward the back of the house, Shayne estimated he was somewhere in the living room, and she frantically muttered into the phone. "He's here. He's in the house. He's going to find me. If the police get here too late, I'm in the bedroom closet."

"Ma'am, they're less than a mile out."

Even as she listened to the dispatcher's calm, steady voice and the promise that the police were near, Shayne roamed maniacally around the closet. She was considering what she could shove into the bag that would give it enough heft for a solid hit when her gaze landed on the curling iron, wrapped in its cord on a small shelf where she kept an overflow of toiletries for when she had guests.

She grabbed the iron, bent down and plugged it into the socket near the built-in dresser, thanking her lucky stars that this large, outfitted closet had sealed the deal on her walk-through with the realtor. She slammed the button on the curling iron straight to the highest heat setting and prayed it would give her the extra help she needed if Rick got to her before the police found them.

"Shayne!"

Rick's booming voice sounded closer, and she estimated he'd cleared the living room and was heading down the hall. Scrambling, she reached for the curling iron, tapping a finger quickly against the barrel to see if it was hot yet.

She certainly didn't want to grip it at that temperature, but she wasn't sure it was primed to do much damage yet, either. But what if she wielded it to smack against him and then pressed the barrel to flesh?

Even as she considered the damage she could do, a deep well of sadness opened underneath the adrenaline.

Who was this person she'd become?

Now wasn't really the time to consider it, but she couldn't fully erase that heavy shot of sadness that curdled nausea in her stomach.

Whatever she wanted to be, right now she was a woman who would defend herself against the enemy.

With that focus front and center, she tapped the iron once more, pleased when it felt much hotter than even a few seconds before.

"Shayne!"

And as Rick moved closer, making noises through her home like an angry bear pawing through garbage, images of Noah flashed in her thoughts.

Had Rick gotten to him first?

Was Noah, even now, lying in her yard because Rick had lain in wait near the kitchen window?

He'd done his level best to remove Noah from Midnight Pass when he was hiding his misdeeds in plain sight, accurately assessing the threat of having such a sharp-eyed team member so close.

But in the weeks since Rick had been captured and then escaped?

It wasn't a leap to assess his deteriorating mental

state and know that his only goal now was to hurt his former colleague.

"You can't hide, Shayne! I know you're here!"

The continued bellowing only made her more convinced Rick had handled Noah in some way before coming into the house. And it made her even more determined to use the iron.

She didn't have time to worry about who she'd become.

She had to worry about the monster who lurked on the other side of the door.

Carefully, she settled the phone on top of the dresser, face up so the dispatcher could hear all that was happening and direct the police as needed.

And then with her dominant hand she gripped the handle of the curling iron and with her other the long cord. She'd leave it plugged in until the very last moment, getting it as hot as possible while still being able to just yank it from the wall so she could move quickly against Rick.

Imagining the jabbing motion she'd use, Shayne felt her breath slow as Rick barreled closer, shouting the whole time.

"I know you're here! It didn't take you long to cozy up with my colleagues, you whore!"

On and on, the insults flew as he stumbled around the bedroom. She heard him drag on the bathroom door she'd closed earlier, then the slam of the shower door. It was only a matter of moments before he'd set his sights on the closet.

She had to time this right. And since she knew he had a gun, she had to use surprise to her benefit. Slam the iron onto his gun hand, stunning him enough to hopefully make him drop the weapon before firing it.

And then she had to go for the face and eyes. It was her only option to hurt him enough to get past him and out to the police.

To Noah.

Oh God, she hoped she could get to Noah. And that she'd find him whole and alive when she did.

In the meantime, she had to focus on getting herself out.

Whole and alive.

Rick wasn't even trying for subtlety, his restless, almost singsongy screaming getting closer and closer to the closet. With her grip firm on the handle of the curling iron, Shayne positioned herself as close to the door, yet out of his immediate vision, as possible.

Her goal was that he had to actually come through the door to find her, and when he did, she'd aim for that gun hand. Knowing he was right-handed, she positioned herself nearest that side of his body, her back to the wall beside the doorway.

And then she braced for impact.

Noah leveled his gun at the lock on the front door and kicked the thick oak even as the gunshot still rang in his ears. He could hear Rick screaming inside the house and moved forward on nothing but adrenaline.

An odd sense of déjà vu filled him as he pushed forcefully into the house, the memories of rescuing Shayne a few weeks earlier eerily similar.

And the enemy was exactly the same.

Rick's stalking echoed through the house like a

drunken bear foraging for food, and Noah gave no thought to taking his time or assessing the situation.

Shayne was in danger and his own idiocy in leaving her vulnerable had put her there.

He wasn't waiting for backup.

A screaming howl of pain boomed from the direction of the bedroom, and Noah crossed through the door just as another shriek filled the air.

Shayne was barely visible in the entry to the closet, but what he could see was her arm flying as she waved something long and pointy at Rick.

Whether due to his lingering injuries or whatever shock she'd given him, Rick had enough sense to put his arms up, even as the howls of pain continued. But Shayne never let up her movements, waving the object in her hand with lethal precision.

Noah lined up his gun, his arms straight and level despite the adrenaline coursing through his system. Even though he had Rick in his sights, the movement of their two bodies made it impossible to ensure he'd get a clean shot on him and avoid any risk to Shayne.

The distinct squawk of police sirens filled the air, distant but growing louder. That noise and the thing Shayne kept jabbing at Rick was enough to get him moving, and he whirled away from Shayne with a hard uppercut to her jaw before racing past Noah through the room.

Noah nearly turned to chase him—would have if Rick had moved a half a second faster—when he saw Shayne slam her head into the doorframe, stumbling hard to her knees.

The same sense of protection that had driven him back into the house kept him moving toward her, will-

ing the arriving officers the job of capturing Rick and
hoping like hell whatever she'd done to the man that had
him screaming in pain was enough to slow him down.

For now, Shayne needed him.

And there was nowhere else he could be.

Shayne heard the heavy sirens and felt Noah's strong
arms wrap around her before her world began to fade.
She struggled to keep her senses, dragging on a large
breath of air, but suddenly everything went black.

When she surfaced, her pulse slammed through her
head and chest, and she struggled to scramble up when
Noah held tight to her.

"Shhh. Hold on there."

"Noah! Are you hurt? Are you burned?" She fought
against his hold, wanting to sit up, only he held her in
place, firm and exceedingly gentle all at once.

"Burned?"

"The curling iron." Her vision wavered, and she
couldn't remember everything. "And before, when you
were outside. Going after Rick. Did he hurt you?"

"Shayne, I'm fine. I'm good." His arms tightened
as he pulled her against his chest. "You hit your head.
Shhh now and try to hold still."

The world was getting fuzzy again, but instead of
that sense of blackness from when she fainted, this was
more of the gentle darkness that consumed you before
sleep.

She had no idea how much time had passed when
she opened her eyes again, but Shayne looked up to
find Noah still staring down at her and heard the dis-

tinct sounds of people moving around. "How long was I out?"

"Only a few minutes." When she struggled again to sit up, he held tight. "Hang on. The paramedics are setting up a board and are going to move you in a minute."

"I don't need—"

Noah shook his head, his features brooking no argument as he stared down at her. "A precaution."

"But Rick. Where's Rick? He's out there. He's got people who are working for him. Helping him. He must. I can't go away, or he'll find me. You can't leave me."

"I'm going with you to the hospital. The whole way. And the police are dealing with Rick."

"They caught him?"

"Not yet, but they're going after him. He left here moments before they arrived."

"Burns. I burned him with the curling iron."

Noah glanced over to where the iron lay on the floor before turning back to her with a smile. "A brilliant idea, by the way. Based on the way he was screaming, you got some solid swipes at him."

That gentle tone and the reassurance that he wasn't leaving her alone went a long way toward calming her racing thoughts. Shayne glanced at the iron. "I knew he was coming after me, so I looked for anything I could use as a weapon. I'm just lucky this closet is big enough to have an outlet in it."

Noah looked up from their position on the floor, his gaze roaming around the walk-in closet. "I think you're equally lucky you're something of a packrat."

"Don't I know it. A lifelong trait I've always been embarrassed about just came in handy."

While she could hardly argue with the final outcome, she couldn't stop thinking about what waited for her on the other side of her bedroom.

Did the cops catch Rick or was he still on the run?

Were there others on the take from him or under his influence who could actually make it easy for him to get away, even if the police did catch him?

And when would he come after her again?

No matter how quickly time had actually moved, from the moment she'd first heard Rick stalking her through the house, every bit of it moved in slow motion for her.

The waiting for him to come through the closet door.

The struggle to burn his gun hand, followed by the even bigger struggle to keep a firm grip on the iron and hit him wherever she could do damage.

And that palpable fear for Noah that filled her the moment she heard him come into the bedroom.

She'd nearly lost her focus at Noah's arrival, Rick's grip on her arm—even as he flailed against the pain of the burns—terrifyingly strong.

But still, she kept stabbing at him. The man she'd once shared the most intimate of moments with in this very room.

"You hurt him, Shayne. Take some solace in that. You hurt him, and you kept him from hurting you. That's a win."

Was it?

Yes, she'd survived.

But she'd let this monster into her life. Into her home. Even into her body.

The dull, steadily thudding self-blame was hard to let go of.

And as Noah stared down at her, a solid, constant protector, she knew she couldn't look him in the eye any longer.

Nor could she erase the shame of what she'd allowed into her life.

Rick hid in a small, concrete culvert about a mile away from Shayne's house, at the edge of her neighborhood. He'd scoped the place out one night when they'd taken a walk after dinner and had remembered it when he'd raced off out of sight of the police.

It had been close, but that echo of sirens had penetrated through the adrenaline and the pain of his fight with Shayne just in time.

Damn it, though—he glanced down at the angry red welts on his forearms and also felt the raw pain from the one she'd landed on his jaw—she'd gotten in some damn fine hits. With a curling iron of all things. Just thinking about it had him rising up from the crouch he was in before he caught himself and ducked back down.

How dare she?

And where the hell had all that moxie come from?

One of the things he'd liked about dating her was how even-keeled she was. She bought his BS excuses like they were candy and seemed genuinely happy to be with him when they were together and not put out when they weren't. She was genuinely low-maintenance and had never given him any indication that she had such wildcat tendencies.

Or the calm ability to burn the hell out of a guy.

What had she become?

He knew he was smarter than others, but he wasn't used to underestimating his enemies. Only he'd done so with her a few times now. She'd cozied up with Ross a lot faster than he'd have expected. But hey, Rick figured, needs must be met and all that.

But something about the burns stuck in his craw. Not only did they hurt like hell, but the up-close-and-personal combat was a sea change. He thought she'd been in hiding licking her wounds, but the demon who attacked him in her closet was a woman primed for battle.

His next step was going to take some advance planning. If he wanted to bring her to Baslikova like some prize, he needed to map this out a bit better because the Shayne he thought he knew wasn't the same woman he was dealing with now.

This meant he needed to come up with another peace offering for Baslikova first. A way to buy himself a few more weeks to figure out how to get to Shayne.

Baslikova's tentacles might go deep in south Texas, but the mob boss didn't have nearly the infrastructure he needed, no matter how many goons and thugs he threw at the situation.

Lucky for him, it just so happened Rick knew which cartel leader owned the corridor that ran straight through Midnight Pass. The man kept his enterprise a closely guarded secret, but Rick had put himself in a position to know, both in his work at the FBI and among the more discreet contacts he'd cultivated on his own.

If Rick moved in and freed up that passage, it would go a long way toward showing his loyalty to Baslikova. It would also give him some cover if he could get the other cartels riled up, thinking the corridor was up for grabs.

And if the cartels got busy duking it out, it would

keep his old field office so busy they wouldn't have time to give Shayne Erickson their full attention.

No one could be two places at once.

Once Shayne was out in the open, away from the Bureau's intense scrutiny and protection, he'd move in and bring Baslikova the prize that would truly prove his loyalty.

Chapter 10

Shayne awoke in a sudden rush of panic, disoriented at the strange room and low lighting. She glanced around, taking in the machines by her side and the over-clean scent in the air. A low hum of activity was audible, even if she couldn't see anything past a pale blue curtain.

She struggled to sit up. Strong hands covered her shoulders, and Noah spoke to her in a quiet tone.

"Hey there, sleepy. Slow down a bit. You're safe here."

"Noah?"

"Yeah, it's me. And you're still in the hospital. You just dozed off for a bit."

"A bit?" She felt so muddled, a sensation she could only remember having once when she had the flu and once when she'd passed out at the dentist after having some oral surgery.

Those experiences had been confusing, but she hadn't

remembered the deep swirl of fear in her stomach as she worked to reorient herself to the world around her.

Turning to face him, she slowly came back to herself. She was in a hospital bed and the low beeping she heard was coming from the machines surrounding her bed. "Why am I here?"

"A precaution to make sure you're okay. Do you remember being checked out by the doctors?"

The morning reconstituted itself in her mind like a picture coming into clarity. The EMTs did stabilize her in her home and brought her to the hospital in the ambulance. Noah had stayed with her as he'd promised, and he'd settled into a seat beside her bed after he was allowed back into the emergency room bay where she'd been taken after arriving.

"You stayed."

"Of course. I promised you I would, and I'm not leaving."

Hot tears pricked the back of her eyes and tightened her throat. "Thank you."

"We're going to find him, Shayne. You're going to come out the other side of this. I promise."

"Does that mean he escaped? That the police didn't catch him?"

"Unfortunately no, they didn't. They sent out the K-9 team as well, and while they caught a scent, Rick eluded them and managed to get away."

"Like a ghost."

Noah didn't say anything, and even with her head injury, she was cognizant that they'd covered this ground already.

Rick Statler was a ghost because he knew how to be

one. He'd been trained by one of the most elite organizations in the world.

"Yes," Noah finally said, nodding his head. "Just like a ghost."

She knew it was madness—and she was still battling those terrible feelings of shame and embarrassment that had assailed her while lying in Noah's arms on the floor of her closet—but she needed comfort.

And more than that, she needed comfort from him.

Reaching out, she felt for Noah's hand where he gripped the railing next to her bed and linked her fingers with his. He responded immediately, holding tight.

It was easy, a simple joining of hands, but in the meeting of flesh, she felt her resolve strengthen. And—maybe—for a few extra moments, the fear of ghosts was held at bay.

"Knock, knock."

Although she didn't let go of his hand, Shayne and Noah turned their attention to the end of her bed, where Detective Belle Reynolds peered around the edge of the curtain. "Can I come in?"

"Belle." Shayne smiled. "Please come in."

The pretty detective was dressed in professional-casual clothes—black slacks and a printed blouse—but they didn't diminish the fact that the look in her eyes was all cop. "How are you doing?"

"I've been better."

"I'm sorry. I understand from the Midnight Pass officers on scene that you sustained a concussion."

"That's what they're saying," Shayne affirmed. "Mild, since I'm fairly hard-headed, but a concussion all the same."

Belle moved around to the free side of the bed, her concern evident. "I'm so sorry we didn't catch him."

Shayne felt the subtle tightening of Noah's hand against her palm before he spoke. "I'm sorry I let the bastard go."

"I'm not," Belle said. "Shayne needed you, and you stayed to help her. We just need to work harder to catch him."

Shayne hadn't gotten the sense any amount of manpower was being spared—by the FBI or by the Midnight Pass PD—so Belle's proclamation was as misplaced as Noah's self-recrimination.

"He's a trained federal agent. He's not going to be easy to catch. Which means," she looked meaningfully between Belle and Noah, "the real problem rests with me. I'm the one who allowed that snake into my house to begin with. I let him get close, and I've somehow triggered whatever madness is now driving him. If we're going to start placing blame, then you need to start with me."

It felt good to get it out, even if the people standing on either side of her immediately began to argue with her.

It was freeing to finally speak the truth.

Noah glanced around the Reynolds kitchen, the big wood table shined to a high gloss. A coffee maker gurgled as a fresh pot finished brewing, and the distant sounds of a baby crying filtered back into the room.

For now, it was just him and Belle at the table, but the long rectangle boasted eight chairs around it, a sign of the size of the family who lived there.

A family who'd quietly given him and Belle space

when they'd arrived at Reynolds Station ranch about twenty minutes earlier.

When the ER doctor had come in and released Shayne, Noah had felt a sudden shot of panic. It wasn't his usual MO, but with the events of the past few weeks, he had to admit that he was stuck and had no idea where to go. The small hotel room he was still living out of until he found an apartment in Midnight Pass didn't feel like the right choice. And Shayne's home wasn't an option until they could get someone out to repair the door.

Belle presented a kind offer, basically an expectation: he and Shayne would come out to the Reynolds ranch and stay for as long as they needed.

He was grateful for it, even as he knew the offer would only highlight his increasing lack of objectivity when it came to Shayne Erickson.

Belle was the consummate professional, but he knew she hadn't missed the way he and Shayne were holding hands in the hospital. Nor would she have missed the fact that he was at Shayne's house when Rick had attacked.

He had a responsibility to protect—their chosen profession meant they all did—but he also knew there were boundaries everyone in law enforcement understood.

And he was edging dangerously close to that boundary.

He couldn't afford to be so on display. To have his increasingly confused emotions out for public consumption. Especially when that consumption was done by a cop.

Or by his team.

The complexity of relying on the Reynolds family also meant Ryder Durant would see the growing bond between Noah and Shayne. And with Ryder's mistrust of Shayne's innocence, it was bound to be awkward.

"Have you slept, Noah?" Belle brought the coffee pot over and filled his mug before lifting the pot high. "This stuff, no matter how high-test, can't fuel you forever."

"Thanks." He turned the mug so he could firmly grip the handle. "I got a bit of downtime. I took the couch last night and slept for a few hours."

"That's not real sleep," she said as she set the pot back on the burner.

"I'll sleep when we catch him."

"And if you run yourself into the ground in the meantime? Shayne's not the only one who's experienced trauma here."

"Hell, Belle, we've all experienced trauma. You think this situation rests easy on any of us? Or that anyone's sleeping with both eyes closed right now?"

"I know that. Of course I know that. And I can confirm my team's not doing any better with any of it. There's a general feeling that this might be a federal problem, but Statler escaped in our town. On our watch. So yeah," she nodded before sipping from a bottle of water in front of her, "I get it."

"You have my compliments, then. Because you're more than keeping up with everyone, and you can't even have the coffee right now."

The announcement of Belle's pregnancy had come shortly after Statler had been taken into custody, and Noah was happy for the detective. He had gotten to know her the year before, when Russ Grantham's crimes had caught the attention of the FBI and he had collaborated with Belle on the case. She was a good cop and a good person, and despite the severe stress of that time, it had brought her back with her first love, Tate Reynolds.

The man hadn't handled her choice to be a cop very well, and it had broken them up years before. So it was good they found a way past that, and to see them moving on to marriage and creating a family.

Some people got that chance, to move on. In the case of Belle and Tate, it was with each other, but others moved on and found a second chance at happiness, too.

They discovered having a life had to do more with caring for another than driving day in and day out, year after year, in pursuit of some cosmic justice that never came.

Or was never nearly satisfying enough.

He'd always believed those were the lucky people. The ones who found a way to not just move on but to thrive.

For all the pain that the Reynolds siblings and their significant others had gone through over the past year, they'd found that path to thriving. A state that only seemed heightened with the arrival of Hoyt and Reese Reynolds's son, William, the month before.

"The water's okay." Belle glanced down at her bottle. "And since my husband sneaks me ice cream every time I so much as whisper I might like some, it's not a bad trade-off."

Noah smiled at that, thinking about the row of coffee machines at the office. "So you're saying I need to put in a requisition for a freezer and stock it with rocky road?"

"Pistachio mint is my drug of choice, but whatever gets your motor humming."

The moment of levity was welcome, but it couldn't

erase the heavy, persistent weight that had settled into his chest at the hospital.

"She thinks this is her fault, Belle. Shayne actually thinks she brought this on herself because she didn't somehow know what a monster Statler really is. A federal agency, a local police department and years of hiding in plain sight never exposed him, either, yet somehow she can honestly think this is her fault?"

Belle reached out and laid a hand over his. It was vintage Belle, that ability to remain a fierce cop and a warm, caring person all in the same package, and he knew what an amazing and rare combination that was.

"Give her time, Noah. Crisis doesn't just show itself in eating copious amounts of sugar and lack of sleep. It shows itself in a myriad of ways, including convincing yourself you had a role in what's happened."

You didn't love me enough, Noah. You didn't fight for me. For us. Tell yourself whatever you need to in order to feel better, but know this is on you.

Lindsey's words, poured out in a rush of anger and tears so long ago, had never really left him or truly gone away.

Belle was right, especially when it came to Shayne and helping her work through this idea that she was somehow responsible for Rick Statler and his crimes. Crisis and stress and strain might be driving Shayne right now, but he had all the patience in the world to help her get through it.

There were times when a person had a role in the bad things that happened to another. He'd lived with that truth long enough, and he knew what it looked like.

What it felt like.

When you knew, way down deep, that someone would still be alive if it weren't for you.

And no amount of soothing words or understanding would—or could—ever change it.

Shayne stared down at the sweet angel sleeping in her arms and couldn't believe her day could end so vastly different from how it had begun. Yet here she was, sitting in the Reynolds family kitchen, holding a sleeping baby who wasn't even a month old and listening to conversation about everything from large animal husbandry to the best ice cream flavors.

Conversation flowed like a rushing river—intense, wild and constant. Yet also underpinned with humor, laughter and care.

She stared down at William once more, his little hand curled into a fist against her breast, and marveled at how a person could start out so perfect. Innocent. Unmarred.

"A sleeping baby always seems to make the world right." Reese Reynolds leaned over, pressing a kiss to her son's head.

"I couldn't agree more. He's so sweet, Reese. So precious."

"Until he's hungry," Reese smiled indulgently down at her son. "Then he's still precious, but I'm not quite sure I'd use the word *sweet* in those moments."

Shayne had seen the full power of William's lungs, and even that precious little face screwed up in anger still hit pretty high on the sweet-o-meter for her.

"I think he's just a man who knows what he wants."

"A trait embedded deeply in his genetic material."

The kitchen had quieted a short while before as Noah, Ryder and Belle went into Belle's office to discuss a few things with her, and the Reynolds brothers headed for the stables to see to a horse who'd been under the weather. Arden and her sister-in-law, Veronica, took off for a quick run to the store for one of the flavors in the ice cream war that apparently wasn't in the large side-by-side refrigerator-freezer.

That had left Shayne, Reese and William to hold down the suddenly quiet kitchen.

"Thank you for having me tonight. After what happened today, I'm not really sure I should be here. That I should be exposing your family to danger."

"Nonsense." Reese shook her head as she settled back into her seat. "You're welcome here always. And while we might look like a bucolic spit of land out here in the country, we've got a whole lot going for us on the protection front. Cameras, security systems and a closet full of tech that could rival NASA."

"It's a shame it has to be that way."

"More than I can say. But it also means that you should feel safe here, Shayne. Protected."

"Thank you."

Silence settled between the two of them, and Shayne used the quiet to focus on William. "He is such a good baby."

"He is. Hoyt and I are lucky that he's made our adjustment to parenthood so easy." Reese hesitated for the briefest of moments, and Shayne got the distinct sense she was weighing her words before pressing forward. "It's hard to see a path to the future when the present has so many challenges. But it is out there. There's good stuff waiting to come your way."

"I want to believe that. Truly, I do. It's just—" Shayne stopped, trying to select the exact words that matched how she felt. "I've had a lot of time to think these past few weeks. And I know that many of those thoughts are steeped in the stress and strain of all that's happened to me. But it's not the only filter."

"What other filter is there? You have been through a tremendous amount of stress and strife. More than most people could see their way through let alone come out standing on the other side."

"I'm also a woman who let a monster into my home. Into my life. What's the old legend? The vampire can't come in unless he's invited?" Shayne shook her head. "It's fanciful, I know. But I also can't erase how I feel. Or how maddening it is to realize that I invited this situation into my life."

"I suppose I see your point, but I also had plenty of stress in my life. I didn't, as you say, invite it in, but that didn't make the confusion any easier to manage. Or the pain of the situation any less.

"Bad things can and do happen, Shayne. That doesn't mean that we're somehow responsible for them. That if we only had some sort of prophetic vision, we could have avoided it. We take the hand we're dealt, and we manage it to the very best of our abilities."

William stirred in Shayne's arms, and she studied his little face, his eyes popping open as he woke up. Bright blue eyes stared back up at her, curiosity stamped into that innocent gaze, and Shayne wondered at Reese's comments.

Bad things did happen. Sadly, they happened every day. But wonderful things happened, too. For all the pain Reese had endured a year ago, with the sad death of her disgraced father, Hoyt and William had also come into her life. She had love and motherhood and a future. And all of it had come from the ashes of pain and terrible hurts.

Tearing her gaze from William's, she considered Reese. "Does something new and wonderful erase the pain?"

"No. It reassigns it, in some way. And it changes how much room it has in your life, but it doesn't erase it. Not fully. I don't know that anything ever does." Reese reached out and took her son's small hand, his grip latching on to her finger. "But that pain also doesn't erase the joy of what comes in its place."

The sound of slamming doors outside the house interrupted them, and Shayne heard Arden and Veronica's voices as they got closer to the house.

"I think the ice cream's back," Shayne said.

Reese glanced toward the door. "A rather fitting end to a long day, don't you think?"

"Baby snuggles and ice cream?" Shayne got the distinct sense that William's attention was shifting to his own meal, and she handed over her warm bundle to his mother's waiting arms. "I think that is a pretty fine end to a day."

Reese stood then to take her son into the other room, but before going laid a hand on Shayne's shoulder. "There is joy, Shayne. A lot of it still to find and so much still to come your way. Today or the past few weeks or even the past few months aren't the definition of your life."

"What if that's the problem? What if I don't know what the definition really is?"

"Then you wait. And you trust that there is an answer. Sometimes it just takes a while to find it."

William let out a loud wail then, his patience for waiting for his dinner at an end.

Reese shot her a wry smile as she patted her son's writhing form. "And sometimes there's a lot of screaming in the process."

Shayne watched Reese go, and only when she had cleared the room with her son did the kitchen door open. Arden was followed by Veronica, tiptoeing into the room.

Arden spoke first, her voice low. "Oh, I love that child, but damn he has a set of lungs."

"I never think I'm remembering just how loud he is." Veronica added, "Then I hear him cry, and I realize yes, he's actually hitting that decibel level."

"He's sweet and he's just hungry," Shayne said, getting up to help them with the grocery bags of ice cream they each carried. Poking at a bag, she added, "Speaking of hungry, did the two of you buy out the store?"

"We couldn't decide," Arden shrugged. "And it's not like it's going to go to waste. Not around here and not with Belle's appetite."

Belle chose that moment to come back into the kitchen, Noah on her heels. "I heard that."

"I meant you to."

Belle swooped in and laid her chin on Arden's shoulder. "Nice try. But it's hard to be offended when you bought two gallons of pistachio mint."

"The worst ice cream ever," Arden and Veronica said in unison.

"More for me, then." Belle already had a spoon out of the drawer and the lid off one of the containers. "Oh wow, that's good."

"What did we just walk in on?" Noah leaned in, his voice a husky whisper in Shayne's ear.

A light shudder raced down her spine at his nearness and the intimacy of his voice so close to her ear. "I think in most quarters it's called trash talk."

"But they're women. Sisters," Noah said, genuine notes of disbelief threaded through the words. "Or sisters-in-law."

Shayne rose to the challenge on that one, turning toward him. "Women can't trash talk?"

"It's… I mean…well…" He stopped. "Well no, not really."

"We heard that, Noah," Veronica shouted over her shoulder as she pulled bowls out of the cabinets. "And we not only trash talk but we're also pretty good at arguing designated hitter rules and whether or not a ball had enough yardage to make a first down."

Noah shook his head. "I stand corrected."

"Schooled, Noah." Arden said, laying a heaping handful of spoons onto the table with a clatter. "It's called getting schooled."

"Consider me schooled then."

Shayne watched all of it in subtle bemusement. The Reynolds family was big and loud and wild about one another, and it showed. That easy familiarity. The silly teasing. Even the affectionate poking at foibles was all done with love and an overarching fondness that was hard to resist.

So she didn't.

Instead, she decided it was time to take the joy of the moment and allow it to take up as much space as the hardships of the day. After all, the day might have started in a way she hoped never to experience again, but it was ending on an incredibly lovely note.

With baby snuggles and ice cream.

With a group of people who welcomed her into their home, no questions asked.

And with a man who reinforced her belief that good existed in the world, steeped in the people who vowed to protect it.

There was joy, also.

And for tonight, she was going to take it. Along with a bowl of chocolate ice cream and the warm, warm gaze of a very, very good man.

Chapter 11

Noah heard the water stop running in the en suite bathroom and diligently fought to ignore the strange sense of intimacy that hung over him like a blanket. He and Shayne had been given a spare room in one of the wings of the large Reynolds ranch house, and he'd already set up several sheets and pillows on the couch that dominated one wall of the bedroom's outer sitting room while she got ready for bed.

He could do this.

He'd spent last night at Shayne's home, and there was nothing about tonight that was any different.

Even if they had spent the long day together, another test of their internal fortitude, physical strength and emotional strain.

But there had been ice cream, Shayne had reminded him as he'd tried to talk over the day with her. *Tried* being the operative word since she'd seemed unwilling to discuss anything beyond the new baby, the vast quantities of ice cream in the Reynolds freezer or a few jokes Tate had made over dinner.

Was she simply processing it all? Or did she just need a break from the mental strain?

He wanted to give her the space she needed but ignoring the day they'd both experienced wasn't necessarily healthy, either.

Maybe because you need to talk about it, too.

That thought struck out, whip-quick as a snake, and Noah recognized it. And in the recognition, realized it was time to own it.

Shayne came out of the bathroom, clad in a T-shirt and shorts, her hair pulled up. She was fresh-faced from her evening ministrations in the bathroom, and he couldn't deny how good she looked.

Or how deeply appealing he found her.

"The Reynolds family are an amazing group of people," Shayne said as she took a seat on the couch opposite him. "Warm, welcoming and really funny. I know Arden well, but before tonight didn't know much of her family beyond passing hellos. They're quite a bunch."

"I feel the same. I got to know Belle last year during the Russ Grantham case but not her family. And then I was transferred out of The Pass quickly after that. They're good people. They've been through a lot the past year but have clearly come out the other side."

"Reese talked about that when we were in the kitchen with the baby. Or maybe better said, she offered a soft suggestion that, in her way, was as indomitable as a shout from the rooftops."

"What's that?"

"She talked about taking joy. And about how we're not responsible for the bad actions of others, even when they hurt us."

"You're not, you know."

Shayne frowned before her back straightened, her shoulders stiffening.

"What's the matter?" he asked.

"Right there. That, Noah. You want to make me feel better with your whole talk track about how I'm not to blame or how I shouldn't feel responsible, yet you can't do the same for yourself."

"I didn't say that."

"You most certainly have. You've said it in your actions and in all you won't say. Your focus on every comment I make when it comes to how I feel about Rick and the time I spent with him being the root of enormous guilt. But you have zero acknowledgment or even understanding that you're doing the same."

Although they hadn't quite shifted over to an argument, Noah felt one brewing. That slow-rolling emotional thunder that made it abundantly obvious a storm was coming.

Oddly, he felt himself primed for it. Because gentle words and quiet understanding no longer seemed like enough.

Based on her reaction, it was no longer enough for either of them.

"What do you want me to say, Shayne?"

"I want you to take the same responsibility you're asking of me. I want you to acknowledge that this isn't one-sided. You keep saying that I've erroneously taken this burden on myself and that I'm somehow trying to manage it all alone. But you've done the same. Ryder Durant has done it. And Belle has, too."

"We work in law enforcement. This is on us."

"No, Noah. This is on Rick. Isn't that what you keep trying to tell me?"

He saw the fire in her eyes and felt the air shift again, zapping with emotional electricity between them.

Maybe she was right.

For all their anger at Rick, it was no longer possible to ignore how much anger they had also directed inwardly. The stress and the strain.

Roiling, frustrated fury needed a place to land.

The words that came out instead tightened his chest and threatened to cut him off at the knees.

"I was married once."

Something in his mind screamed and clamored for him to pull back the words, yet now that he had started, Noah didn't know how to stop the confession.

"Once?"

"Yes. We were married for eighteen months until the day she came home and told me it was over. And three days, later she was murdered."

Shayne's gaze went wide at his description of Lindsey's death, but it didn't diminish the raw sympathy that infused her voice. "Oh, Noah. I'm so sorry."

"Yeah, see, it's funny. Those words. 'I'm sorry.' That's the first place anybody goes. They're the first words anybody has. And it's not that I'm not appreciative, or that I think you're saying those words in vain, but the only filter I hear them through is a guilty one."

"But why?"

"Because I'm the reason she's dead."

* * *

Shayne searched Noah's face for any sign that what he said was exaggerated or possibly overblown from living with it over time, but all she saw was the bleak knowledge of what he believed.

"What happened?"

For a long time, Noah remained silent. So long that Shayne feared he was just going to get up and leave, embarrassed at the outburst that had him confessing this aspect of his past.

So when he finally did speak, she was determined to give him the floor and even more determined that he have the space to get it all out.

"I began dating Lindsey about two years after I got into the Bureau. It's an intensive job, and it's something I wanted for as long as I can remember. So while I dated, it wasn't something I made a very high priority in my life."

He stilled, scrubbing a hand over his cheeks. She heard the light scratch of his day's growth of beard and wondered at the absolute bleakness that had settled deep in his brown gaze. At the horrifying memories that swirled there, even now.

"But I met Lindsey through a friend at the Bureau. We dated a few times, and it was fun and more enjoyable than the dates I'd been half-assing my way through. And then we both realized pretty quickly that there was something more between us. We were compatible, and we enjoyed each other's company. She lightened me up, and for a while, it was a heady experience. For as much as I wanted the Bureau job, it's a grind and it gets to you. We're not exactly dealing with easy cases or people who inspire a lot of confidence in the human race."

"I can see how that would be trying. And I can also see how someone who provided a reprieve from that callousness and cruelty would be valuable beyond measure."

When he only nodded at that but didn't elaborate on what else made Lindsey special to him, Shayne got the first inkling the relationship might have had serious bumps. Committed to letting him get the full story out, she gave him the space to continue.

"The dating got more serious, and we were together for about a year when I proposed. Her friends were all starting to get married, and she mounted increasing pressure for us to move in that direction."

"Did you want to get married?"

"I wanted to stay with her, so in some ways yes, I did." He shook his head. "But in others, no, not really. I loved her, but I wasn't in the same hurry to move us toward that milestone."

It was a reality of dating when you were younger, Shayne knew. That pressure to start the next phase of your life. To begin building a future with another person.

It also sounded like an insurmountable burden, weighted with a heavy urgency, when she looked back on it now.

When it was a welcome next step—for both parties—it was wonderful and happy and life affirming. But when it was simply about keeping up appearances for the sake of what others thought?

Not so much.

Wasn't that part of what she'd realized about her relationship with Rick? Putting his psychopathic tendencies aside, she had been more excited about being *in* the relationship than she had been with the person she was in the relationship with.

It was a tough admission but an honest one.

"But you got married anyway?" she finally asked Noah, pressing him forward with his story.

"We did. And for a while, it was a happy thing. We had the whirlwind of parties and the activities with our friends who were also getting married, and life just sort of moved us along. But my work got more intense as well. I was in the San Antonio bureau at the time, working my way up. And I got put on a really big case. A gang running a money-laundering scheme was increasingly taking shape, adding some sex trafficking and illegal gambling to round out the business."

"More inspiring tales of the best of humanity."

"Exactly."

Her reiteration of his earlier point was enough to draw a small, sad smile, and he nodded at her assessment. "And these dudes running this ring were some of humanity's finest, let me tell you. I was low man on the job, but I was making a name for myself. I uncovered a clear connection between the ring and a few underground gambling parlors and helped on an op that removed three women from a sex-trafficking operation.

"It was good work. Challenging work but satisfying when I realized it was making a difference. It was only three women, sure, but to each of them, getting out of that hellish existence meant everything. And it reinforced for me why I was doing this job and why it mattered."

"I'd have thought Lindsey would agree with you. That she'd have believed she was married to someone who worked every day to help others. To give them a better life."

"On the surface, she did. She preened to her friends about how hard I worked and how proud she was of me. And I believe she was proud. I don't think that was just lip service. But she was also terrified for me and about what I was doing. Or what little of it I could talk about."

"Did she tell you she was afraid?"

"No. Instead of talking to me about it, instead of working through it together, she found solace elsewhere."

Shayne was sorry the woman was dead, but a shot of anger also filled her chest at such a callous action. Holding it back, recognizing on some level her anger wasn't welcome in this moment, she pressed on.

"You didn't know any of it?"

"Not until it was too late. The damage to our relationship was too great, and she told me she wanted out and that she didn't want to be married anymore."

Shayne considered all he'd told her, and while she was sorry that his relationship hadn't worked out or that his wife hadn't been able to find a way to overcome her fear for him, she couldn't understand how that could possibly relate to Lindsey's death.

Or why Noah felt so responsible for any of it.

"It's sad that things didn't work out. Truly, Noah, it is. That life inexperience that pressed her to want to be married to keep up with others was the same inexperience that prevented her from talking to you and telling you how she felt.

"But I'm not sure I understand why you're responsible for that? Or why you need to take responsibility for someone who wanted to marry you yet couldn't talk to you about how she felt."

"Because I'm the reason she was murdered."

"But how? You didn't share your case files with her or talk about the specifics of your work. How was she possibly exposed to any of that?"

"I kept the confidences of my job, never sharing the specifics of my cases. But she read some texts I got one night while I was out of the room. She put two and two together with a news story that had just broken in the area about the women who'd gotten out of the sex ring, and Lindsey talked to her lover about it. He was a friend of an acquaintance of ours, and it turns out that acquaintance was also one of the low-level operatives in the gang."

Shayne finally saw where this was going, and it horrified her to think that idle gossip had wrought such damage.

Worse, that it could inflict such devastation on a life.

"That guy came after her?"

"He did. He was going to come after me, but he didn't know she'd already set our breakup in motion. I basically spent three days holed up at the FBI office, licking my wounds and never leaving, not even once. When he couldn't find me, he decided he'd bring a prize home to his organization and killed Lindsey instead."

"Oh my God. Noah."

She reached for him, but he was already up off the couch, pacing the room in front of her. "She didn't do anything wrong, but she paid a horrible price."

"She did suffer, Noah. Needlessly. But she also put her faith in the wrong people. That's terribly sad, endlessly so," she rushed on when she caught sight of his face and the misery stamped there. "But it's not on you. You're not responsible for that choice."

"I'm the reason she's dead. Nothing can change that."

While she could understand his regret, it was impossible as an outsider looking in to see how it was truly Noah's fault.

Bad circumstances, yes. And a situation that existed because of his job, another yes.

But he didn't cheat on his wife. He didn't read texts not meant for him. Nor did he pull the trigger.

Sadly, based on whatever he'd built in his mind over the years, he didn't see it that way. However he'd chosen to emotionally protect himself, it was rooted in the idea that he had to take ownership for this terrible crime.

That he had to be the one to pay for it.

As she considered the man sitting before her, the one she'd come to know over the past few weeks, Shayne understood that it would be difficult for him to get past this. It would be hard for anyone, but knowing the deep level of responsibility Noah took for his work and for the team around him, it would be ridiculous to think this was something he could easily get past.

Yet how could he ever move on if he was mired in this pain?

Noah walked the length of the barn and took comfort in the softly whickered greetings of the various horses. Several had bedded down already, but a few were interested enough in their new visitor to put their heads over their stall doors and greet him with a mix of curiosity and welcome.

It had been Tate who'd given him the code to the barn,

acknowledging him in the kitchen with a soft hello after Noah had fled the guest room.

No, he corrected himself, after he'd fled Shayne.

He didn't regret telling her about Lindsey. He was a man who knew how to keep his own counsel, and if he hadn't wanted to discuss it, he'd have left the subject alone.

Only on some level, he wanted Shayne to know.

Maybe he even needed her to.

"They're even more willing to listen to your late-night secrets if you feed them a few sugar cubes." The voice was quiet, and Noah was shocked anyone had managed to sneak up on him. But when he whirled around to face Arden Reynolds, he admitted she'd done just that.

"I'm sorry if I disturbed anyone by coming out here. You've all been more than kind to host us for the night."

She extended a hand and dropped a few cubes into his palm before turning toward the nearest horse and offering the taste of sugar. "Sweet boy," she crooned to the horse. "You enjoy."

She moved down the line and offered the same to the next horse peeking over its stall door before turning back to face Noah. "And there's no such thing as disturbing anyone around here. Between a newborn and eight adults, all of whom are dealing with something of their own at any moment in time, our house doesn't exactly rest peacefully each night."

"I know you all had some troubles over the past year, but I thought those were well past and settled?"

"Some?" Arden raised a lone eyebrow. "You're a kind man, Noah, but I'd say the Reynolds name has basically equaled trouble for the past year."

"Yes, but those times are past," he persisted. "You all should be able to rest easy in your own home."

"Well, that day might come someday, but it's not here yet. So in the spirit of someone who knows the value of a late-night equine listener, please know I'm happy to lend a human ear, too."

Noah busied himself with his own sugar cubes, debating the wisdom of sharing his thoughts since the whole reason he'd come out here in the first place was to find solitude.

He managed to delay the inevitable for a few minutes with the sweet treats for the horses, but by the time he turned back to an expectant Arden, he knew he couldn't hold back.

"She thinks it's her fault. This situation. Rick. His stalking her at her home. How can she think that? Any of it?"

Once again, for a man used to keeping his own counsel, Noah was saying an awful lot this evening.

Add on how hypocritical it felt to voice those thoughts to Arden, especially on the heels of his confession about Lindsey, and Noah knew he wasn't making a bit of sense .

"Of course she does. We humans are a funny lot under the best of circumstances. We take ownership for stuff we have no control of and precious little ownership of the emotions we actually wield as weapons to hurt others."

"But she's a smart woman, and she knows fact from fiction. How can she possibly take ownership for the actions of a madman?"

"Because she shared her life with him. She had sex with him." Arden held up a finger to signal to wait a minute before she pressed on. "She was contemplating a future with him. Finding out the man you saw that way is a murderous bastard with a side of psychosis will shake anyone."

"But that's on him."

"And it's on her, too. Until you understand and recognize that, you and Shayne will continue to be at cross-purposes."

Noah didn't say anything, just let Arden's well-considered arguments hover between them.

He wished like hell, though, she hadn't brought up the sex part.

He was a grown man and had no problem thinking of women as having their own sexual freedom and agency. But damn, the thought of Shayne and Rick together left something dark and ugly swirling in him. It wasn't fair and it wasn't rational, but he hadn't quite been able to see his way past it, either.

In her admonitions, he sensed Arden recognized that, too. It didn't paint him in a particularly favorable light.

And deep down he knew he didn't deserve any sympathy if he couldn't get his head out of his ass on this issue.

"She can't see past all the judgment and self-directed anger she's putting on herself, Noah. So you have to let go of your own anger on the subject because if you don't, all you're going to do is add to the problem."

"What I think doesn't matter. And it shouldn't matter. I'm one of the agents assigned to protect her. That's my job, and it's all she should expect from me."

"You know, Noah, there's usually an earthy undertone in this barn, but there aren't normally any piles of bullshit lying around."

He couldn't have been more surprised if Arden had punched him. And because he wasn't ready with a comeback, she plowed right on through.

"You care about Shayne. It's easy to see, and it's not something you should have to hide from or excuse."

"She's the job."

"Yeah, well, maybe she can be more than the job. We all deserve a shot at that. Ryder and I got that shot. Belle and Tate got that shot. You're no exception."

"I'm not that man, Arden."

The youngest Reynolds sibling looked about ready to argue when she seemingly thought better of it.

"I'm a yoga instructor. I've made the practice of yoga one of my lifelong goals. I'm nowhere near where I want to be, but I show up every day, focused on improving. On learning. And on working toward the best version of myself, both in body and mind."

"Ryder speaks well of your work. He's proud of you."

"He's also a chicken who won't get on a mat with me and do his own practice."

"Well, I'm sure—"

"That my fiancé is afraid of bending himself like a pretzel and falling on his face? Yes, most likely. But that's not the real reason he doesn't come."

Since Noah had seen Ryder in a weight room at the FBI gym as well as his athleticism and endurance out in the field, he was having a hard time picturing Ryder afraid to do yoga, but Arden clearly had a point to make, and she'd set him in his place a few times already. Allowing her to make it was in his own best interest.

"The reason I'm telling you this, Noah, is because the things we are afraid to do take on any number of excuses in our mind. And until we actually do the thing—

that thing that makes us scared and afraid of physically falling or even proverbially falling—we never move ahead."

As metaphors went, hers made her point. But he still felt honor bound to defend Ryder.

"Your fiancé is one of the best field agents I know. Maybe he just doesn't want to do yoga."

Arden waved a hand. "It's beside the point."

"Then what is the point? Of all this or any of this?"

"The point is we don't live when we're afraid. We don't take risks when we're afraid. And we don't even do the basic maintenance work when we're afraid."

"You're not really talking about yoga, are you?"

She let out a long-suffering sigh, one he had no doubt she used on her three older brothers often. It was surprisingly effective, even without a blood tie, and it forced him to stare in the face of that irrationality he couldn't quite seem to shake.

And recognize that it really had no place in whatever was happening with him and Shayne. Or, frankly, in whatever didn't happen, either.

He just needed to let it go.

And for all her sighing, Arden was sweetly gentle when she did finally speak.

"I'm talking about a lesson it took me far too long in my own life to learn. I'd probably still be living a half-truth myself—believing I was making my way in the world and constantly blathering on and on about the body-mind-spirit connection—if I hadn't learned it a few short months ago when Ryder came into my life."

"But you believe in the body-mind-spirit connection, right?"

"Of course I do. But I believed it for other people. I

never believed it for me. Even after Ryder showed up. Even after I knew I was in love with him, I was still afraid to believe it could be possible for me."

"Some people just don't get a happy-ever-after."

"True," she nodded. "Some don't. Which is why when one is being offered to you, you'd better not be an ass and ignore the gift."

Without waiting for his response, she turned on her heel and headed for the exit. It was only as she hit the doors that she turned around. "The horses really do make great listeners. So stay as long as you need and get it all off your chest, Noah."

She gave him a little wave before heading out the door, her last words drifting into the night. "You'll feel better for it. I promise."

Chapter 12

Shayne lay in bed for a long while staring at the ceiling and thinking about Noah's talk of his dead wife before she swung out from under the covers and headed for the door. He'd disappeared a while ago, and she was secretly grateful for a bit of breathing room as she took in all he'd shared.

Then she'd grown bored with her own thoughts, determined to take some action.

Veronica had shown her a small office earlier when she'd brought them up to the spare bedroom and had offered use of the laptop and internet connection if either of them needed it. As she'd lain there, tossing and turning and full of her own thoughts, Shayne landed back on her idea from a few days before.

It was time to reach out to her sister.

Leaving the guest room and padding down the hall

to the office, she quickly logged into her email account.
Unsure of what to say, she started with the obvious.

Hello, Caroline. I wanted to reach out with a bit of an
update. I know I've been bad about showing it, but I've
missed you.

Shayne reread the opening and nearly deleted it when
she stopped herself, opting to leave it alone. She wasn't
writing pretty platitudes. She did miss her sister. And
to be honest, Shayne knew, she'd missed Caroline for
far longer than this current situation in her life.

I know we spoke shortly after my kidnapping, but I
found it necessary to go off-the-grid for a bit. I'm working with the FBI since I've realized that's not the best
way to stand my ground and get past this. I'm staying
with a friend and her family in Midnight Pass. they've
offered protection and shelter, and I'm safe.

Shayne stopped writing and considered her next
steps. And knew there was only one thing she wanted.

I'd like to talk again if you're free. whatever time works
best for you. I don't have a cell phone right now, but
you can get a hold of me through my friend, Arden
Reynolds, or you can email me if you'd like to talk.

Shayne added Arden's number and hit send before
she could stop herself. She was strangely affected by
sending the note, an odd mix of anxiety and hope in
her chest.

Would Caroline respond?

Did she even want her to?

For all her deep need to talk to her sister—and her

belief that Noah would stand by his promise to keep
Caroline safe—there was still concern about involv-
ing her sister in the disaster that was her life right now.

But there was also the increasing panic that she
needed to warn Caroline about what was happening.
Although she'd said very little about her family situation
to Rick while they were dating—yet one more sign she
hadn't shared with him all her innermost thoughts—she
had still mentioned that she had a sister.

And while Caroline had been given a full debrief by
the FBI on the kidnapping and all that had happened
to Shayne, with the specific instruction that she, too,
needed to watch out for herself, Rick had proven himself more dangerous than any of them had suspected.

Which made a conversation not only prudent but
necessary.

And if she were really honest with herself, she wanted
to talk to her sister about Noah.

The jumbled feelings—ones she had no business
having—weren't going anywhere and having a sister's
shoulder to cry on would be helpful as Shayne navigated this new wrinkle in her life.

While she harbored significant embarrassment and
guilt over her relationship with Rick, she wasn't so far
gone that she somehow thought she should spend the
rest of her life alone. She deserved to find someone and
deserved to find love.

But so soon?

Up until a month ago, whether the relationship had
been fully satisfying or not, she'd been in one. And although she'd had doubts, if asked directly, she'd have
said she was happy with it. That was, of course, before

her significant other kidnapped her and threatened to kill her.

But before that? She thought wryly.

She'd been all in.

Although she'd known people throughout her life who could end one relationship and move quickly into the next—and she envied them that ease—she'd never really succeeded in managing that.

Which made these feelings for Noah confusing and exciting, all at once.

All while being deeply inconvenient.

This simply wasn't the time to pursue a relationship. That went double when it came to falling for the federal agent who'd made it his mission to protect her.

"What are you doing up?"

The subject of all that confusion stood in the doorway of the office, his gaze steady.

"I'm emailing my sister. I've been meaning to, and since I couldn't sleep, I figured it was a good time to contact her."

"I'm sure she'll be glad to hear from you."

Shayne wasn't entirely sure about that but thought he was sweet to say so.

Misguided, perhaps, but sweet all the same.

"We'll see. I just hope she responds."

Noah frowned before pushing himself off the door frame and coming to stand beside her at the desk. "Look, Shayne. About before—"

She wanted to tell him not to worry about it. To put any concern about the sad conversation they'd had about his dead wife out of his mind. That it was a quiet moment of sharing that didn't mean anything beyond a few minutes of solace with another human being. Nor did his deeply sad story have any bearing on the situation they presently found themselves in.

But she couldn't.

And she refused to let him think that he could get away with assuming he had a role in the poor woman's death and then not even consider Shayne's own concerns about the outcome of her time with Rick.

They were both right, and they were both wrong.

She'd spent a lot of time alone thinking about that fact after he'd made his excuses and escaped from the guest room.

"What about before? Because I'd have liked the opportunity to respond to what you'd shared, but you ran away instead."

"I didn't run." He maintained his level gaze, but she didn't miss the way the hand cocked on his hip tightened, his fingers digging into the material of his jeans. "But it is a painful memory, and I needed to get a bit of air."

"I've no doubt of that. The whole story was awful and terrible, and I'm sure it doesn't get less so, no matter how much time passes."

"No, it doesn't."

"Nor does it make any sense to continue beating yourself up over what happened to Lindsey."

He looked prepared to argue, and Shayne was about to let him when something leaped inside her chest. A small spark quickly caught flame, and she realized that she was done letting things happen around her.

She'd recognized the men and women of the FBI were doing their jobs every minute of every hour that they questioned her.

She'd also recognized that Ryder Durant was doing

his job and playing all the reasonable angles when he gave her the stink eye over pizza, his suspicions of her still abundantly evident.

She'd even recognized that the Reynolds family was doing their duty to her friendship with Arden and the very real intricacies of Ryder's job by allowing his field boss to stay in their home.

But damn it, she was done giving everyone her gentle, patient understanding.

When was she going to get a bit of it in return?

She wasn't guilty, and she wasn't conspiring with Rick. Her entire life had been upended, and she was done playing nice about it.

"What I don't understand or appreciate is how you can continue to mire yourself in a relationship that came to an end, by all accounts, more than a decade ago and not give me a moment's grace over my feelings about Rick."

"He's not worth your feelings."

"That's not for you to decide!"

The words were out like a shot, and she caught herself by surprise at the immediate anger coalescing like liquid fire in her veins.

Leaping up from her chair, she crossed the room, suddenly grateful for the huge Reynolds ranch house and the fact they had the guest wing all to themselves. Because there was a fight brewing, and Shayne had to admit, it was one she relished having.

Especially when Noah spoke in a calm, placating tone.

"Taking on the sins of a madman isn't worth it, no matter how much you want to believe you're at fault.

You can yell and rant at me all you want, but I'm not going to indulge that line of thinking."

"Indulge me?" Shayne practically vibrated at the insinuation Noah somehow needed to coddle her and pander to her feelings.

"Yes, indulge you. At some point, you need to open your eyes and see this entire situation for what it is. A bad actor who used and abused his position of authority. He didn't care who he took out in the process, nor was he about to let anyone get in his way."

"Big words from a man who can't stop licking his wounds long enough to look around and see life has moved on."

It was raw and it was rude and monumentally unfair, but if she had to take it on the chin, then so did Noah.

If her behavior was about wallowing in embarrassment then he needed to be called out, too, because his wasn't any better.

And if the sentiment underlying all of it was that they had a real, genuine attraction to one another, and it was time to move on past old loves, then she'd push there, too.

And she was done sitting back and not taking what was right in front of her.

With that foremost in her mind, she made the last few steps to Noah, wrapped her arms around his neck and took.

Noah let the wave of need and want and sheer unbridled desire wash over him like a benediction.

He wanted Shayne.

And it increasingly didn't seem to matter why he shouldn't want her because he did.

His job? His past? Their current situation?

None of it mattered when the woman was in his arms, her mouth pressed to his, heat flaring between them with pure, pulsing energy.

The heavy heart that had carried him out to the stables lightened as he held Shayne in his arms, and he recognized the truth of the moment. She brought something to him that felt a lot like air and breath and healing.

And—maybe, just maybe—a fresh chance to move beyond the pain of Lindsey's death.

He'd never fully be free of it, but he'd carried the guilt for so long it had become a living part of him, like another appendage or a new organ. One that had become rotted from the self-recrimination and remorse.

And the very real knowledge that he couldn't be the man Lindsey had needed him to be.

Was he destined to repeat the same mistake?

Despite the strange moments that had pulled them together, Noah knew that his time with Shayne was different. Being with her was different, even if he accounted for the fact that they didn't fall into this situation by dating.

Quite the opposite, actually.

Shayne Erickson was a material witness he'd initially vacillated between condemning as an accessory to nearly treasonous behavior and anxiously trying to prove wasn't guilty.

One his colleagues still questioned as to her guilt or innocence.

Yet in some strange way, he recognized her, too. Knew her. Believed on some level that there was something between them.

Was he deluding himself?

Even as he asked himself the question, Noah ran his hands down her spine and pulled her closer, their bodies flush together.

Whatever was here between them was real.

Misplaced, yes.

Out of time, without question.

But real? Absolutely.

"Shayne," he whispered against her lips, his hands roaming over her slender form. She was still so thin, the weeks of hardly eating while in hiding taking their toll. Yet there remained an inner strength to her.

A spine of steel that had seen her through.

That would continue to see her through.

It called to him and only added to his fierce determination to see this case through. To ensure she came out the other side whole and ready to thrive in the world once again.

Oh how he wanted that for her.

"We fight when we talk too long," she whispered against his lips. "Let's just keep kissing."

Since he had no response for that, he did as she asked, pulling her close once more and sinking into the moment.

Noah wasn't a fanciful man, and he saw the world in black-and-white. This trait had served him well in pursuit of the bad guys, but it made navigating the more nuanced aspects of life a challenge.

And everything about Shayne Erickson was about nuance.

She'd forced him to look at his work through a filter, and he wasn't used to doing that. He had no interest in wrapping a case just to close it, and he worked them to the very best of his ability, but he'd always sustained himself on the understanding that people did right or they did wrong.

When they did wrong, they were apprehended and justice was meted out to match the crime.

He knew Shayne was innocent of working with Rick—knew it down to his toes—but he had precious little to prove that fact.

Yet he knew.

And for someone who wasn't used to operating solely on instinct, it scared him and made him question himself. The woman made him lose his balance, and he was both intrigued by the sensation and scared he'd never get that sense of equilibrium back.

Or that he'd want to.

With that thought firmly echoing in his mind, he pulled back, lifted his head and broke off the connection.

Her lips were glossy from their kiss, slightly swollen, and her eyes were wide, that vivid blue drawing him in. She considered him, and Noah was shocked to realize how on display he felt and how deeply open to her scrutiny.

That anger and frustration that had driven her to kiss him had faded, replaced with a level of understanding he wasn't sure he deserved.

"We've been through a lot the past few days," she said. "It hasn't just been me."

"You've borne the brunt of it."

Her gaze narrowed slightly. "I think that's all a matter of perspective."

Since she'd defended herself with a hot curling iron

and ended up with a concussion, he would give her the edge, but at the same time, he was humbled by her point.

"Maybe it is. But thank you for understanding."

"You're not superhuman, and no one expects you to be, least of all me." She laid a hand on his shoulder. "Maybe that's the real takeaway from all of this. That even when we push ourselves and try our hardest to drive to the best outcomes, we're not always successful."

"Success in this instance is keeping you safe."

"That's one aspect, but it's not all. Catching Rick is important. For you and your colleagues. For the safety of Midnight Pass. And for the overall safety of the people who are ultimately impacted by the drug corridor he's doing his level best to keep open. That's important work, Noah. And it's way bigger than one person.

"I allowed myself to forget that for a while, but being here, seeing how the Reynolds family is working toward building a new life for themselves, it brought it back to me."

Yet again, she simply awed him.

How many people could stare down a very clear threat to themselves and be so open and understanding of how that threat affected others? Because while all that she said was true, none of it diminished the fact that Rick was after her.

The man's reasons might be his sick, twisted own, but his determination was clear to everyone.

"You don't deserve this, Shayne." Noah reached out and stroked the soft skin of her cheek. The space was hollower than in the headshot of her that hung on his board at the office, the weeks of stress and strain since her kidnapping taking their toll, but even that couldn't diminish her inner radiance.

Or keep him from seeing that while she had a sur-
face-level beauty that was obvious, the depths of who
she was shined from her with the true loveliness that
was Shayne.

He bent his head, unable to resist her once more,
when Ryder's voice filtered down the hall mere moments before he moved into the room.

"Noah. We got a hit."

Shayne leaped back from her close proximity to
Noah, her wide-eyed expression shifting between him
and Ryder and back again.

"How close is he?"

Ryder eyed Shayne with that same thin veil of distrust Noah had seen at the office the day before but said
nothing. Instead, he just pressed on with the details.

"Caught on camera at a small drugstore two coun-
ties over."

Noah stared at the large set up of monitors in Belle's
office and considered the video Ryder had already cued
up and replayed a few times. They currently had it on
pause as Noah and Ryder conferenced in with Brady
and two other field operatives.

The temptation had been great to send out a team
immediately to canvas the area around the drugstore
where they'd gotten the footage, but the speed with
which Rick was in and out and the fact they couldn't
get a handle on him after he left the small store—either
on foot or in a vehicle—made a middle-of-the-night
search less than useful.

Instead, they were trying to focus on the clues they
could glean and use the next day in a surprise attack.

"He's hurt," Brady reasoned, his features set in hard

lines visible even in their video conference. "It's the only reason he risked going in there at all."

"There's another clue, too. Your intel says the owner of the drugstore just put the cameras in a week ago. Statler's staked out every place he's been using to stay off the radar. Going in there and not registering the cameras means he's not just injured but in a lot of pain."

"Shayne got him good this morning with the curling iron." Brady's grim features broke into a smile at that. "I'd love to have seen that one."

Noah had seen it, and he still had the mental scars from fearing she'd be hurt, but he understood Brady's underlying point. And the fact that Shayne's willingness to fight back so hard was a genuine point of pride.

That didn't even make a dent in Ryder's demeanor or attitude, Noah acknowledged as he glanced over at Durant.

They made a few more plans, agreeing to meet at nine in the office before shutting down the video call.

The end of the call didn't reduce any of the tension in the room, but Noah opted to let it lie and see if it dissipated or if he and Ryder would finally have it out. He moved closer to the screen and tapped a few keys to watch the video again.

Rick came into the drugstore, his gait stiff. He wasn't moving erratically, but he was clearly in pain. He kept his face averted for much of his time in the store, but they caught a clear visual when he checked out. And, when they'd zoomed in earlier, they'd seen the items on the counter were bandages and antiseptic ointment.

"He's definitely hurt." Noah tapped a few keys to bring the quadrant where Rick's face was into a close-up view on the screen. Some markings on his face, consistent with the curling iron burns Shayne managed to get in, were visible along his jawline.

"Shayne did a convincing job on him."

And we're off.

Ryder had remained quiet through most of dinner, but that had been easy with the boisterous conversation in the Reynolds kitchen. Noah had noticed, and he was quite sure Arden had, too, but Ryder's lack of conversation hadn't made much of a ripple in the evening.

But Durant didn't like having Shayne in the house, and he obviously didn't appreciate the kiss he'd come across in the small office upstairs.

Of that, Noah had no doubt at all.

"Convincing?" Noah turned fully from the screen to look at Ryder. "I'd say it's hard to be anything else when you're fighting for your life."

"Or turning on the one you've been in league with all along."

Noah recognized the jab and nearly responded with a few of his own when something held him back, his conversation with Arden in the stables ringing in his head like a five-alarm fire.

The things we are afraid to do take on any number of excuses in our mind. And until we actually do the thing—that thing that makes us scared and afraid of physically falling or even proverbially falling—we never move ahead.

"This isn't about Shayne, is it?"

"Who else is it about?"

"You, Ryder. You know what you almost lost a month ago in that safe house. You know how close Rick came to doing unspeakable harm to Arden."

"Don't psychoanalyze me, Ross. You're the one cozying up with the suspect."

"You've never given me a concrete reason, not from the very first, why you think she's guilty."

"You don't have much better to claim that she's innocent," Ryder shot back. "Nothing more than your dick."

That was nearly the last straw, but Noah held in for one more round.

Because if he couldn't set the right example—if he couldn't keep his head when one of his own was hurting—then he didn't have the right to call himself a leader.

"Actually, I do. The tech team's scoured her electronics top to bottom. She was kidnapped for more than two days by the man you're claiming she was in league with, and her medical examination after that kidnapping indicated she was dehydrated and nearly in shock."

Ryder looked ready to argue, but Noah pressed on.

"After that roller coaster of fun, we gave her hell for four days of intense questioning, after which she went on the run and lived alone, hiding out and basically living on granola bars and diet soda. Oh, right, and the last thing. The man you claim she's colluding with has tried to kill her three times in less than forty-eight hours.

"So yeah, Ryder, I do have some real, tangible reasons I think she's innocent. And not one of them have a damn thing to do with my dick."

Ryder shook his head, even as some of the militance faded from his tone. "You've lost your focus, Noah."

"I've found it, Ryder. We all have. We've all got a common enemy here, and it's not Shayne Erickson."

"You want her."

"And you wanted Arden. Did it keep you from doing your job?"

"Hell no."

"Then why can't you see your way toward giving me the same respect?"

Ryder hung his head at that, and Noah finally saw a break in the clouds. But when Ryder's voice came out in a choked whisper, Noah recognized they might have finally broken through to rock bottom.

"Arden was kidnaped and manhandled and held in that safe house like a caged animal. It kills me, Noah. Freaking kills me every time I think of it. And I can't stop thinking about it."

"You love her. And you're going to have to work through this together."

"I know, man." Ryder dragged a hand through his hair. "I know."

"And Shayne?"

"All those things have nagged at me, but not just to spite her. She spent a lot of time with Statler, and we needed to cover our bases there."

"We needed to and we did. And if it makes you feel any better, she's beaten herself up over that time she spent with him far more than any of us have."

"Arden said as much." Ryder blew out a hard breath. "If it makes you feel any better, Murphy thinks I'm a dumbass."

"You talked it over with your K-9?"

Ryder gave a small lopsided grin at that. "I know he's a dog, but I talk, he listens. It works for me."

"And he regularly tells you you're an ass?"

"In his own amazing doggy way, he does. Even if he is mad as hell at the world for that not-so-little-anymore demon Arden has brought into the house." Ryder shook his head once more before falling heavily into one of the desk chairs scattered around the room. "And to think I was the one who encouraged her to get him."

"You're responsible for the devil's spawn who terrorized the kitchen all through dessert?"

"In a way. I just took Arden out to the farm where Brennan Gabriel trains K-9s. Newman didn't make the training program, so Arden adopted him."

Noah considered the rambunctious Belgian Malinois he'd met since arriving at Reynolds Station. "That dog was going to be a K-9?"

"No, like I said, he didn't make the program. That's on him. But the excessive spoiling we're dealing with now? That's all my fiancée. The only one who can keep him in line is Hoyt. My future brother-in-law was special ops, and the dude can conjure up a layer of scary I can only envy. He's the only one who can get the dog to chill out."

"An impressive feat."

"It's the family I'm marrying into. What can I say?"

As Noah thought about the boisterous dinner and the sleeping baby and the wily puppy, he understood why Ryder was struggling.

When a man found everything, it took a hell of a lot of courage to not live in constant fear of losing it.

"I think it's time you shut this off and went and spent some time with your fiancée."

Ryder pointed to the screen, still frozen on the close-up of Rick. "But we need to prep for tomorrow."

"We're prepping in the morning. That's soon enough."

Ryder was nearly to the door when Noah stopped

him. "Arden told me something tonight. It was something I needed to hear."

"What's that?"

"We don't live when we're afraid." Noah walked over and laid a hand on his friend's shoulder. "Don't be afraid of losing this, Ryder. Be amazed and grateful for what you've found."

Chapter 13

Shayne blinked against the bright sunlight streaming through the windows and glanced around the unfamiliar bedroom. Unfamiliar but welcoming, she admitted, as the events of the prior day filled her thoughts.

She was at Reynolds Station and, for the time being, safe.

Giving that a moment to sink in, she deliberately took a deep breath and stretched.

And, knowing the threat was still out there, came back to her senses and took stock of how she felt. Her head came first, and considering she was diagnosed with a mild concussion the morning before, she was pleased that she only had a slight headache, more a pesky throb than anything truly debilitating.

Shayne moved on next to the overall state of her body and figured overtired muscles were a small price to pay for doing hand-to-hand combat with a madman in her closet, so again, she'd take the slight inconvenience.

And then she considered her heart.

She and Noah had shared a lot yesterday. And his story about Lindsey's death had been more emotional and more challenging than any physical threat they'd faced. Even now in the clear light of a new day, the reality of what he'd lived with haunted her.

Along with the reality of how much guilt he still carried over his late wife's death.

For as much as she hadn't wanted anyone to tell her that she, too, was carrying guilt over Rick, she had to admit that Noah's story had given her a new perspective. And while she wasn't fully past her own feelings, hearing his story had given her a new way to look at what had happened with Rick.

Reese's kind guidance had helped, too.

Bad things can and do happen, Shayne. That doesn't mean that we're somehow responsible for them. That if we only had some sort of prophetic vision, we could have avoided it. We take the hand we're dealt, and we manage it to the very best of our abilities.

It was hard-won wisdom, and it had been obvious that Reese admitted such personal feelings out of a deep desire to help.

And in that sharing, she'd given Shayne more than she could possibly know.

Pain also doesn't erase the joy of what comes in its place.

In her kindness and in the quiet moments of sharing the sweetness that was her baby son, Reese had given Shayne something she had been missing for a while.

Certainly, since her experience with Rick, something

had been missing, but if she were being honest maybe even before that. All the way back to when she was young and they lost her brother.

Life for her had changed so irrevocably that day. And while grief did that to a person, it hadn't just left a wound on her heart, it had done irreparable harm to her relationships with her family.

But there was still joy to be found. Armed with that new perspective—and maybe if she were lucky and really tried to work on her relationship with her sister—she'd find some healing.

With Caroline in her thoughts, Shayne remembered the email and headed to the office to check. She logged into her email account, and a hard clutch gripped her heart when she saw the unread message.

YES, I WANT TO TALK TO YOU, AND I WANT TO SEE YOU. I'LL CALL AT EIGHT. I MISS YOU, TOO.

Short. Sweet. Direct. And totally Caroline.

With a lightness she hadn't felt in much too long, Shayne headed back into the bedroom to get ready. The women of Reynolds Station had banded together and offered her a wardrobe selection that gave her a lot of choices for the day. Without checking the impulse, she picked up the pretty yellow-and-blue sundress Veronica had provided.

Time to go find some joy.

Shayne felt a tug at the bottom of her dress and looked beneath the kitchen table to find Newman chewing on the hem.

"Newman! No!" She pulled gently on the material, afraid to tear it, but he quickly saw it as a game.

Only when Hoyt stalked over from where he was cooking a heaping pile of bacon at the stove did the dog drop the material and put his head between his paws.

"You didn't even have to say anything," Shayne whispered, afraid to make too much noise and spoil the moment.

"The scary eye of Hoyt has spoken," Arden intoned in a deep, eerie voice from across the table.

"Eyes don't speak. And you need to get that dog into training," Hoyt gave his sister a pointed glare as he took up his place again at the stove.

"He is in training." Arden offered up the half-hearted argument before patting her lap to distract Newman's attention and get him beside her chair.

"Then double your classes," Hoyt shot back before turning to focus on his bacon.

"My mother always said God made puppies cute for a reason." Arden's expression was thoughtful as she leaned down to rub a chastised Newman's head. "To talk to Ryder, you'd think Murphy came out like Venus on the clamshell, utterly perfect and potty-trained to boot."

As if on cue, Ryder and Murphy came into the kitchen. Without missing a beat, Ryder joined right into the fray. "Murphy is the perfect dog and always has been."

Arden tilted her head back as Ryder leaned down for a kiss. When he lifted his head, a wicked grin stole over Arden's face. "God made you cute for a reason, too."

"Right back at ya, namaste."

Their focus on each other made Ryder's shift in attention a bit startling. Especially when his gaze landed on Shayne's, unmistakably direct. "Shayne, I owe you an apology."

"Oh, well, um… I'm sure you don't."

"I'm quite sure I do." Ryder glanced around the kitchen before seeming to come to a decision on a light shrug. "And I'd best get to it."

He came around the table and took the seat next to her. "I know I've put a lot of scrutiny on you since the kidnapping, and you deserve better. Especially after it became very clear that you were as blindsided by this whole experience as the rest of us."

Whatever animosity she'd sensed up to now had vanished, replaced with a warm sincerity that made Shayne soften toward Ryder. It was a bit daunting to have so many eyes on her in the kitchen, but hard to resist the genuineness she saw in Ryder.

Yet one more reason she truly liked the man.

She'd been happy for Arden from the start. Before things had gone so darkly wrong, she and Rick had met up with them while out on a date, and they'd shared a round of drinks together. Shayne had recognized Ryder's innate worth immediately. She'd liked him even more when it became clear that he made her friend wildly happy.

But this?

A man who knew his mind and also knew how to say he was sorry?

It was a whole other level of sweet and good and kind and decent.

"If you'll excuse us for a minute, I would like to talk to Shayne in the other room."

Quiet murmurs and head nods greeted Ryder's request, and in under a minute, Shayne found herself being escorted into the large Reynolds den and seated on a couch near Ryder.

"I am sorry, Shayne." He tilted his head in the direction of the kitchen. "That wasn't just lip service for my family."

"Thank you."

"Noah and I talked last night, and he forced me to acknowledge a few things that I hadn't been ready to admit, least of all to myself."

Again, that sense of what a good and decent and honorable man Ryder Durant was came through, but underneath it all, Shayne saw something else. A man confident enough to admit a mistake.

It was a rare trait in anyone, but to be faced with someone who worked a job where confidence in one's decisions literally meant life or death, it was refreshing to realize he could still admit when he needed to reassess a former opinion.

"Thank you for telling me. But can I ask what changed your mind?"

"Noah." Ryder took a hard breath but continued on. "I was blaming you for the fact Arden ended up kidnapped."

"Oh."

As answers went, it made a shocking amount of sense.

And if she considered his position, she could see where he was coming from.

Whatever horrors she and Arden endured as Rick's kidnapping victims, Ryder had to come through the other side of the door.

Without any assurance the woman he loved was still alive inside.

Once again, the shocking complexity of Rick's web of deceit showed another glistening strand of evil. His lies and his malevolent choices had laid waste to lives, the ones immediately touched by his crimes as well as those touched by the ripple they created outward.

Wasn't that the real horror of his behavior? The sheer magnitude of what he'd wrought?

"I appreciate you believing in me. I'm not quite to the place where I'm okay with everything that happened, but I am beginning to realize just how many people have been touched by Rick's malice. And just how deep that betrayal goes."

"You were betrayed the most. It took me too long to realize that."

"I'm not sure this is a contest any of us want or need to win. He did a number on everyone, Ryder. And as his colleagues, you, Noah and the others all need time to work through this too. To process it and make sense of his lies."

"Then it's my turn to say thank you."

Murphy chose that moment to come into the room, and Ryder smiled as the chocolate lab came to sit beside them, leaning his large body against the couch. Ryder petted his head and on down over his powerful shoulders. Murphy leaned into the attention and camaraderie.

There was trust there but affection, too.

Wasn't that also what Rick took away?

That sense of calm and a safe harbor where you not only trusted the people you were with but believed they only had your best interests at heart.

It made her earlier thought even more powerful.

"You and Murphy had to come through that door, Ryder. At the safe house. Not knowing what awaited you or what you would find when you did. That's an immeasurably heavy burden. Please give yourself time to heal."

"It's my job."

She saw the hard lines of conviction, set deep in his face. "It's your job when strangers' lives are on the line. It's a whole other matter when it's someone you love."

Murphy looked up at her, a sweet strength in his eyes, and Shayne used the dog's focus to leave Ryder to process the intense moment. Laying a hand on the dog's head, she rubbed her fingers over the hard skull, down over the softness of his ears.

This dog had saved her. In a very real way, she knew as she petted him that things in the safe house could have gone entirely differently if Murphy hadn't come straight into the house, attacking Rick the animal's sole focus.

Did he understand that?

Or was he just a sweet boy who was able to forget all that after the danger was over and the command to heel and retreat was given?

There was no way of knowing, but Shayne did know she was deeply grateful for the fact that Murphy had come through that door.

Ryder and Noah, too.

Shayne heard her name coming from the direction of the kitchen before Arden cleared the doorway, her cell phone in hand. "Your sister is on the phone."

"Oh yes," Shayne quickly remembered the agreed-upon time from her email with Caroline. "Thank you."

She took the phone but not before turning to look at Ryder. "Thanks again, Ryder. For everything."

"You're welcome." He pointed to the phone. "Now go take that."

Shayne didn't wait another minute. She lifted the phone to her ear as she headed back toward the stairs and the guest room.

"Caroline. I'm so glad you called."

Noah had left early to pick up breakfast for everyone. A small but necessary thanks for the Reynolds family's hospitality. So it was a bit unexpected to find the kitchen full of nearly everyone except Shayne when he returned, several dozen breakfast tacos in hand.

After the quick confirmation that Hoyt, Tate and Ace had already been out riding the ranch for the past two hours, he had to admit that however much of an early riser he considered himself, he had nothing on the Reynolds men.

He'd used the drive into and back out of Midnight Pass to mentally prepare for his morning meeting with his team. The extra bag of tacos that he'd left wrapped in the car, nestled under a blanket in a cooler, would hopefully make up for the late night and the early morning start to get right back into it.

Everyone thought better on a full stomach.

And when the situation was as grim as theirs with their ex-boss, every little bit helped.

What was Statler's end game?

The fact the man had allowed himself to get caught on camera was a major red flag. It meant Shayne's defense with the curling iron was not only the right move, but harmful enough to drop Rick's defenses another notch.

They'd use that.

At this point, if the man got a hangnail, they'd use it if they could find an advantage.

But Shayne did some damage.

A shot of pride filled him again at the image of her fighting Rick off. Especially when he considered how much he'd needed to convince her to make that drop out of her office window less than twenty-four hours before she did hand-to-hand combat with Statler.

She was inspiring.

And he saw her growing strength, at direct odds with the quiet, angry, nearly emaciated woman he'd discovered holed up in that deserted office complex.

Reese intercepted him at the kitchen table, a serving platter already in hand. "We'll put the tacos on the plate."

"They're not going to last long enough for a plate," Tate Reynolds teased his sister-in-law as he snagged three foil-wrapped tacos straight from the bag.

Ace chose that moment to stride into the room, his broad frame edging Tate away from the table. "Save some for the rest of us."

"Seriously, babe," Hoyt came up behind his wife, his hand already snaking around her for the bag. "Who puts breakfast tacos on a serving platter?"

"People who want to eat a nice breakfast with company."

"He's company?" Tate said around a mouthful of food, his head tilted in Noah's direction as he dropped into a seat.

Reese just shook her head and walked the serving platter back to the cabinet. Noah distinctly heard a muttered "heathens" from her, and he made a point to pull a few tacos out just for her, handing them over when she returned to the table.

"Saved you a few."

Her smile grew broad before she shot her husband and brothers-in-law the stink eye. "Ah, thank you. A true gentleman in our midst."

Although he didn't want to seem obvious about it, Noah had immediately wondered where Shayne was. He waited until Reese was settled in the seat beside him, delicately unwrapping the foil from her taco, before he said, "Has Shayne been down yet?"

"Up and ready to meet the day. She and Ryder were in the other room for a bit. He made a rather inspiring apology."

Although Noah was sorry to have missed it, he was glad Ryder had given Shayne the apology she needed and deserved.

"She was okay with it?"

"I think so. She seemed to be when they went into the other room to talk a bit. And then her sister called Arden's phone, and I think Shayne went to take it upstairs."

A lot had happened in the forty minutes he'd run to town, bought out the breakfast counter at the taqueria on Main and come back to Reynolds Station.

Important things.

Necessary things.

He unwrapped his own taco, well aware Shayne needed the time with her sister and he needed fortification for the day.

But once he finished his breakfast, he would take a few up to the room they'd shared. And they'd map out the needed next steps to visit her sister.

"I overheard a bit of their conversation," Reese said around a small bite of taco. "I needed to tend to William, and I know it's not my business, but I was touched by her guidance, and I think she had wisdom for Ryder that you could use, too."

"Oh?"

"I know Arden and Ryder have been through a lot." A long sigh escaped her. "We all have this past year. But I never thought about the situation from an outsider's perspective. And what Shayne told Ryder really hit me."

"What did she say?"

"She said that Ryder had to stand on the other side of the door at the safe house where she and Arden were kidnapped. He didn't know what awaited him, and there's a burden there. One that takes time to heal from."

Noah recognized the truth within Shayne's repeated words. Even more, he understood how much it meant that the woman could still see and understand those risks to others when her life was so deeply endangered.

And yet, it was their chosen profession. The responsibility and oath they took each and every day to make a difference.

"It's the job."

"Maybe so." Reese laid a hand on his arm, her touch firm against his skin. "But that doesn't mean it's easy."

Wasn't that what Lindsey had never understood?

For as difficult and challenging as his professional choice was, it was still his choice. One he made consciously, every single day.

"You should go up and talk to her. I'd expect she's done with her call by now."

"Are you sure?"

"Of course I'm sure." Reese smiled. "Besides, I need

to yell at my husband and brothers-in-law to save some of these tacos for the rest of the family."

"Hey!" Tate argued across the table with a mouth full of food.

"Don't *hey* me." Reese shook a finger. "This is your second breakfast, I'll remind you."

"But it's tacos," Ace said in a tone that could only be classified as a whine.

Noah had long recognized the importance of making a strategic exit and figured it was time to make his. Grabbing two more tacos off the pile, he pushed out of his chair.

Before leaving, he couldn't resist laying a hand on Reese's shoulder. When that pretty green gaze lifted to his, Noah realized there was only one thing to say.

"It sounds like there's a lot of this going around this morning, but thank you."

She laid a hand over his. "You're welcome."

Rick lay in the small hunting cabin just outside Mesa Creek. The place was nothing more than an oversized room, and he was holed up on a cot in the corner. But it was all he had, and besides, he'd dealt with worse.

But not for a very long time.

Not until everything went sideways with that traitorous bitch he'd considered his future partner.

"Damn it to hell and back," he moaned out loud at the pain racking his body. All he needed was some rest.

Was that too much to ask?

He closed his eyes, willing the rest that seemed elusive to steal over him. He'd checked and rechecked the cabin a few times and knew it was safe, even if he could swear he heard noises nearby.

He'd faded in and out of sleep for the past hour, but something kept pulling him away. Tugging him from an already fitful sleep that was more tiring than restful.

Over and over, he felt the stab of that hot brand against his face and neck, his hands and arms. The welts had hurt the day before, but he'd crashed hard and ignored them. But now, the loss of adrenaline and a day's worth of injury had left them raw and blistered, an added pain overlaid on his existing problems.

He considered the stash of drugs he had in his backpack. He'd used up all the antibiotics, but he still had the cream the FBI docs had used on him.

Did he get up?

Or just stay here and hope sleep took him under for a few hours?

He'd nearly done just that, sporadic images filling his mind of Shayne and branding irons and a dog leaping for his throat until his light sleep was interrupted when the cabin door exploded off its hinges, wood splintering and flying in the direction of the cot.

Rick sat straight up, the last of his adrenaline reserves pumping through his system as he scrambled from the bed to face the threat head-on.

He watched as an elegantly dressed man with a camel-colored coat over his shoulders stepped into the shack, a couple of his thugs following him through the door.

Blue eyes so pale they were nearly clear stared him down from across the room as Vasily Baslikova considered him. Although the man's face was an impassive mask, Rick sensed extreme displeasure in that blank slate. "This is your living quarters now?"

The words were quiet.

Precise.

And somehow louder and more ear-splitting than the shots that splintered the door.

"I'm in between my mansion and my yacht at the moment," Rick ground out.

"Humor, Mr. Statler, doesn't become you."

Rick eyed the door and considered the pain that was rapidly returning to his body, only briefly held at bay with that adrenaline push.

He couldn't make a run for it, and Baslikova didn't look in the mood for humor—or being tested—even if Rick had the strength to try.

"Why are you here?"

"I'm hiding out from my old employer since they sicced a mad dog on me."

Baslikova flicked a hand. "Circumstances you created with your laziness."

Lazy?

Indignant rage swelled up in Rick's chest, quickly curdling as the man stepped closer. His intense scrutiny ratcheted up a few more notches. "And those burns on your face? Those aren't from a dog."

The question that was actually a statement of fact hovered there in the small space between them. Again, Rick briefly considered making a run for it, even as he cursed the fact that it simply wasn't possible for him right now physically.

There was a time it would have been easy. Natural, even, to outmaneuver whomever got in his way.

Until Shayne. And Noah. And this ridiculous bastard standing in front of him who knew too much and demanded even more.

"You still have not answered my question, Mr. Statler. Why are you still here living in this hovel?"

Rick knew there was nowhere he could run that Baslikova wouldn't find him, but he could make a damn fine go of it.

Yet even knowing that, he'd stayed in Midnight Pass.

He was still here because of Shayne. Because she owed him. At first, he thought she was destined to come with him, to make a life with him, but now he knew better.

She was the offering that would allow him to take his spoils and live in peace for the rest of his damn life. Retirement might have shown up a bit sooner than he planned, but he had a solid nest egg, and he'd make the best of it.

More than the best, he figured as he imagined his future stretching out in front of him, a life down in the islands somewhere.

But before that imagined new life could become a reality, he needed to get out of this one.

"I have connections. I'm not without resources, despite my change," he glanced around the room with pointed disdain, "in circumstances."

"Your bravado knows no limits, Mr. Statler."

Rick stared into Baslikova's dead eyes and lied his ass off.

"I've worked long and hard to build what's mine. You think I didn't make backup plans?"

"Your planning hasn't been stellar so far."

"An unforeseen set of events. And a woman who betrayed me with a seemingly biddable I."

Something sparked in those dead eyes. Not life, exactly, but a stirring of interest. "Women are rarely biddable."

"We'll agree to disagree there." Rick considered the ideas that had been building and taking shape in his mind. "I thought I'd give her to you. As a peace offering. But I know it's not enough."

That flicker of interest didn't fade, but the flat response didn't quite suggest interest, either. "I have plenty of women."

"Yes, true, which is why I recognized you deserve something more."

Baslikova simply continued to stand there, his breathing so light as to be nearly imperceptible. "You already owe me more. Losing your position doesn't change that."

"I owed you unfettered access to the corridors through Midnight Pass. What I have to offer is better."

A slight guffaw echoed from across the room, where Baslikova's two thugs exchanged glances.

Rick shot them a pointed glare before turning his attention back to Baslikova. "My deal's with you. Not them."

That silent stare didn't waver, but after a few beats the man did wave a hand. "Outside, please."

The thugs quickly departed, but their physical absence didn't mean they weren't close enough to do damage. Especially with loaded guns and the gauntlet of a broken door spilling over the threshold of the cabin.

Besides, Rick figured, running was no longer an option. His injuries had seen to that. One more thing he could lay at the feet of Shayne and Noah.

So he turned back to Baslikova and prepared himself to make a deal.

"All I could get you before was a drug corridor without eyes. There wasn't a damn thing I could do about the tax to pass through it. Now that I'm working for myself, I can get you the whole package. We'll remove the cartel who owns the passage, and it'll be yours."

"That's a big offer for a man who can't subdue one small woman."

"It's a promise."

"The management of the passage is a closely guarded secret."

"One I know."

Rick recognized his miscalculation the moment the knife was at his throat.

He'd believed offering up the ownership of free passage through Midnight Pass would prove his loyalty. He hadn't calculated on the opposite.

"You've been holding out on me, Mr. Statler," Baslikova twisted the knife to draw blood and pain. "You will give me the name of the cartel owner if you value what little is left of your life."

Rick had always enjoyed poker. The strategy of it all. The bluffing. The figuring out another player's tells.

Baslikova had none.

What little he'd been able to study of the man—and it had truly been little—had indicated the bastard had such a grip on himself that there was absolutely nothing to read.

Which meant there was only one way to play this.

"Kill me and you won't have the name you need."

"There are other ways to get what I need without killing you."

In that moment, the absurdity of it all came flooding back to him. The K-9 attack in the safe house. The weeks on the run nursing injuries that refused to heal.

Even Shayne's slash-and-burn with the curling iron had left its marks.

He had nothing left to lose, and his body was fast betraying him.

"I won't last very long, and you'll still be out a name." Rick never broke eye contact. "If you want that corridor, you're going to need my help to get it."

That steady, empty stare never receded, but Rick recognized a small moment of victory as Baslikova pulled the knife from his throat.

And knew he had won this round when the man gave a small nod. "Let us set up a plan. And tell me more about this woman. I believe you called her a peace offering?"

Chapter 14

Shayne watched the darkened expanse out the passenger-side window and wondered, not for the first time, if she was bringing horrible danger to her sister's door.

Caroline had insisted she come, and Shayne still wanted the comfort of being with her family, as well as her sister's extensive computer expertise. Yet as they drove closer and closer to Austin, Shayne grew increasingly concerned she had made the wrong decision.

Ryder Durant had apologized, after all. He no longer thought she was the enemy, and she had to believe that between him and Noah they'd bring the rest of the FBI field office around to that way of thinking, too. Her fear that their desperate need for a scapegoat made her an easy target wasn't quite so urgent any longer.

Even if the top brass in DC were still a wild card.

It was the same point Caroline had made when they spoke.

"You can't be sure, Shayne. An apology is nice, but until this guy is in custody there's no way you can trust the FBI. You can trust me."

"But it's still dangerous."

"I'm dangerous, too."

That thought had lingered, long after she'd hung up the phone.

It had lingered even after Belle sent one of her deputies with Shayne to pack a bag at her house. She'd continued to think about Caroline's words while she and Noah had shared an early dinner with the Reynolds family before setting out on the drive to Austin. And she'd thought about it long after she and Noah had negotiated driving shifts on the impromptu road trip.

I'm dangerous, too.

Her baby sister.

A baby sister she really didn't know. Not as an adult woman.

"You've been quiet, but you're not sleeping," Noah gently interrupted her thoughts as he reached for his cup of coffee in the console between their seats.

"A lot to think about."

"That I believe. But you had a lot to think about before getting in the car, and you weren't this quiet." He took a slow sip of the coffee. "Want to talk about it?"

"I know I've pushed for this, but now that we're heading to Caroline's, I can't help worrying I've put my sister in danger."

"You have."

Shayne gasped, shocked at how hard it was to hear her fears put into words.

"But that doesn't mean it's the wrong choice."

"How can you say that? Damn it, Noah, why didn't you tell me this before we left? We should turn around."

"No, we shouldn't."

She sensed he was trying to keep things level and even, but several days of running on fumes had left his voice scratchy and deep, with a weariness settled in under that core of strength he worked so hard to maintain.

"Why not?"

"The field office in Austin has been alerted and will be watching out. I hate to break this to you, but your sister has been in danger since this whole thing went down when you were kidnapped and Rick escaped, but she's doing fine. Better than fine, if her technological skills are as strong as you claim."

"That's only because Rick's in Midnight Pass, and by all accounts, he's working alone. How could he come after both of us at once?"

"He couldn't. And since all his activities have been focused on you, and he's continued to give every indication his focus is The Pass. We've had no need to increase protections on your sister because the threat hasn't been anywhere near her."

"Which means I'm bringing it to her."

"It means you're hunkering down with your family while we try to get this monster captured and in federal prison for the rest of his life."

Shayne recognized all those points, but nothing could quite remove the sudden dread at what was to come.

When it was just her dealing with this, she found a way to keep her panic in check. But the idea of bringing her family into it was a whole other level of fear.

They drove on quietly, each keeping to their own thoughts. As she considered the past few weeks, Shayne finally had the courage to ask questions that had been lingering.

Maybe it was the darkened world outside the SUV. Or perhaps the late night and the tiredness creeping in.

Whatever the reason, it was time to dive deep.

"Why is he able to do this?"

Noah glanced over, drawing his gaze momentarily off the road. "Do what?"

"Keep escaping. I know he's a trained agent, but he's hurt and he's isolated. Yet he keeps getting the upper hand. How?"

"I wish I knew."

"That's not very comforting." She side-eyed him. "Nothing about this conversation is."

"What do you want me to say? You and I have spent nearly three days like this, on top of weeks of Statler eluding us. I'm as sick and tired of this as you are, and I don't have any answers anymore."

He reached for his coffee before seeming to think better of it. On a shake of his head, he turned to her quickly and gave her a small smile. "Sorry. Long day."

"Bad meeting today?"

"*Fruitless* is probably a better word than *bad*."

She reached for her own cup of coffee in the center console and took a fortifying sip. "Top brass still upset?"

"And getting madder by the day."

Although he'd worked hard to hide it, Noah had carried an uneasy frustration all through dinner. But she noticed it had taken a distinct shift since they'd gotten in the car.

For the past several days, he'd been focused. Frustrated with the lack of progress but focused all the same. But now…

There was an edgy layer of anger that hadn't been there before.

"Want to talk about it?"

He shrugged and from where Shayne was sitting, it looked like the weight of the world lay on his shoulders. "The top brass is not happy he's still out there. Pressure is mounting by the day, and it's not like it's been easy going up to now."

"They should be upset. They trained him and put guns in his hand. They gave him access to intel and promoted him. They should be a hell of a lot of mad."

"Well, like other unpleasant things, that mad rolls downhill."

That fact only reinforced why Noah was on board with Shayne working with Caroline. Egg on the face never looked good on anyone, and the top brass in DC had enough for a facial.

"It never ends, does it?" She asked softly.

"What part?"

"All of it. The endless stream of bad actors. You work hard to get rid of one, and you get three more."

"I wish I could tell you it wasn't the case, but it is."

"Then why do you still beat yourself up over Lindsey?"

She hadn't intended to ask that question. Nothing of the sort. Noah had shared his past, and while it only increased the growing feelings she had for him, she refused to force him back into that place over and over.

But why should he continue to pay the emotional cost for something he didn't do?

"She was my wife, and I brought this danger to her door."

"She cheated on you and shared the private details of your work with the wrong person. How is that your fault?"

"Look, Shayne. It's late and I'm not interested in explaining myself."

His eyes never left the road, but she saw the cords in his neck tighten as he obviously fought to keep control. Saw the way his hands remained firmly gripping the steering wheel as well.

He wasn't unaffected by this.

Not in the least.

"I'm not asking for an explanation, Noah. I'm telling you that it's time to let this go. Or you're going to be as worthless and useless to the FBI as Rick is."

The lights of a large gas station and rest stop beckoned out of the right side of the vehicle, and without saying a word, Noah took the exit. Her words lingered, scattershot and still ricocheting off the interior, dangerous and deadly, but he said nothing. Just navigated off the interstate and into a gas bay, stepping out to operate the pump.

She wasn't sure what to say, the strange silence unlike anything she'd experienced in his presence up to now.

Noah Ross might be a lot of things, but one to dismiss a confrontation hadn't been on her list.

Strong, stoic and capable, yes.

Willing to ignore danger to himself to protect others, oh yes.

But dismissive and silent? Hell no.

She slammed out of the car, heading for the well-lit

all-night market. She'd use the ladies' room and get herself a new coffee. She might even buy those packaged doughnuts that not only lacked any whit of nutritional value but also had enough chemicals to likely take a month off her life.

And damn it, she'd enjoy it.

She finished her personal business and headed for the wall of slushy machines. Powdered mini-doughnuts were one thing. Did she dare fill her system with enough processed sugar to send her into shock just looking at the machines?

What the hell.

She poured one for herself—blue raspberry—and in a small act of apology, she filled a large cola one for Noah. All that sugar was still only ninety-nine cents for a jumbo cup. The worst thing he could do was take two sips and wash the grime off his tire rims with it.

Topping both cups with plastic lids and reaching for two straws, she nearly tumbled into the large man at the end of the counter.

"Oh, I'm sorry."

He stared down at her, clear blue eyes in a hard-lined face. His nose looked like it had been broken more than once, and when he smiled, she noticed the chipped edge of one tooth. "No problem, miss."

His English was thickly accented, and his smile was warm, almost appreciative, but something sent a shiver down her spine all the same. He was…oddly compelling. Large. Well-muscled.

And strangely terrifying.

She only nodded and grabbed her drinks, heading for the exit. Something hard and heavy pounded in her veins as she waited to pay and then all the way back to the car where Noah waited for her.

"Everything okay?"

"Fine."

She handed over his drink. "I thought you might want a bit of a pick me up."

He stared down at the frozen drink, the corner of his mouth tilting up. "How come you got blue and I only got a soda?"

"You want blue raspberry?"

"Not particularly."

"Then what's wrong?"

"Just curious why you thought I'd only like a drink that's brown."

He handed her the keys before ducking back into the SUV and exchanging the soda for his nearly empty coffee cup. Tossing it in a nearby trash can, he pointed to the doors. "Please get in and lock up. I need to make a quick stop, and we'll be on our way."

"Okay."

Shayne did as he asked, then used the private moment to watch him walk toward the store. The fluorescent overhead lights cast long shadows behind him, only further accentuating that impression of the long, tall Texas lawman, keeping order in his town.

He was such a difficult man to figure out.

That overarching sense of honor and authority hid so much dark. Deep shadows he refused to share or untether himself from.

Yet for all those shadows, he could still smile. Still make jokes.

And even be oddly offended she didn't think him whimsical enough to enjoy a blue drink.

* * *

Now back in the SUV, Noah took a sip of his drink and avoided wincing as a shocking amount of sugar raced through his system.

He took it as a win Shayne had thought of him at all.

Especially with the way she stomped off when he'd pulled in silently for gas.

But damn it. He didn't want to talk about Lindsey. Didn't want to hear how he should be over it by now and how she betrayed him and how none of it was his fault.

Because, somewhere deep inside, Noah had begun to wonder if all the time he'd spent this past decade in waves of guilt was…wasted a bit. He didn't deserve to be fully free of the guilt—he wasn't a good husband when they were married. He loved his wife, but he wasn't there for her. And while his job was intense and difficult and challenging, he hadn't been there even when he was with Lindsey.

And that was totally on him.

I'm not asking for an explanation, Noah. I'm telling you that it's time to let this go. Or you're going to be as worthless and useless to the FBI as Rick is.

It bothered him to admit it, but Shayne had a point.

"I'm not holding onto Lindsey's memory over any sense of anger or guilt for the actual events that led to her death," Noah began.

It wasn't a lie. Or not entirely. Because if he were honest with himself, while sorry for the outcome, Lindsey had brought some of it on herself. It had taken him a lot of years to get to that point, but he had done the hard emotional work and it was true.

She was a sweet woman, but she'd gone into their marriage with a rosy view he never promised her. And instead of talking to him about her frustrations, she'd found the attention she craved elsewhere.

He didn't believe she deserved to die, but he had learned how not to take all of the blame for it, either.

"What are you holding on to then?"

"I wasn't a good husband. I never lied to her about the demands of my work, but when I did have free time or personal time, I allowed work to dominate those moments."

He broke off, reconsidering. "Or said another way, I chose work over her in the moments where I should have put her first."

"You're right. That is on you."

He should have been startled by the honesty, but he had to admit that was just Shayne. Straightforward. Honest. And not afraid to speak her mind. Although he had no desire to compare her to Lindsey, this conversation proved how starkly different the two women were.

"I am sorry things didn't work out," Shayne said. "And I'm more sorry than I can ever say that she was the victim of such horrible violence."

"Me, too."

"But I'm glad that you might have an opportunity to come out the other side of this."

"The situation with Rick has churned it all up. Old feelings. Old memories." Noah reconsidered and realized that the truth of the matter went far deeper. "Actually, you're the reason those memories have been all churned up."

"Me?" That lone word was nearly a squeak, and she took a quick sip of her drink. "How does it have anything to do with me?"

"You've made me wonder, Shayne. About things.

About what I want. And about what it means to be in a relationship with someone who understands you and values you just the way you are.

"You strike me as a woman with that talent. And I think it's rather rare."

The interior of the SUV grew quiet, the only sound the persistent hum of the road flying past them beneath the wheels.

He considered saying more but knew there wasn't much else to say. Shayne had opened his eyes. All those days, reviewing his case board in the conference room and staring at her picture and remembering the woman he'd carried out of the safe house, he'd sensed her innocence somewhere deep inside.

Oh, he couldn't have said she was innocent then, but he saw something there.

Felt something.

And the woman he'd gotten to know in the time since had only reinforced that strange instinct that kept telling him to trust her. And believe in her.

And maybe, by believing in her, he'd come to believe in himself.

"You've made me wonder, too."

"What do you wonder about?"

"I don't form relationships easily. I don't know if it stems from my childhood or if it's just the way I'm wired, but it took a lot to let Rick into my life. To be comfortable letting him into my life."

"But you did it. You gave him that space."

"Yeah, I did."

"I'm sorry he betrayed the trust you gave him."

"For the past month, I've been so angry. And then

something interesting happened. It started when you came to my office, and it's been building ever since."

"What's that?"

"I thought I was in this alone. And you and the Reynolds family and now Caroline. You've all helped me see that I'm not."

She took a quick sip of her drink, and Noah sensed she was fortifying herself for something.

"I do value you, Noah. And I think all the things that make up who you are include a strong sense of self and a strong sense of what it means to do what's right. Those are equally rare traits. I think that if circumstances were different, you'd be the sort of man I'd let into my life."

She hesitated before rushing on.

"And unlike with Rick, I would be able to get comfortable with the idea in no time at all."

Noah took in her words, allowing them to settle into his mind. He heard them on repeat, both what she said and, even more, all that she implied.

By the time they rolled into Austin around two in the morning, those words had done a damn fine job of settling into his heart, too.

Chapter 15

The overhead light on the garage winked on as Noah pulled into Caroline's driveway. Shayne had managed to doze off for a few hours, and upon waking about twenty minutes outside of Austin, she realized Noah had handled all the driving since they left Midnight Pass.

Shayne was already out of the vehicle and around to Noah's side as he stepped from the SUV. "Why did you let me sleep? I could have taken a turn."

"We're both tired. And since you did fall asleep, I hated to wake you."

The temptation to lecture him on sharing the load was strong, but she was still struggling to process the things they'd discussed on the drive and that subtle awareness of him that had only grown steadily larger. More insistent.

And then it didn't matter because the garage door

went up and Caroline ran out of the house and straight to Shayne.

"You're here. And you're okay." Caroline held her in a tight hug, and Shayne clung to her sister, quickly realizing just how much she needed this.

How much she needed the comfort and the love of her family.

Caroline pulled back, her bright blue gaze roaming over Shayne's face. "Those are some exhausted circles under your eyes."

"Thanks." Shayne forced a dry tone before smiling broadly. "You look amazing."

And she did. The quiet, somewhat mousy appearance her sister had cultivated through college had vanished. In its place was a lovely vibrance that spoke of life and verve and an effervescence Shayne remembered from when they were young.

"You look happy."

"I am." Caroline's face fell. "Though I'd be a lot happier if my sister wasn't arriving at my house at two in the morning with an FBI escort and a madman snapping at her heels."

And just like that, outward fashion choices aside, the real Caroline was there.

Blunt. Honest. And not one to BS anybody.

"Let's get the bags, and I can introduce you to Noah."

Shayne made quick introductions after they got into the house and recognized that while his polite, yes-ma'am polish was on full display, Noah was running on fumes.

Caroline obviously recognized it, too, because she deftly moved them toward the guest room in her small single-story ranch house.

Still reeling from the car conversation, Shayne pivoted quickly. "Why don't you give this room to Noah, and I'll bunk with you."

"Of course," Caroline said, her voice serious even as Shayne saw a slight smirk just before her sister ducked her head.

As she and Caroline were walking to the opposite side of the house and to her sister's bedroom, Shayne realized that smirk had come home to roost.

"Even dead on his feet he's dreamy. A small fact you left out when we spoke this morning."

"He's an FBI agent, and he's protecting me. He could look like a movie star, and it wouldn't matter."

"He damn near does. The compelling sort that draws the eye and eats up the screen, far more interesting than the average pretty boy."

Since it was impossible to argue the point, Shayne only pointed toward the bed. "While I will be very happy to discuss Noah tomorrow, I'm crashing hard."

"Lay down. I've already reset the security system, and I also spoke with a local FBI team earlier today. They've got a patrol coming through the neighborhood every hour or so."

"That's good," Shayne said, unable to smother a yawn.

"I'll see you in the morning."

"Where are you going?"

"I need to do a bit more work, and then I'm coming to bed myself."

Shayne was exhausted and knew it wasn't the time to start a serious conversation, but she couldn't let the words go unsaid.

"Thank you for letting us come here. For taking me

in. I know we have a lot to talk about. Or I have a lot to tell you and even more to apologize for."

"Shaynie," Caroline came closer. "There's nothing to apologize for."

"Yeah, there really is. And tomorrow, when my head's clear and I've had some sleep, I promise to tell you all of it."

She had the vague sense of being tucked in but fell hard into sleep before she could even say thank you.

Rick tossed back a few pills and willed them to take some of the blazing pain away. As he'd expected, Baslikova refused to leave him at the hunting cabin, so he and his thugs had taken Rick to their compound.

Blindfolded, of course.

He chafed at the restraints and the subtle innuendo that he was a guest when he knew damn well he was a prisoner, but the counter full of drugs in the bathroom and the large bed had gone a long way toward easing his mind.

Baslikova had the upper hand, but he was a hell of a lot more welcoming host than Rick's old bosses had been when they dragged him into FBI custody.

And besides, Rick still had a hand to play, courtesy of their discussion about the drug corridor into The Pass. If that deal wasn't enticing in some way, Baslikova would have already put a bullet in Rick's head himself, so there was still room to maneuver.

He closed his eyes and waited for the pills to do their job, dragging him into the same oblivion of his first dose earlier. Only it didn't come.

The pain did dull, but the full drop into unconsciousness remained elusive.

Where was Baslikova getting his information?

The question had Rick sitting straight up in bed. The man seemingly knew everything, yet it made no sense how. Rick had the FBI office on lockdown. They had minimal weak spots, and the one he knew of had helped in his escape.

So where was the intel coming from?

Because no matter how rich or influential or connected, no one could be everywhere at once.

Yet Baslikova had read his every move. No, Rick shook his head, now trying to clear his thoughts as the drugs finally began to do their work. The man had anticipated his every move.

It was uncanny, and it went well beyond the woo-woo vibes the man managed to give off with those snake eyes of his.

Rick fell back against the bed, the move jarring enough to press at his still-healing side wound. The move was also enough to have his head hitting the pillow, the scrape of fabric across his facial burns searing through him.

This brought him right back to Shayne.

He knew all the people at the FBI who were vulnerable. Hell, he'd cultivated files for years on who could possibly be used to his advantage should it be necessary. And while he'd managed to collect a solid dossier up in Boston, his time in The Pass hadn't borne much fruit.

But Shayne...

He'd accessed her tech.

And Baslikova hadn't reached out until Rick had started accessing that tech.

Was Shayne the reason the mobster had found him? And how he continued to find him?

One more betrayal in an endlessly long line of them.

And to think he'd believed he and Shayne had a future. That they could find a way to be together after Rick broke free of The Pass. After they got far away from here and he put that stashed-away bank account to good use.

Whatever lingering feelings he had—and there weren't many since he'd seen her working with Noah—vanished in that moment.

Shayne Erickson was the enemy—a traitor to the core.

He couldn't wait to lure her out in the open.

And then he was going to kill her for her betrayal.

Noah grabbed his phone from the bedside table and glanced at the screen.

Ten o'clock?

He shot straight up in bed, scrambling for his clothes.

How had he overslept? He could have sworn he'd set the alarm. Hell, he knew he had. Right before he fell into the bed and collapsed after that drive.

A soft "hello" from the other side of the door drew his attention away from the hunt for his gun—he had remembered to stow that properly, right?—and he hollered an abstract "Come in!"

"Good morning." Shayne had two mugs in her hand. "I thought you might like a cup of coffee."

"I overslept."

"I know."

Noah stopped the hunt for the gun and turned to stare at her. "What?"

"The alarm went off around six this morning, and

I happened to be up. When it wouldn't stop, I came in here and turned it off for you."

"Why'd you do that?"

"You mumbled it was okay."

"I was asleep!"

Shayne frowned. "What's the problem here? You haven't slept in days and then added the strain of an eight-hour drive last night, which you insisted on doing all by yourself. You're entitled to some down time."

He knew it was unfair of him to take his frustration out on her, but hell, what if someone had come in? If he was so out of it that he'd slept through a clanging alarm, what else could he have missed?

"I'm trained for this."

"You're a human being, and it's about time you acknowledged that. One who has been running on fumes for weeks, no less." She marched forward and handed him his coffee. "It's a few extra hours, Noah, not a week. Deal with it."

She was nearly back out the door when he stopped her. "Thank you for the coffee."

"You're welcome."

The dress she'd worn yesterday was gone, and in its place were more of the workout clothes he'd admired her in before. Despite his better judgment, he couldn't help but notice the gorgeous curve of her backside as she marched out of the room, and he was suddenly helpless not to follow.

Her sister's ranch house was small, and the guest room he'd slept in was off a long hallway. He passed another room clearly set up as Caroline's office, and then they were in the large open living room that dominated the center of the house.

"Thank you for letting me sleep."

"Sure. Fine." She stood against a long bar counter that separated the living room from the kitchen and stared at him. "Really, Noah, it's fine. It's been a long few days, and we're both tired. Go back and make your calls and do whatever it is you need to do."

He glanced around. "Where's your sister?"

"She said she had a few errands to run. She checked in with the agent assigned here and let her know what she was doing and where she was going. I expect she'll be back sometime this afternoon."

"I'll call Agent Daniels myself and check in."

"It's fine, Noah. My sister's not a prisoner, and she is running her own business. She had to make a client visit. Chill."

When Shayne put it that way, he couldn't help but feel a bit off. Aside from waking like a grumpy grizzly bear, he realized she had a point. Caroline wasn't a prisoner, and she'd followed the protocol they'd asked her to. He could hardly argue.

So why did he feel like doing just that?

"Why were you up at six this morning?"

She took a sip of her coffee before setting it on the counter behind her. "I'm blaming it on that horrendously poor choice of a blue raspberry slushy. Between the sugar and the caffeine, it's a wonder I slept at all."

"You need your rest as much as I do."

"I'll try to remember that next time I decide to make bad choices at a gas station mini-mart at midnight."

The signs were all there. A brewing fight and a subtle layer of antagonism neither of them seemed capable of pulling back right now.

He needed to walk away. After all, he was the one

who'd snapped first, and she was entitled to some quiet time of her own. Besides, he had work to do and the office to call and Durant to check in with.

Which made the fact that he very carefully set his mug down on the coffee table in front of the couch a surprise. One he figured he should pay attention to or change course from, only he had no interest in doing that.

Moving with determined purpose, he crossed to where Shayne still stood at the bar, a weight hanging over her that made it a wonder she was still standing.

And even then, he didn't back away.

He needed to.

But it was obviously well past the time of making rational decisions. So instead, he went on instinct and something else.

Something that felt strangely like hope.

Without stopping to check the impulse, he moved straight into her, drawing her close in his arms and pressing his mouth to hers.

Despite what felt a lot like sluggish movements on his part, he must have been faster than he realized because she seemed shocked by the sudden kiss. A shock that didn't stop her for long as her arms went around him, one forming a tight band around his waist and the other reaching up from behind, clutching his shoulder.

The kiss was hard and fast, a hot merging of lips and teeth and tongue that showed no indication of being sluggish or slow. Instead, need spread between them like wildfire, quickly consuming them.

"Noah?" She whispered against his lips, even as she kept finding a way to kiss him.

"Hmmm?"

She lifted her head and stared at him with an intensity that nearly took away his breath. "Please tell me your defenses are down far enough that we're going to do more than kiss."

It was one of the oddest conversations of his life—and certainly the strangest one he'd ever had in the realm of sex—but Noah found all he could do was smile.

"Do you want to do more than kiss?"

"Yes. I want that very much."

"So do I."

He had no idea how less than five minutes before he'd been on the verge of picking a fight, but when Shayne reached for his hand, taking it in hers and leading him toward the guest room, Noah knew there was nothing to be done for the confusion.

A smart man knew when to keep his mouth shut and take a gift that was offered freely.

And while he might have started his day off groggy, slow and more than a little dense, he was fast catching up.

Shayne wasn't sure what had changed or why, but one minute she was fantasizing about sawing Noah's moody, irritable head off with the blunt end of a butter knife and the next she was kissing him as if her life depended on it.

And maybe it did.

The achy yearning that had only grown stronger with each day she'd spent with Noah Ross had threatened to pull her under.

And the desperate need to do something about it had finally become too overwhelming to ignore.

That morning, as she'd stared down at his sleepy

form batting a hand against the end table to find his phone ringing an alarm, she'd felt something deep inside break wide open. He was her protector, and he'd driven himself to exhaustion he was so focused on keeping her safe.

The very least she could do was give him a few extra hours of sleep.

It was natural and easy and as she'd stood there, giving herself the quiet opportunity to watch him, unobserved, for a few precious moments, Shayne had acknowledged the truth. She had no idea how it had happened, but in an impossibly short period of time she'd fallen for him.

Hard.

And she didn't know what that meant for her or him or the future that stretched out in front of them, but she damn well knew what she could do with today.

Today, she could be with him.

Today, she could take solace in being in his arms.

And today, she could take the sweet oblivion of mindless sex with a man who captivated her on every level possible.

"Shayne, are you sure?" Noah had wrapped his arms around her, following her into the bedroom, his lips nuzzling the exquisitely sensitive skin beneath her ear.

"I'm very sure." She turned in his arms, pulling him back for a kiss as her hands snaked to the waistband of his gym shorts. In deference to being in her sister's home and, presumably the need to be prepared for any eventuality, he'd slept in gym shorts and a T-shirt. Sculpted muscle was hot and hard under soft cotton, and Shayne worked the material up over that hard stomach and solid chest before pulling the T-shirt fully over his head.

She gave herself a moment to simply revel in the well-defined man standing before her. He was long and lean, but just as she'd recognized when he'd saved her outside her office and again in her home, that build was deceptively strong, made up of corded, ropey muscle.

The desire to continue looking warred with the need to feel him, and she finally gave in to what was obviously mutual impatience. In the span of a few heartbeats, they'd shed the rest of their clothes and she stood before him naked.

Never could she have imagined this moment, especially coming off the pain of such a horribly damaged relationship with Rick. She didn't share herself easily with others—her mind or her body—but this didn't feel rushed. Oh, she was impatient for him, but in a deeper sense, it seemed she'd been waiting forever for Noah.

And now he was here.

More importantly, thoughts of Rick had no place in this room.

Firmly parking memories of her ex, she reached behind them to close the door and then kissed him as they worked their way to the bed. The sheets were still rumpled, and as he laid her down onto the soft cotton, Shayne could still feel the imprint of his body heat from sleep.

That heat, coupled with the intimacy of his naked body against hers, was nearly her undoing, and she held him close as he drifted kisses from her lips, over her jaw and down her neck. A sense of wonder permeated through her as he kept up that steady rain of kisses over her skin, coming to a stop at her breasts. She felt a moment's hesitation when he stopped, his gaze hot on her body, before he stared up at her.

"You're beautiful."

"You make me feel that way."

"No," he shook his head, a tender reverence reflecting deep in his gaze. "You are beautiful. Outside. Inside. All of you."

"Thank you."

He refocused his attention, his kisses growing bolder as he pressed his lips to her breast before taking a nipple into his mouth. Shayne felt a hard tug echo through her body, pleasure flooding her veins and coiling deep in her core.

Oh yes, she wanted him.

The play of his mouth over her sensitive flesh grew more intense, the deep draw of his tongue against her breast drawing sensation after sensation, spiking pleasure and need in equal measure.

Her body came alive under his attentions, feelings she didn't even know were possible springing to life beneath his touch. Care and consideration met and merged with eager yearning into a potent combination that had all the power of a building storm.

And as those dynamic sparks of energy filled her veins, she was desperate to give him the same pleasure. To make him feel the same. Shifting, she rose up over him, kissing a path of her own over his body. A light dusting of hair covered his chest, and she marveled at the contrast of masculine to feminine as she made an erotic path over his pectoral muscles and on toward the thickly corded muscles of his stomach.

His erection pressed hard against her stomach, and she reached for him, taking him fully in her palm while pressing her tongue against the ridges of his abdomen, enamored with the barely leashed strength in the firm lines of his body.

Shayne allowed those erotic moments to spin out, one after the other, faster and faster as the urgent need flared stronger and higher.

His hard exhale and labored breathing as she worked his erection in her hand sent shockwaves of pleasure through her. That bold declaration of his pleasure—all because of her—was the sweetest victory. One she would have drawn out and savored if not for his sudden shift of their positions.

"Shayne—" Another heavy exhale ripped from his lungs as he uttered her name. "I need you."

"Yes." She lifted a leg, rubbing her calf against the back of his leg and reveling in the feel of the thick press of his body against her core.

It was only as she felt him move, teasing her flesh, that she remembered protection.

"Noah."

Abject disappointment flooded her as she realized she didn't have anything with her, and she could hardly go raid her sister's home looking for condoms.

"What?" A gentleman to the core, he sensed her question and stilled immediately. "What is it?"

"Protection. I don't have anything."

His sexy, unfocused gaze sobered immediately, and if she weren't so desperate for him, she'd have laughed at the quick change in his demeanor.

"I'm sorry. Oh wow," he shook his head as he moved off her to the edge of the bed. His long arms snaked out for the duffle he'd set nearby, and she was once again grateful for his size and strength.

"Those are some long arms, Agent Ross."

He grinned at that, the smile carefree but fleeting, before coming back up with a condom in his hand. "The only side benefit of being a beanpole throughout high school."

"It's an impressive skill."

"I'd like to think I've developed a few more."

Her hand closed over the condom, eager to rip open the foil, when the lingering lightness in his eyes faded.

"Just so I don't seem like an opportunistic weasel, I didn't pack those."

Shayne sensed something important in his words even as she tried to keep up.

"What do you mean?"

"I don't normally pack condoms in my work bag. I mean, I didn't have them on me. Or packed. But I found them last night when I pulled out my gym shorts."

Intrigued now, despite the urgency of the moment, Shayne could only stare down at the small packet in her hands before glancing back up at him. "Magically appearing condoms? That's a new one."

"Not quite so magical when they come with a cheeky note. You can thank Arden later."

Whatever Shayne was expecting, a proactive stash of condoms from her friend was not it. Unbidden, a hard shout of laughter rolled up from down deep and spilled out in a happy burst.

"She did not!"

"I can show you the note."

"Later." She pulled him close, still smiling as she kissed him. "You can show me later. For now, all I can do is be grateful and put to very good use all the flex-ibility I've gained from her yoga instruction."

He whispered against her lips, "Then remind me to thank her, too."

And then there was nothing else to say, only to feel.

The moment he was sheathed in the condom, she guided him into her body, reveling in the long, slow, very self-assured strokes as he buried himself inside her. She gave herself a quiet few seconds to take in the simple joy of the moment, that initial joining that felt it had been predestined in some way.

Maybe it was, she thought, as she gave in to the whimsy of the idea.

And then he began to move and all thoughts fled, nothing but feeling in their wake.

The pleasure built, steady and sure, and Shayne gave herself up to it.

Gave herself up to him.

And as pleasure crested, then broke over them, Shayne had a startling revelation. She hadn't just fallen for Noah. She'd fallen in love with him.

Deeply, irrevocably, impossibly in love.

Chapter 16

Noah wasn't sure how it had happened, but he'd fallen asleep again. Which wasn't entirely true, he thought as he reached for his ringing phone. He knew why he'd fallen asleep.

He just couldn't believe the reason he'd fallen into a deep, satisfying sleep had actually happened.

Only it had.

His reason had taken form and shape as Shayne, who had stayed in his bed all morning and into early afternoon. He should feel guilty about it. Somewhere in the back of his mind, he tried to muster up a shred of that guilt as he answered the phone, but he was coming up woefully short.

"Ross."

"Agent Ross. It's Megan Daniels."

"Agent Daniels." Noah sat up, settling the covers

over his waist. Agent Daniels was keeping an eye on Caroline.

"I wanted to let you know we've asked Miss Erickson to remain in her office, and I've put two officers on her protection detail. Your team alerted us to the increasing threat from Rick Statler."

"Threat?"

"He made contact with the field office fifteen minutes ago."

Noah lifted his phone from his ear, a message already visible in his missed calls. "Damn it. I missed the call. I'm at Miss Erickson's home with her sister."

He avoided adding anything, and it had only been fifteen minutes, but damn it, how did he miss it? Even as he cursed himself, he knew the call was likely what had interrupted his sleep and had him waking up in the first place.

"Is Miss Erickson okay with the direction?"

"She's fine. Concerned about her sister, but she's more than willing to wait with us until the threat is neutralized."

"Let me call my office, and I'll follow back up. Please wait for further direction."

"Of course."

Daniels disconnected with brisk efficiency, and Noah was already dialing in Durant.

Noah barely gave Ryder the chance to answer the phone before he dived in. "What's going on?"

"Statler made contact."

Although he knew it had only been minutes since Ryder's phone call and voicemail, Noah couldn't help but curse himself some more. They'd been working on this case for weeks, and he had put in his own personal time for months before that trying to prove that Statler was dirty.

And he missed the call.

Not because he was doing his job or protecting the house or working through logistics with Shayne, but because he was asleep.

After sex.

Ignoring another wave of regret, Noah snapped out questions. "What do we know?"

"The call was traced to Texas. We couldn't fully triangulate where, but he's still in the state. We're sure of that much."

"Did he say what he wanted? Give any indication why he hasn't skipped out yet?"

"He talked in circles, Noah." Ryder hesitated, collecting his thoughts. "It was weird. I worked with the man for a long time, and he was never anything but confident. Almost pompously so.

"But this call? It makes me think he's had a lot of time on his own, nursing some pretty serious injuries. He didn't sound like he was in his right mind."

Noah considered Ryder's assessment and realized it was entirely possible that Rick was beginning to break. Between the injuries he had sustained from Murphy, and the burns Shayne had managed to inflict, Statler was in bad shape.

"Did he give any indication of his plans? Anything threaded through or under the rambling we can use?"

"Not really. But he's angry. And he's definitely planning something."

Noah sensed a brief hesitation. "What does 'not really' mean?"

"We barely caught it initially, but Brady's replayed

the call several times. In one of Rick's rambling moments he slips and says 'we.' It was just once, and it could have been just that. A weird slip as he caught a head of steam. But it's a possibility."

We?

Who could he be working with?

The team had done a solid sweep of the office. They'd scrutinized anyone who'd been in the field office for the past year as well as several years before that. Anyone who might know Rick or who could have come under his influence. Other than the bribe he'd used to escape, they didn't find anything.

The big bosses in DC had cleared everyone, too.

So who was Statler working with? Who'd he have his hooks in?

"What else did he say?"

"Nothing other than that he'd call in six hours."

"That's specific. Did he say why?"

"Nope. Just said six hours and to sit tight."

They made plans to connect in an hour, and Ryder promised to send the recording of the call immediately. Noah was already reaching for his laptop when Shayne walked back into the bedroom.

"I fixed you some lunch." She smiled. "Gotta keep your strength up."

"I'll eat later. There's been a development."

"What happened?"

"What happened is I got distracted and missed a call from Ryder. What happened, is that the Austin office is keeping your sister in place in her office, under protection."

Her gaze widened at the mention of Caroline, but she remained steady.

"What does that—"

He cut her off before she could ask anything else. "I lost my focus, Shayne, and that's deadly. I shouldn't've done it."

"I'd say we lost our focus together."

Although she kept her voice level, even, it was impossible to miss the anger. "It was a few hours, Noah. A few precious hours. I think we both earned it."

"I can't afford that sort of extravagance."

She stared at him across the room, and despite all they'd shared, she was now miles away from him. Maybe not physically, but the emotional chasm was enormous.

"You go ahead and think that. You think it all you want. It's obvious I'm not going to convince you otherwise." She set the sandwich she'd fixed on the corner of the small desk in the guest room.

But her parting shot before she turned and left lingered long after she was gone.

"Sometimes we need to give ourselves a chance to let go, or we risk losing everything."

Damn infuriating man.

How was it possible she'd just spent a significant portion of the past few hours making love to Noah, and now she was wondering if it even mattered?

And to hell with that, she mentally chastised herself. Of course it mattered. It mattered to both of them, and she damn well knew it.

Whatever anger she had at his reaction to missing a call from work, none of it had to do with how he felt about her. If anything, she recognized, it was because he gave into what was between them that he was angry.

Foolish man.

Grabbing her phone, she called Caroline, her sister answering on the first ring. "I'm okay."

"Me, too." Shayne quickly affirmed before letting out a choked laugh. "Is this what our lives have come to?"

"Not forever, Shaynie. But today? Yeah, it's what we're dealing with."

"How can you sound so even-keeled about this?"

"Knowing there are two FBI agents standing outside my office door and another one focused on communicating updates about my safety helps."

Shayne took some comfort knowing her sister was literally flanked with protection. "That does make me feel better."

"What about you? Are you okay?"

"No, but not because of any danger." She considered spilling all of it before belatedly remembering where Caroline was calling from. "Do you have me on speaker?"

"No."

"I had sex with Noah."

"Hot damn. And probably well overdue."

"Caroline!"

"I'm just calling it like I see it. It's obvious you have feelings for him. And I don't think they're unrequited or one-sided, either."

Her sister's observation caught her short. "You could see that? In the five minutes it took us to get the bags out of the car last night and fall into our respective beds?"

"It wasn't the amount of time but the way you looked at each other. There was a concern there and a partnership between the two of you. It's hard to miss."

"Well whatever was there vanished instantly when Noah missed a phone call from Ryder."

"He's scared, Shayne."

"Scared? I don't know about that. But he is angry, at himself most of all."

"Of course he is. But he's angry because he's scared. We all are. We care about you, and the person who's after you has made it abundantly clear he's not going away until he does harm."

Once again, Caroline's ability to cut to the chase and say the thing that was hard helped Shayne really see the problem.

"I'm sorry, Caroline. So, so sorry."

"What are you sorry for? You didn't ask for this. You had no idea Rick was capable of this."

"No. I'm sorry for us. I'm sorry for all the wasted years when I didn't see past my own grief or my frustration with what we went through as a family."

Caroline was quiet for a moment, and for all her normal directness, Shayne got the sense her sister was framing her thoughts.

"It was so hard when Todd died. Mom was already upset about losing Dad, and then she lost her child. And we lost our brother. It was so very hard to figure it all out and who we were anymore."

"You can't possibly be giving me a pass on it?"

"Not a pass, but I've had a lot of time to think. And maybe just a chance to look at it all as an adult. But it's been the thought of possibly losing you that has helped me realize all we've done is waste a heck of a lot of time being angry."

"I've realized that, too."

She had.

Wasn't that one of the hardest things she'd had to come to grips with during all those lonely days with nothing but her thoughts in her office? All the years that she had missed with her sister, living and laughing and building an adult relationship with the family member she still had.

"Are you sure you're okay?"

"Yes, I'm fine. I'm following directions, and I'll do whatever I need to do until this is over."

"Thank you. And when it is over, you and I are doing something. Together."

"I'm holding you to that. And just so you know, I'm thinking a spa weekend with the works."

Tears welled hard in her eyes, and Shayne was unable to hold them back. "I think that would be wonderful."

Although she was reluctant to hang up, Shayne sensed the need to prepare, too. Whatever was going on, whatever Rick had planned, they needed to be ready. She swallowed back the last of her tears, washed her face and put on a fresh outfit. Most importantly, she made sure her sneakers were on. The memories of being in bare feet the other morning when Rick had attacked at her home—and how vulnerable she'd felt while waiting for him as he stalked through the house—had left a mark.

She refused to be vulnerable.

And she wanted answers from Noah on however much they knew now.

The sleepy lover she had left in bed less than an hour ago had been replaced with a sharp-eyed agent when she walked back into the bedroom.

He paced the room on his phone while images ran

on a loop on his laptop, which sat on top of the small desk Shayne still remembered doing her homework at in high school. He'd made an effort to make the bed, the covers set in neat lines so that it didn't look as if anyone had slept there, and she didn't miss how his duffel bag was set neatly on the end of it.

It looked like she wasn't the only one prepared.

She heard him speak to who she assumed was his team but only caught a vague sense of the words. Things like triangulation and setting traps and possible bad actors lending support to Rick's efforts. It was fascinating to listen to, even if she didn't fully understand what it all meant.

But did it matter?

What she did understand was that Noah was in charge.

What she also understood was that he had a fascinating ability to listen, take feedback and revise his approach based on whatever he heard in reply.

How could someone so gifted—so able to lead as well as work within a system like the FBI—be so shortsighted? He was entitled to a life. To a few precious moments each day to himself. She didn't just think that because they had been together, those moments spent with her.

She thought it because it was true.

How many years had she wasted, wrapped up in her own head and unable to get out of it? Wasn't that the amazing part of the conversation she'd just had with Caroline? They had a long way to go, realistically she knew that, but they had made a start.

And with it, Shayne finally had an opportunity to know her sister again. To build a relationship with one of the people who knew her best. It was a precious gift, and she wasn't going to squander the opportunity.

For all the pain she'd experienced since Rick came into her life, his actions had somehow—miraculously—given her Caroline back.

She waited until the end of the call before she addressed him. "Where is he?"

"We don't know. Somewhere in Texas, but other than that we can't get a sense of where he called from."

"He's hurt. Do you think he's that far from The Pass?" When Noah only shook his head, she pointed to the bed. "Is there a reason you're all packed?"

"An escort is coming to pick us up, and we'll take the FBI plane back to Midnight Pass."

"We're leaving?"

"We need to. I need to get back, and I'm not leaving you here."

Shayne's head was spinning. They spent all night driving here, and they were just turning around and going back? What happened to getting Caroline's help? The support they'd agreed she needed so that Shayne didn't become the FBI's scapegoat.

"I'm staying."

"No, Shayne, you're not. We need to get back."

Whatever they had shared earlier had vanished so completely she wasn't even sure she was looking at the same man. "You've said it more than once. I'm not in your custody."

"Maybe not, but I need you with me. I need to know that you're safe."

"But I can stay here. Go do what you need to do, and I'll hunker down for a few days. There's already protection assigned and in place. You said yourself we were good to stay with Caroline. That getting out of town was the way to get out of Rick's immediate orbit."

"You're not safe anywhere!"

The outburst was so unlike Noah, or anything she had observed up until now. And in that explosion of emotion, laced with raw fear, her sister's words came back to haunt her.

He's scared.

As she stared at this brave, stoic man who stood all alone, her heart trembled before breaking in two. And then she moved, purely on instinct.

It was all she had left.

She wrapped her arms around his waist.

He stood there stiffly for a few moments—heartbeats, really—before his arms came around her. "I need to know you're with my people. The ones that I trust all the way. I need to know they have your back, just like I do."

She thought about the relationship she was so eager to build with her sister, but only nodded against his chest.

"When do we leave?"

It turned out that leaving required a significant amount of logistics, input from his office and the Austin field office and a surprisingly serious negotiation with Caroline Erickson.

"Of course I'm coming with you."

Shayne had been arguing with her sister for the better part of the past hour, but Caroline would not be deterred. Agent Daniels had brought the woman to the small private airstrip south of Austin where they would depart back to Midnight Pass.

"You need to stay here," Shayne argued. "It's not safe to come with us."

"I'd say it's not safe anywhere. So like it or not, you've got a shadow."

Noah shifted away to give the two women privacy and answered a call from Durant.

"We're about ten miles out and cleared for landing. We've got plenty of fuel, so as soon as the plane's turned around, you'll board and we'll be on our way."

"Looks like we're going to be a party of three, not two," Noah said.

"Let me guess. The sister's giving you a hard time?"

"You could say that."

Although to be fair, a hard time wasn't the perfect description. Only now that she'd been pulled into things, Caroline Erickson wasn't content to leave her sister's safety fully to someone else.

If it didn't end up adding to his logistics nightmare, he'd actually be grateful for the intrusion. Keeping Shayne occupied with Caroline for the next few days would give him the space to finally take Statler down.

Because no matter how elusive the man had been, Noah felt the net tightening. They were too close, and Rick's increased instability had to work in their favor. The team had already set up and tested the equipment for his expected call later.

They were going to get him.

In the meantime, he sighed. They needed to stretch a bit on expanded protection detail.

It was uncanny, Noah thought as he considered both women where they stood near the large bay window that fronted the airstrip. While they certainly looked different if you knew them, with a bit of physical distance you not only took them for sisters, but you could mistake them for twins.

Both had that long, lush blond hair, and they were slim yet carried a strong, regal bearing. Caroline was slightly bigger, but he suspected that was only because Shayne hadn't fully regained her weight after spending far too many days living on granola bars. Caroline's face was a bit more angular as well, and her eyes were a shade of grayish blue he'd only ever associated with the ocean in a storm.

But yeah, they were clearly sisters. Even their physical movements as they argued were similar. Each of them used their hands to punctuate their gestures and exhaled when frustrated so that small wisps of hair around their face blew in the light shifting of air.

If the situation weren't so dire, he might have taken more joy out of the moment.

If only they could get past this. Get Rick caught as well as anyone who was acting with him.

If only…

Noah moved toward the window as he saw the plane descending for touch down. At the arrival of this team, Noah took his first easy breath and moved back to the women.

"Plane's almost here."

Shayne nodded toward the window before turning to Noah. "I'm going to run to the restroom."

"There's a bathroom on the plane."

"I appreciate that but I need to use the one here. I'll be right back."

He briefly considered stopping her and recognized how dumb he'd look if he didn't let her go to the bathroom. There were agents all over, inside the airport as well as on the incoming plane. And the bathroom was thirty yards away.

"You're really coming?" he asked Caroline.

"You're stuck with me."

"We can keep her safe."

"I'd like to see it for myself."

He might have argued if not for the earnestness in Caroline's face. For all her bravado, the woman's sole focus was her sister's safety. And as determination glinted in her eyes, Noah admitted to himself that since they had brought this fight to her doorstep, it was hardly fair to ask her to step away now.

"I'm not just dead weight. I can help."

Although he was tempted knowing how expert Caroline's skills were—and they could use all the help they could get—Noah wanted her to focus on Shayne.

"I know that, and there may come a point where we need that help. But for now? I need you to focus on your sister."

"She doesn't open up very easily, you know."

The sudden change in conversation was oddly expected. "That's not really my concern."

Caroline's gaze narrowed. "I'd say it's very much your concern, whether you want to admit it or not."

Wherever she was going with this, now was not the time for the conversation, both due to their current physical circumstances and the fact that he simply could not give headspace to what had happened between him and Shayne.

"I have a job to do. That's where I need to place all my effort right now."

Caroline's gaze was unwavering, and while she kept her thoughts to herself, her poker face fully intact, he couldn't quite shake the idea that his response was lacking.

"Perhaps you should get to it, then."

At that clear dismissal, Noah looked around, suddenly realizing Shayne hadn't come back. "Where is she?"

Caroline glanced toward the far edge of the terminal. The space wasn't big, and they should have seen Shayne by now. "I'm not sure. Let me go look for her."

Although he'd wanted her to wait and use the restroom when they got on the plane, Noah honestly didn't see a threat in this place. It was small and contained, and there were agents everywhere.

So why did he suddenly feel so untethered? And so convinced something had gone sideways?

Caroline ran back from the direction of the bathroom. "She's not in there."

"What?"

Agent Daniels and her colleagues who had escorted Caroline moved in closer. "What's going on?"

"Shayne's gone." The words ripped out of Caroline's throat like gunshots. "I just looked for her, but she's gone."

Noah raced to the windows at the back of the airport, to the ones that didn't face the airstrip.

And as he stared down at the large black SUV, he caught the edge of a flailing sneaker just as a body disappeared into the backseat of the car.

Chapter 17

Shayne was gone.

Snatched out from underneath his nose as well as three other agents.

Noah raced out to the front of the airport, the SUV nowhere to be found by the time he hit street level. Within minutes, Ryder, Brady and the rest of Noah's team had swarmed the private terminal, flanking him on the sidewalk where people were dropped off.

"Walk us through it." Ryder was calm and focused, a contrast to the writhing, live-wire energy coursing through Noah. He started to describe what had happened when Caroline neatly swooped in. She gave an overview of the past few minutes before Noah added in what he'd seen in the SUV and that lone sneaker hanging out the door before Shayne was fully pulled into the car.

Agent Daniels had already started on an APB on the SUV, and she and several team members had headed out in pursuit.

And still, none of it changed the fact that Shayne was gone.

Kidnapped practically right in front of him.

The past days with Shayne flashed through Noah's mind, one after the other like a mental movie. From that first moment when she opened the door to her office, peeking warily out from behind it, to just that morning when he lay in bed with her wrapped in his arms.

Had it really only been a few days since he grabbed that extra sandwich at the sub shop on a hunch?

How had she become so important in so short a time?

Because no matter how many times he had told himself that this was a job and that he needed to maintain his focus and catch a killer, Noah knew deep in his heart that it was so much more.

Despite his every inward objection, he had fallen in love with her.

Those memories of Lindsey that had been so close to the surface filled his mind's eye again. That horrifying day when he had discovered the news of what had happened to her. And in the memory, he recognized something else.

This wasn't the same.

He would regret, for the rest of his days, that he had created an environment where Lindsey couldn't talk to him about her fears or her anger or her disappointment about their marriage. But because he didn't know the depth of her unhappiness, he couldn't be there to save her. Couldn't help her out of a bad situation.

This wasn't the same, he reminded himself again.

He wasn't letting Shayne go. He was going to do everything in his power to see they got her back safe and sound.

"Noah." Caroline moved up next to him, her laptop open. "I need to show you something."

"What is it?"

"Shayne. I'm tracking her."

"You're what?"

Caroline gave him a small, unrepentant grin. "What can I say? I didn't really trust the FBI."

Never before in his career had Noah felt so grateful to have his profession so thoroughly dismissed. "How did you put a tracker on her?"

"I put it in her sneaker last night. I wasn't going to use it unless there was an emergency, and I would've told her eventually, but I figured she might be better off not knowing."

Noah moved beside her, his eyes lasering in on the screen and the small dot that moved steadily toward Austin.

"You're amazing."

"I'm counting on you to be the same. Now let's build a plan to take the bastard down."

Shayne struggled to calm her breathing, the cloth over her head upsetting but not stifling. And when she finally did slow her racing pulse, she realized that she could still breathe.

Oh God, how did this happen again?

And while it was tempting to blame this on Rick, the male form that had grabbed her coming out of the ladies' room wasn't Rick. Aside from the fact that she knew of the man's injuries and recalled his lumbering stiffness when he'd attacked her in her home, the physical heft of whoever had snatched her was different.

Taller. Broader. And clearly not sporting debilitating injuries if the fluid movements of his body were any indication.

"Where am I?"

The interior of the car was quiet, no one reacting to her words.

They'd already changed cars, the backseat where she had been unceremoniously dumped at the airport replaced with another after they'd screeched to a hard stop. She'd been dragged out then and moved and, despite her struggles, stuffed into a different backseat. One that was plusher, the rich scent of leather enveloping her, as they drove farther and farther from Noah.

She asked one more time where she was before giving up. Whoever had captured her wasn't inclined to answer questions. And she wasn't inclined to waste her breath. Whatever intimidation they were determined to mete out, she was equally determined to resist.

She had come too far.

Wasn't that the real lesson in all of this?

For as horrible as it had all been up to now, she had survived. And she was not going down without a fight.

The trip ended without warning, the big SUV slowing before coming to a stop. The same rough hands that had maneuvered her into the car came around and dragged her back out. Her hands were already zip-tied, and her captor's grip was firm on them as he perpwalked her into a building.

She had no idea where she was, but that industrial smell of large buildings—a mix of cavernous, stuffy air and cleaning chemicals—rose up to fill her nose. And as she was half pushed, half led to a room, she prayed that she could figure something out.

Because no matter how much he wanted to save her, Shayne had little hope Noah would even know where to start looking for her. Unless they'd realized she was gone in time to see and pursue her kidnappers—and things had happened so fast she hadn't even had time to scream—how was he going to find her somewhere in the entire city of Austin?

Hopelessness threatened to swamp her, and Shayne forced air in and out of her lungs.

She wasn't incapable. She had her mind, and she could bargain for her life. Whoever this was clearly knew she had a connection to Rick. The FBI had spent long enough believing she had sensitive documents. Why not use that same assumption if there were bad guys who wanted in on Rick's territory?

She'd bargain and use the explanation that she had computer files in her home and encrypted on her machine.

Her mind whirled with possibilities as she was pushed forward.

When she felt herself being maneuvered through a door, the air around her changed. It wasn't quite as dank, and she had a sense of being in a smaller room, though she couldn't explain why. But the combination of the passage through the door and the change in smells let her know she'd been taken somewhere new.

That scent of antiseptic cleaner had faded, and in its place was a thicker, heavier odor that assaulted her senses. It hovered there around her, seeming to fill the room.

But she was only able to place it as her captor dragged the cloth covering off her head.

It was then that she knew.

And saw the blood that surrounded Rick's body where he lay dead on the floor, a bullet hole in the center of his head.

Noah worked with the team to quickly evaluate where Shayne had been taken. He wasn't surprised to find her location was identified as a large warehouse area, but he was surprised when they uncovered the property's ownership.

"Rick managed to snag himself warehouse property?" Ryder asked. He and Caroline were in the backseat while one of Agent Daniels's team members drove them north.

Straight to the blinking light that was Shayne.

"No, no," Caroline said, tapping the top of Ryder's computer. "You need to dig further. It's a decoy."

Ryder turned to her. "How do you know that?"

She just smiled. "It's my job."

"What is your job exactly?" Ryder asked.

"Watch." Caroline went to work on her computer, the keys humming as she dug for information. Despite the tension and his insane concern for Shayne, Noah couldn't deny how incredible it was to see an obvious master at work.

But that smile of triumph, so similar to her sister's, clutched his heart.

"There." Caroline pointed to the screen. "That's your man. High Value Trucking and Shipping."

Noah turned that over in his mind. It was such a generic name, it shouldn't have rung any bells, yet it did. Pulling out his phone, he quickly tapped into one of their Bureau databases, hunting for the company name.

As soon as he hit the link, the pieces fell into place. And suddenly it all made sense.

The frantic undertones of Rick's call that morning. The "we" reference. Even the rambling that was so unlike the man. Statler had made an alliance with the wrong person.

"So that's who you're in with, you bastard," Noah whispered under his breath.

"Who?" Ryder asked, looking up from his computer. "Who's High Value?"

"Vasily Baslikova."

"Oh hell."

Noah nodded and recognized they needed to do an immediate regroup. Baslikova had tentacles all over the country but had recently put his focus on the south. His roots went deep, and he was rumored to be merciless in going after what he wanted.

He'd also managed to rather craftily escape capture.

If the man had Shayne, he wasn't going to let her go easily. Nor was he going to be easy to attack.

And whatever he imagined awaited them at the warehouse had suddenly morphed into a nightmare.

Shayne fought the rising waves of panic and tried to avoid looking at Rick. What had possibly happened? How did he go from being the resident bad guy to ending up with a bullet in his head?

And who were these horrible people who had her?

Did the FBI know Rick was working with somebody?

After all the time she and Noah had spent together over the past week, she had to believe if he had been aware of Rick's connections, he would've said something.

Which meant this would be a surprise to them, too.

An ambush, actually, if he was even able to find her.

They were the FBI. She'd come to the assumption that they had the capability to track the SUV that had taken her from the airstrip.

But what if they did find her and had no idea what they faced on the other side?

Feeling her breath sticking in her chest, Shayne forced herself to breathe slowly. The horror of seeing Rick wasn't going to go away, but she needed to stay in the moment.

She needed to figure out how to handle this.

When she'd been dropped into this room, her captors had stayed behind her, ripping the blindfold off and leaving before she could see them. So now she had to figure out who they were. She had to keep them talking long enough to put her plan into action.

It was a sound approach and a good plan.

Until the slender man with the white-blond hair walked into the office. Two large men walked in behind him, flanking him, and she recognized one of them on sight.

"You! From the rest stop last night."

The man only nodded, but she saw the supreme pleasure that lit his face at her recognition.

A pleasure he obviously didn't dare share with his boss based on how he kept his profile averted from view.

The man with the reptilian eyes focused fully on her. "Miss Erickson. Welcome."

"Who are you?"

"That's not your concern."

While Shayne was hardly expecting him to give her his name, rank and serial number, she was surprised he didn't share his name. "What should I call you then?"

"I think *sir* will be fine."

Her mind scrambled with ideas of how to play this, including everything from acting like a smartass to behaving with nonchalant cool. Somehow, though, she quickly discarded each idea.

Whoever this man was, it was clear he was not someone to trifle with.

She flicked a glance down to Rick. Something dark and oily unfurled in her belly, but she went with instinct, playing an angle. "I see that you disposed of the trash."

"I suggest you consider it an example." Those creepy dead eyes also flicked to Rick's body before returning Shayne. "A promised outcome, if you will."

"Well I have no interest in ending up the same, and I can't say I'm sorry he died."

"Cold words for a woman plotting with him."

She nearly argued, almost choking on the words, when she reconsidered. Did this man actually think she was in league with Rick?

Could she use that?

"Loyalties have a way of changing."

"I'm not easily amused, Miss Erickson. Nor will I be played a fool. You spent quite a bit of time with the FBI this past week."

"Loyalties, sir." She emphasized the name he gave her, pushing the slightest bit of cheek into her voice. "They're always shifting."

Might as well go down swinging.

She saw interest spark ever-so-slightly, and Shayne had a modicum of hope he might keep her alive for a while. It wasn't a stay of execution so much as waiting to see if she might be useful, but she'd take it.

And she was determined to find a way for him to think she wasn't just useful, but essential to whatever he had planned.

"Use me as bait."

Caroline's words rang through the interior of the SUV, and Noah was torn between hearing the woman out and dragging her straight to FBI headquarters in Austin to put her into lockdown until this was all over.

"You know it's a great idea." Caroline kept pressing.

"How is it a good idea?" Ryder asked. "You're putting yourself in serious danger and adding to the possibility the whole thing goes sideways."

"Or we're taking advantage of possible confusion. Those goons think they picked up my sister, but she was dragged quickly out of an airport bathroom. What if I go in and say I'm really Shayne? You can wire me up and find a heap of evidence all at the same time."

Noah didn't want to dismiss the idea right away because Caroline had made some excellent points.

But none of it changed the fact that they were blind to the situation.

"We have no idea what Shayne has already said to them. Nor do we even know if anybody will buy it. Statler knows who she is, Caroline."

"Do you honestly think he's still alive?"

Noah considered Shayne's sister, her cool-eyed stare steady and fierce as she left that verbal bomb hanging out there.

He equally understood that each minute they dithered on they were losing time to form a much-needed plan.

"We have no idea if he's outlived his usefulness or not, but we have to consider all the angles."

"So worst-case assumptions?" Caroline probed.

Noah got a sense Caroline hadn't asked a question she didn't know the answer to and was rewarded when she turned her computer around.

"Is that Rick Statler?" She tapped the lower corner of what looked like a grainy video feed.

"Where did you get this?" Ryder was already leaning forward to get a better look, but Noah didn't because in that grainy feed he saw all he needed.

Shayne sat on a chair with her hands tied behind her back.

Vasily Baslikova and his goons stood over her, clearly interrogating her.

And Rick Statler lay dead on the floor beside her.

Shayne stared down at Rick's body and, again, fought a shudder. She knew she was locked in here with him as a tactic to break her down, but damn it, it was working.

She thought she might have made a dent with the whole switching loyalties bit, but at this point who knew? She couldn't discount the overwhelming sense that she was some sort of pawn in whatever game was being played.

Why, for instance, had Rick been killed?

It had obviously been beneficial to keep him alive up until now. What changed?

Even as she asked herself the question, Shayne had her suspicions. It was his insistence on coming after her.

The attack at her office and then the attack at her home. Whatever had driven him before now, the past few weeks had only reinforced the fact that Rick had gotten sloppy.

A state that would be very difficult for an associate who expected obedience.

The door opened and the thug who had followed her into the mini-mart stepped into the office. "Would you like something to drink?"

"A water please."

He crossed to a small fridge in the corner of the room, and Shayne considered what she'd learned so far. It wasn't much, but she had begun to piece some of the hierarchy together. The way the two goons flanked the man with the snake eyes. That subtle flash of pride this one had shown when she recognized him from the night before.

"Who's your boss?"

"If you have to ask, then you don't need to know."

"Convenient and thoroughly unhelpful."

She might not be willing to sass the other guy, but with this one she was more than prepared to test boundaries.

And, oddly, was rewarded with a big smile as he crossed back to her. He flicked open a large knife and Shayne fought to keep her composure when the cool steel ran over the back of her hands. But when he finished, she was free, her arms out of the zip ties.

"You've got spirit. I like that." He handed over her water before glancing down at Rick, a sneer on his face. "He didn't deserve you."

Shayne nodded in Rick's direction, even as she tried to keep her gaze from lingering too long. "He liked being the big boss and throwing his weight around. I can't imagine that went over well with your boss."

"My boss can take care of himself."

"Oh, I'm sure he can. And I'm sure it helps that he has a big guy like you to watch his back."

The man stiffened, but Shayne sensed she scored a point. "This is a difficult business. He needs to protect himself."

"So that's why he has to tie defenseless women up?"

"You don't act defenseless."

The comment hung there like a flirtation, and Shayne decided to leave it for now. This one seemed strangely vulnerable to her sweet words and subtle innuendo, but she didn't want to overdo it.

Which made the knock on the door a welcome interruption.

The second goon poked his head through the door. "Would you come here, please?"

Shayne's new friend looked obviously confused by the summons, but walked outside the door, closing it in his wake. Although she couldn't hear all the specifics, especially through their accented English, she did catch a few words.

"Did you get the right one?"

"Is that the sister?"

"Baslikova is going to kill us."

Sister?

They thought they picked up Caroline instead of her?

Although her knowledge of the players was woefully lacking, the first spears of hope alighted in her chest. If they thought she might be Caroline, someone must have put the idea in their heads.

She was damn sure they wouldn't have come up with it on their own.

Which only left one question.

Where was Noah?

Noah had no idea what Caroline actually did for a living, but between her computer hacking skills and her ability to mimic her sister, he was ready to give the woman a wide berth.

She knew things.

And he'd worry later how she came by her knowledge.

"We made contact. And Baslikova is pissed that his men might have picked up the wrong woman."

"I know what you need me to do. I know the play, Noah. We've been over it and over it."

In fact, they'd only reviewed it a few times, their lack of options pushing the entire mission into high gear. Ryder had already taken external detail with the other field agents, and Noah was on point with Caroline to actually get her into the building.

They would do this.

And they would be successful.

They had to be.

Ignoring those creeping moments of doubt that had nagged at him throughout the preparations, Noah focused on Caroline. "Well then, make me feel better and let me walk through it again. If anything happens to you, Shayne is going to kill me."

"And if anything happens to Shayne, I'm going to kill you, so we'll be even." Caroline hesitated, the bravado she had worn for the past several hours dimming. "Nothing can happen to her, Noah. It just can't."

"I know."

"This is going to be fine. It'll all work out. And we're going to bring those bastards down."

While he appreciated her enthusiasm, he was well aware anything could happen on an op. And when you had one this hastily put together, with an enemy known for his craftiness, it left a lot of room for concern.

"Okay. Walk me through it again."

Caroline nodded, her focus absolute. "I'm going to march right up to the warehouse. I'll have all my tech with me. And I'm going to ask why the hell they took my sister and not me."

"Tech that we've rigged for you."

"Yes, of course."

"You can work it as seamlessly as you can your own?"

The serious facade fell, and she gave him the fish eye.

Oddly, that shot of confidence made Noah feel better. Their sting operation wasn't much of one, and God knew there was a tremendous amount of risk, but they had to try.

Because there was no way Shayne could stay inside that place for one moment longer.

Although she played dumb when Snake Eyes and his men came back into the room, Shayne had had plenty of time to cycle through what she knew. And knew it was time to start bluffing.

Really hard.

She had no sense if she was right, but based on what she had overheard through the door, she got the impression some outreach had been made claiming the wrong woman had been kidnapped from the airport. It was an interesting strategy, and Shayne worked through idea after idea as to how she could play the trio to further seed that doubt.

What did she have to lose?

They were going to kill her anyway if she didn't get out of this situation. It was a sobering thought, but she needed to stay sharp.

So as the men filed in, she smiled broadly.

And prepared to play her sister.

Chapter 18

The Austin FBI team outfitted Caroline with a wire, a rigged laptop and a quick change of clothes that mirrored the outfits Shayne favored. Leggings and workout tops, with her hair fluffed to diminish the view of her face on camera.

There was no more time to wait.

Noah climbed into the waiting SUV that would take him around the back of the warehouse, where Agent Daniels's team had already staked things out. Caroline had proven herself extra valuable when she managed to disable the same cameras she'd used to spy on Shayne, and also helped set up the FBI's tech lead with a steady feed.

They had done all they could.

It was time to act.

Noah was quiet as they drove to the back entrance to

the warehouse and considered all Caroline had discovered on the interior cameras. Baslikova had two thugs with him, and there was a heat signature coming out of the front quadrant of the building. They assessed at least ten bodies, but there had been little movement in the entire time Shayne was there. Odds were, based on the close quarters, the people in that room were related to sex trafficking, and Daniels had already called in colleagues to help manage that part of the op.

If they were going in, they were going to get as many people out as possible.

Caroline had been fitted with a small camera in a heart pendant necklace and a microphone attached inside the intricately curving gold. The necklace would get them a full recap of the op in addition to each agent's body camera, and Noah knew the intel and evidence would be invaluable.

He considered the maps they had reviewed, and he mentally walked through the floor plans in his mind. They'd bumped the floor plans up against the camera angles Caroline captured on her hacked feed, and he'd mentally mapped his route to Shayne.

Agents would follow behind him into the building.

His sole focus was getting Shayne and Caroline to safety as quickly as possible. The rest would subdue Baslikova and his men before rescuing the women who'd been trafficked.

He allowed the chatter in his earpiece to fade into the background, his mind tracing over that route. And all he could think about was getting to Shayne.

As they pulled into position, the past several days flew through his mind on a loop. But the image he kept coming back to was Shayne hanging from her office window, too afraid to jump.

How far they had come in so short a time.

Caroline might be taking the overt risk by heading into the lion's den, but Noah had watched Shayne carefully on the feeds. She was holding her own, against a threat she didn't know or understand. And all with Rick's body lying mere feet from her.

Yet she hung in there.

He saw the straight line of her back, the hard set of her shoulders and the clear determination that etched itself on her face.

She was a warrior.

And as he prepared himself to defend her and her sister, Noah prayed he could keep them safe.

Shayne heard her sister's voice and was both relieved and panicked.

How dare Noah let her come here. How was it possible in any circumstance that the FBI sent a civilian into a situation like this?

The thug who'd gotten her the water dragged Caroline into the small room, and Shayne wondered how she could be so blindingly mad and so desperate to see Caroline all at once?

"You're here!" Caroline rushed to her, clearly avoiding the use of names. "I've been worried sick."

Even though she was pushed into the room, Caroline's hands weren't tied, and her arms went around Shayne immediately.

"Why are you here?" Shayne whispered fiercely against her ear.

Caroline hugged her extra tight before pulling back,

all while overtly ignoring the question. Her sharp, aware gaze landed on Rick, and she let out a long, low moan. "He's dead?"

The moan turned into a keening wail, and even knowing what Caroline was up to, Shayne had to give her sister credit for making it look real.

"How did this happen? How long has he been gone?"

Caroline shot one determined look toward the thug before going from actively convincing to really selling it. But when she dropped to her knees and laid her head on Rick's chest, her arms wrapping around him as she continued that low keening moan, Shayne couldn't quite hold back a shudder.

Caroline leaped up, her tone accusing as she stalked toward the thug. "What have you done to him?"

"Shayne—" Shayne started in with the switcheroo tactics, dragging on her sister's arm. "It's okay."

She deliberately kept her gaze off of the thug but knew they'd both hit their marks when he made a quick excuse to leave.

Once they were sure he was gone, Caroline was back on her feet, shaking off that quick interlude with the dead. "Eww, that was gross. But it was about time the ass was good for something."

"I don't believe you did that."

"Desperate times and all that. There's backup coming."

"Noah's here?"

"Noah and all the rest of them. You've got a cavalry on the other side of the building."

"Shhh. They'll hear you."

"Tech's all handled." Caroline smiled proudly. "And since I came in with 'your tech,'" she put air quotes around the description, "they're going to be jammed up even further with the little program I added to attack the Wi-Fi."

"I mean this in the very best way, but you're scary."

"I'm efficient. There's a difference."

Caroline took tight hold of her hands, pulling her to a standing position. "Come on, we need to be ready to get out of here."

"They're not going to let us walk out of here."

"No, but we need to be ready." Caroline bent down to inspect Shayne's legs and ankles. "Have they tied you up anywhere?"

"Just on my wrists before. But that guy took them off when he got me a bottle of water."

Shayne glanced around, and while she wanted nothing more than to leave, she also wanted to know more. "Who are these people?"

"A very nasty group of foreign mobsters who've been trying to get a toehold here in Texas. And apparently they've been doing a damn fine job of it. The head guy's named Vasily Baslikova."

"These are the people Rick was in with?"

Every time she thought it couldn't be worse, Shayne realized that it was. But knowing what they'd done to her was enough to finally accept the truth.

Whatever lingering traces inside her wanted to believe that there was something decent about Rick Statler finally died.

It was humbling and freeing all at once.

Caroline took her firmly in hand, pulling her toward the door.

"What are you doing?" Shayne hissed.

"We need to get out of here. There's backup to support us, and what are they going to do, just shoot us right in the middle of the warehouse?"

"It's a distinct possibility."

"Not until they figure out what's on my computer they won't."

Shayne held tight to Caroline as they exited the door of the small office. It was shockingly freeing to get a breath of air that didn't include the scent of Rick's blood.

Even if Shayne's more methodical expectations proved true over Caroline's bravado.

"Leaving so soon? We're just getting started."

Shayne and Caroline turned in unison to face the man with the snake eyes.

Noah heard the exchange through his earpiece and held his position on the other side of the door. The tech lead had kept them informed of what was going on with a steady stream of updates from the camera feeds, and Noah nearly ignored all protocols and run straight into the warehouse when he heard Caroline had brazenly walked them out of the office where Shayne had been locked up.

It was only with the quick add that they were all right and engaging Baslikova in conversation that Noah waited.

He knew that whatever evidence they got in the next few minutes could mean cutting the man and his organization off at the knees.

At Shayne's expense?

The question haunted him, and he was torn between duty and the reality that leaping too soon could endanger them even more.

But damn it, she was a civilian and so was her sister. She shouldn't be involved in this.

Just like Lindsey.

The thought struck so hard Noah felt it slam into his solar plexus, and he nearly bent at the waist. Strangely, Reese's repeated words from Shayne the day before rang in his ears, blanketing him in a layer of calm.

Shayne said that Ryder had to stand on the other side of the door at the safe house where she and Arden were kidnapped. He didn't know what awaited him, and there's a burden there. One that takes time to heal from.

Now he was the one outside.

And the woman he loved was on the other side.

Shouts echoed in his earpiece, affirming it was time to move.

With the order, everything else faded away. The floor plan came up like a map in his head, and Noah charged through the back door.

He had one goal.

He had to get there in time.

Shayne knew Noah was there before she even turned around.

The menace of being stared down by the soulless man with the snake eyes had held her in a trance as Caroline wove a spell of questions designed to trap the man even further for his crimes.

But the near war-cry from Noah was what pushed her into motion.

Their time together seemed to fold in on itself, the same orders he'd shouted when he rescued her from her office suddenly driving her actions.

You will move.

Had it really only been a few days? It felt like a life-time, and in some way, it had been. And as Shayne did move this time—no order required—she wrapped a tight arm around Caroline and raced for Noah.

Agents swarmed in around them, filling the space and setting a shocking number of guns directly on Vasily Baslikova and his men.

Shayne ignored them all.

She had two goals entwined into one outcome. She and Caroline would get out alive. And she'd wrap her arms around Noah in triumph that this was all finally over.

When she saw one of the agents swiftly maneuver her sister out of danger, her first goal was cleared.

And as Noah came fully into view, Shayne moved directly to him, wrapping her arms around him and sinking into his hold.

Noah held tight to the woman in his arms, the certain knowledge that things could have gone in a wildly different direction coursing through him in hard, pounding beats. He continued to keep an arm around her on the ride back to the Austin bureau office and on into the night when they finally took the plane back to Midnight Pass.

He even held her close when they arrived to an entire welcoming committee of Reynolds family members.

When they were finally alone, standing outside her newly fixed front door, Noah took a step back.

She was okay. Better than okay, he admitted. She was safe, and the threat to her life had been vanquished.

She could really live again.

"This is where I leave you."

"Noah—" She stopped, obviously confused. "Wait? What?"

"The past week has meant more to me than I could ever say. But I can't do this."

Something hard glinted in the depths of her clear blue gaze, and Noah felt that look straight through to his midsection.

"So this is it? You're turning tail and running?"

"I'm not turning away from anything. I got you back here, and you're OK. I came through the door, Shayne. And I'd do it a million times over to know that you were safe."

Her gaze softened under the bright lights of her porch, but she didn't back down. "That's only half the battle, you know."

"What is?"

"Coming through the door. I realize that now." She laid a hand on his shoulder. "It's staying, Noah. It's making the commitment and staying, every day, even when it's hard. Even when your every dream isn't being fulfilled. Even when you're struggling to have the tough conversations. That's what Lindsey didn't understand."

"I'm the one who didn't understand it."

She shook her head. "No, my dear man. You've taken the responsibility for it, but in the end, it's not yours to bear."

"I don't know how to do this."

"I'm not exactly a bright shining example, either. I haven't had anything but a surface conversation with my sister for the past decade, and my last boyfriend was a psychopathic killer." She moved in closer, her arms wrapping around his neck. "I'm not a good bet."

"Could have fooled me."

"Love me, Noah. Stay with me. Build a life with me. I promise you, I'll stay, too, and we can figure it out together.

"Let go of the ledge, Noah. I promise, I'll catch you." She lifted her lips to his, whispering against his mouth. "Because I love you."

Whatever he'd been holding onto for so long seemed to fade away into dust.

Not because it was no longer important, but because he'd found the future that made everything in his past finally make sense.

"I love you, Shayne."

"Then please kiss me. We do a lot better when we're kissing. There's no room left to argue or fight."

Since she was right and she loved him, Noah did as he was told.

He kissed the woman he loved.

The woman he'd love forever.

* * * * *

*Don't miss the previous books in
the Midnight Pass, Texas series*

The Cowboy's Deadly Mission
Special Ops Cowboy
Under the Rancher's Protection
Undercover K-9 Cowboy

Available now from Harlequin Romantic Suspense!

COMING NEXT MONTH FROM

♦ HARLEQUIN
ROMANTIC SUSPENSE

#2219 PROTECTING COLTON'S BABY
The Coltons of New York • by Tara Taylor Quinn

ADA Emily Hernandez's life is at risk—so is the child she's carrying. Her much younger former lover, PI Cormac Colton, is willing to play protector to Emily and father to his child. Will their unexpected family survive, or will Emily be silenced for good?

#2220 CAVANAUGH JUSTICE: DETECTING A KILLER
Cavanaugh Justice • by Marie Ferrarella

When NYC detective Danny Doyle finds DNA remains tying Cassandra Cavanaugh to the victim, the determined investigator jumps at the chance to crack her cousin's cold case. If only the detecting duo's chemistry wasn't off the charts...and a serial killer wasn't targeting both of them...

#2221 HOTSHOT HERO IN DISGUISE
Hotshot Heroes • by Lisa Childs

An explosion in a Lake Michigan firehouse has exposed Ethan Sommerly's secret identity. Which means the target he avoided five years ago is now on his back again. Local Tammy Ingles is the only one he can trust. As the danger increases, is Tammy's life now on the line, too?

#2222 UNDERCOVER COWBOY DEFENDER
Shelter of Secrets • by Linda O. Johnston

Luca Almera and her young son found a safe refuge at the highly secret Chance Animal Shelter. But when a deadly stalker targets Luca, undercover K-9 cop Mark Martin will risk his life *and* his heart to keep the vulnerable single mom safe.

HRSCNM0123

HARLEQUIN
PLUS

Announcing a **BRAND-NEW**
multimedia subscription service
for romance fans like you!

Read, Watch and Play.

Experience the easiest way to get
the romance content you crave.

Start your **FREE 7 DAY TRIAL** at
<u>www.harlequinplus.com/freetrial</u>.